THE DALE OF DESPAIR

A LUKE TREMAYNE ADVENTURE

THE DALE OF DESPAIR

A NORTH YORKSHIRE MYSTERY
1659

GEOFF QUAIFE

Copyright © 2019 by Geoff Quaife.

ARPress
45 Dan Road Suite 36
Canton MA 02021

Hotline: 1(800) 220-7660
Fax: 1(855) 752-6001

Ordering Information:
Quantity sales. Special discounts are available on quantity purchases by corporations, associations, and others. For details, contact the publisher at the address above.

Printed in the United States of America.

ISBN-13:   Softcover   979-8-89389-191-1
           eBook   979-8-89389-190-4
           Hardcover   979-8-89389-964-1

Library of Congress Control Number: 2024914530

THE LUKE TREMAYNE ADVENTURES

(In chronological order of the events portrayed)

1648-9	The Irish Fiasco
1650	Chesapeake Chaos
1651	The Black Thistle
1652	The Angelic Assassin
1653	The Frown of Fortune
1654-5	The Spanish Relation
1656	The Dark Corners
1657	The Garden of Deceit
1657	Lady Mary's Revenge
1657-8	Murder In the Maghreb
1658	A Queen Besieged
1659	The Dale of Despair

Characters

Luke's Inner Circle

Sir Luke Tremayne	Retired major general, landowner, and magistrate
Lady Matilda Tremayne	His wife
Capt. Peter Frost	Steward, lawyer, and bookkeeper
Harry Green	Former corporal, now Luke's valet and bodyguard, and later bailiff

Tenants and Servants of Abbey Grange and Inhabitants of Abbey Dale

Janet Bates	Wife of former steward of Abbey Grange

The Catholic Families

Charles Ogden	Deputy steward and reeve
Simon Snigg	Bailiff
Emma Snigg	His wife, sister to Timothy
Matthew Foxton	A tenant farmer
Mark Foxton	His nephew
Elizabeth Foxton	Missing daughter of Matthew
Timothy Carver	A tenant farmer
Mary Carver	His wife, daughter of Charles Ogden

The Protestant Families

Robert (Robbie) Dutton	Constable, wealthy farmer
Roger Dutton	His brother, Whitby merchant
Teresa Dutton	Exiled wife of Robert
Edward (Ted) Unsworth	Rector
Richard (Dickie) Unsworth	His uncle, cobbler and leather worker

Johnny Harland	Shepherd, brother of Mother Harland and James
James Harland	Landlord of the Three Roses
Abigail and Phyllis Harland	Washerwomen, daughters of James
Mother (Tamsin) Harland	Elderby white witch, midwife and herbalist, sister of Johnny and James
Nell Briggs	Richard's housekeeper, daughter of Billie Briggs, the miller
Alice Eades	Sister to Tim Carver and Emma Snigg, wife to William
William Eades	Tenant farmer, blacksmith, cutler

Others

Kit Jagger	Moorland gang leader, former Royalist soldier, publican of the Pilgrim's Rest
Rowland (Roly) Jagger	His cousin and assistant
Margaret Vernon (lady)	Sister to Barbara Dutton and Grace Swan
Elinor	A barmaid at the Pilgrim's Rest
Lancelot Keeley	Whitby lawyer
Captain Welby	Officer attached to General Lambert
Colonel James	Officer attached to Sir Thomas Fairfax
Nicholas, Lord Ashcroft (alias Colonel Smith)	Commander of the king's bodyguard and Royalist emissary to republican leaders
Sir Evan Williams (colonel)	Former military intelligence, now governor of York Castle, commander of government troops in Yorkshire

Referred To

Billie Briggs	Miller, father of Nell
Stephen Bates	Lawyer, brother to Thomas
Giles Dutton	Father of Robert and Roger

Barbara Dutton	Giles's wife, mother of Robert and Roger
Martin Snigg	Simon's father, once bailiff
Agnes Ogden nee Jagger	Wife of Charles, sister of Kit
Clare Snigg nee Ogden	Wife of Martin, sister of Charles Ogden
Arthur Garnettr	Previous rector of Grange Dale
Cecilia Garnett	Widow of Arthur
Grace Swan	Robert's aunt, onetime inhabitant of Nighby hamlet, sister to Margaret and Barbara
Arthur Swan	Grace's son
Peregrine Leigh (sir)	Former lord of Abbey Grange
Thomas Bates	Missing former steward of Abbey Grange

Real Historical Characters

Thomas Fairfax (sir)	Former commander of the New Model Army
John Lambert	Former deputy to Oliver Cromwell but dismissed for not accepting a hereditary protectorate; tried to seize power after collapse of government in 1659; troops deserted
Charles Stuart	King in waiting
George Monk	Cromwell's military governor of Scotland, appointed commander in chief of all English troops
John Thurloe	Head of intelligence
Thomas Scott	Thurloe's successor

1

ON HIS RETURN FROM the North African and Portuguese missions, Luke was initially surprised that the transfer of power from Oliver Cromwell to his son, Richard, had occurred with the minimum of trouble. This optimism was quickly dispelled. Luke, who had served Oliver Cromwell as a cavalry commander, secret agent, bodyguard, troubleshooter, and latterly as a special envoy, always believed that a just England could only be ensured by a united and dominant army.

It only took brief discussions with several of his comrades to ascertain that the once-united army, without the firm hand of its old commander in chief, Oliver Cromwell, was disintegrating. Only a few of the generals and junior officers, foremost of whom was George Monk in Scotland, maintained the position of a professional army, willing to obey the commands of whichever government was in power.

The majority of Oliver's high command led by Generals Desborough and Fleetwood wanted to increase their influence over the government and reverse the increasing reliance on conservative civilians. They worked to recreate a military republic. Many of the troops who had little faith in a Cromwellian hereditary protectorate or in their current high command were looking to Oliver's former but dismissed deputy, John Lambert, to seize power. Vast numbers of junior officers and men were fed up with their officers and resented the failure of the Cromwellian protectorate to proceed with radical reform and introduce real democracy. They reactivated the democratic demands of the levellers. Finally, there lurked in most branches of the army a residue of religious radicals who wanted to take religious reform to extremes and reintroduce the rule of the saints.

As these divisions became obvious and various sections of the army confronted one another, encouragement was given for an inevitable Royalist insurrection and invasion.

When Luke reported on his two missions to Whitehall, the loss of Oliver Cromwell hit him surprisingly hard. Instead of a friendly chat with the ruler of England who had concluded many of his earlier assignments, he had a formal debriefing with Oliver's surviving secretary to the Council of State and head of intelligence, John Thurloe.

Thurloe thanked Luke for his efforts but candidly admitted that he had no idea whether any of Luke's recommendations would be adopted in the developing fluid political situation. He admitted that the current government did not know where it was heading and was losing support by the day. Most serious of all, the bedrock on which the government had rested for over a decade, the army, was increasingly divided.

Luke took Thurloe's view on the state of the military as the opportunity to tender his resignation from the armed forces and the service of the protectorate.

"I am not surprised. You served the late protector well over fifteen years, and I imagine you want to retire into private life and perhaps marry that delightful widow, Lady Matilda Lynne," Thurloe said.

"Yes, it is my intention to marry Matilda and retire into a quiet country existence," replied Luke.

"That may not be possible! Oliver has left you a new mission from beyond the grave."

"How so?"

"He has left you an impressive wedding present. When he announced your knighthood and promotion to major general, you were sent to North Africa immediately. He had no time to inform you that with the knighthood, he had bestowed upon you a number of estates and added your name to the list of county magistrates."

"Are these estates to be found in my native Cornwall or the adjacent west country or in Lady Matilda's Kent?"

"None of those places. Your estates are in Yorkshire, covering most of one of the dales, Abbey Dale, which leads up to the northern moors. In addition, you have been appointed one of the magistrates for the northern riding of that county."

"The late protector always had an ulterior motive in any acts of generosity. What is wrong with these estates? Are they a hot bed of Royalist activity, religious fanaticism, or uncontrolled criminality?"

"Probably all three. Oliver saw your appointment as the first step to bringing law and order to that part of the benighted north. Given your background, there was undoubtedly a security issue involved, which, following his death, may be much more serious now than it was."

"I am to tackle whatever I find solely on my civil authority as a magistrate?"

"As such, you can nevertheless call on the local militia and any garrison troops in the area. The nearest are at York Castle, where your former deputy and then successor in military intelligence, Sir Evan Williams, has recently been appointed governor."

"One of Oliver's last acts as ruler of England was to send his last two heads of military intelligence to Yorkshire," mused Luke.

"Yes, it must have had some significance for our late protector," commented Thurloe.

"I may have difficulty in convincing Matilda to move north."

"No need to hurry. The estates have been without a resident squire for over a decade. They have been run by a government-appointed steward who fed the rents and income from them straight into the government coffers. Since those properties were formally transferred to you about six months ago, the income from them has been placed into an account in your name held by Sir Evan. On the basis of six months' revenue, you will soon be a very wealthy man."

"I will discuss this unexpected development with Matilda. My current feeling is that we will continue to live in the south, but at some time after the wedding, I will go north to organise my new estates."

John Thurloe handed Luke a large folder. "This contains most of the paperwork relating to your knighthood and appointment as magistrate. Anything else you need wll be handed to you by Sir Evan."

Six weeks later, Luke married Matilda in Canterbury Cathedral, a wedding celebrated for the next two days at Matilda's home, Greytowers, in Kent. It was a small wedding attended by a few of Luke's comrades from his various missions. He took the opportunity to offer his most recent deputy, Capt. Peter Frost, who had returned from Portugal with him, the position of steward. Prior to his military service, Peter had been a lawyer, and during his time at the consulate in Lisbon, he had become an experienced bookkeeper. Luke also recruited a former corporal, Henry Green, overtly as a valet but, in reality, as a bodyguard. Luke was entering an unknown and possibly hostile territory.

Eight weeks on, Luke, Matilda, and Peter sat in an antechamber of York Castle with the governor, Sir Evan Williams. He handed over to Luke the remaining papers pertaining to the transfer of Abbey Grange and associated properties. Evan explained that Luke's estates consisted of the large manor of Abbey Grange, which occupied the lower reaches of Abbey Dale to its confluence with Pickering Beck. As one moved up the dale in a northerly direction, associated properties dotted the countryside. Most of the land on Abbey Grange was currently worked by tenant farmers whose rents made the owner a very wealthy man—an income supplemented by the direct farming of cereals on the better land and sheep farming on outlying properties and on the moor itself. The lands at the head of the dale and onto the moor, while legally owned by the squire of Abbey Grange, consisted of a number of hamlets and isolated farms that had not paid regular dues to their nominal landlord for some time.

All the lands had for centuries been under the control of the Cistercian Abbey, which introduced sheep to the area, animals that continued to dominate the economy of the region. With the dissolution of the monasteries by Henry VIII, the abbey lands were bestowed on one of his supporters, Peregrine Leigh. His descendants held the manor until the last squire, another Peregrine, was removed by Parliament more than a decade earlier for twice taking up arms against it.

Luke interrupted, "Am I taking over a manor of solidly Royalist tenants?"

"Difficult to say! Most of North Yorkshire is Royalist, but Abbey Dale had some strong supporters of Parliament, no doubt created by the general dislike of the Leighs, the last of whom was hated by his Protestant tenants. The Leighs are Papists."

"What is the exact position in regard to the outlying lands? Did the Leighs cease to exert any control?"

"Yes, and it has been made worse over the last decade when the parliamentary-appointed steward made no attempt to exact rents and other dues from any of the outlying areas."

"Tell me about this steward!"

"There are mixed reports about Thomas Bates. Some claim he bribed the local parliamentary officials to give him the position at Abbey Grange and that he did not transfer to government coffers all the income he gathered on its behalf. On the other hand, he actually increased income from the manor. Have Captain Frost carefully audit his books! You may be able to find if any money was illegally siphoned off."

"Is there anything else I should be prepared to face?" asked Luke.

Evan gave a weak smile. "Where do I start? Feuds amongst the tenants, general lawlessness in the moorland areas of your estates, and the dominance of superstition, diabolic practises, and unexplained murders, disappearances, and mysteries. Given your past expertise, the late protector must have chosen you specifically to restore order to this lawless area. I have heard it referred to as the dale of despair."

"How do we get to Abbey Grange?" asked the practical Matilda.

"In good weather, ride or coach to Malton, and then follow the valley of the Pickering Beck north to its confluence with Abbey Beck, and then proceed up Abbey Dale to your manor house."

Evan turned to Luke, saying, "As the weather is bad, I would leave Lady Matilda and her retinue here in York until you are well settled at Abbey Grange."

"Is there anyone that I can rely on in Abbey Grange or within Abbey Dale generally?" asked a dispirited Luke.

"Most of the estate officials are appointees of Bates and may reflect that man's strengths and weaknesses. The one man who has a good reputation in the area, at least in the eyes of the magistrates, if not the locals, and who had nothing to do with Bates, is the constable of Abbey Dale parish, a wealthy yeoman and tenant farmer, Robert Dutton. He spent most of the war here in York Castle. He is one of us. The local rector, Edward Unsworth, is also a strong supporter of the Parliament and the protectorate and for a time was chaplain to Sir Thomas Fairfax. He faces many difficulties as the dale harbours a large number of Papists, accused but never proven witches, and assorted criminals who associate with the moorland brigand, Kit Jagger. Jagger continues to control the upper reaches of the dale. He will challenge your authority at every opportunity."

"Evan, how do you know so much? You have only been in York a few months," observed Matilda.

"When I discovered that Luke was to take over the manor, I made enquiries and discovered that the widow of a former rector of Abbey Dale, a Cecilia Garnett, lived in York Minster. I extracted everything I could from her still-functioning memory."

"Unsworth! Why would a chaplain to Sir Thomas located in the wealthy and comfortable West Riding of the county finish up in an isolated, partly moorland parish on the other side of the county?"

"According to my source, when Sir Thomas ceased to be commander in chief of the parliamentary army and became obsessively critical of his former deputy, Oliver Cromwell, Edward Unsworth publicly rebuked Fairfax for what he saw as traitorous tendencies. He was dismissed and could only find a position well away from the Fairfax influence in the parish of his birth. Ted Unsworth is a local lad with an unsavoury reputation."

"You have certainly made me aware of the difficulties I face. Is there any good news?" asked Luke.

"Apart from any personal attributes you have, your appointment as magistrate will give you immense power in the local area. That part of North Yorkshire has not had a resident magistrate in decades. You might be confronted with a backlog of built-up conflicts and tensions at your initial petty sessions. Dutton should be of great help to you in this regard."

With Lady Matilda and her maid servants remaining in York, Luke, Peter, and Henry Green moved up the Pickering to its confluence with Abbey Beck. Eventually arriving at Abbey Grange, Luke was amazed at its opulence. His prejudiced view of Yorkshire men as penny-pinching, austere recluses certainly did not apply to the former lords of the manor, the Leighs.

2

L UKE EXPECTED TO BE met by the steward, Thomas Bates. This did not happen. They were welcomed instead by a small man with cropped hair in which the original ginger was now overwhelmed by a dominant silvery grey. He was dressed entirely in black and introduced himself as Charles Ogden, deputy steward and reeve. He was accompanied by a large much younger man with a blotchy red face and a disconcerting vacant stare. He announced that he was the manor's bailiff, Simon Snigg.

They exuded mediocrity. Ogden seemed an obsequious toady, obviously maintained in a role for which he was ill suited, while Snigg looked somewhat simple, verging on the village idiot. Perhaps Luke's lifetime in the military had put him out of touch with the typical rural villager?

He thanked Ogden for his welcome and immediately asked the obvious question, "Why is not Mr Thomas Bates here to welcome me?"

"I don't know" was the sheepish response.

"Where is he?" demanded Luke sternly.

Snigg answered. "Sir, none of us know. He supervised the preparations for your arrival over the last few days. He moved his wife and possessions out of the manor house and into a substantial cottage on the edge of the estate, which had been the home of the steward in the days of the Leighs. When he did not appear this morning, we all assumed he was in the cottage, adjusting to his new living conditions."

"And was he?" asked Peter.

"No! When I went to the cottage a few minutes ago to tell him you were seen coming up the dale, all I did was upset his wife. Thomas had not returned there the previous evening. She assumed he had stayed here overnight, attending to any last-minute arrangements that had to be completed before your arrival."

"What did you do then?" asked Luke.

Ogden responded, "I sent a man to find the constable, who replied that given your imminent arrival, he would await your coming and consider your opinion as what should be done. I would expect him and the bigoted rector to arrive at any time to pay their respects."

Luke was given a tour of the building, a large H-shaped, double-storied edifice. The house had been built largely from the masonry of the old abbey that had been progressively demolished. He was introduced to the limited staff of the manor, some of whom had been acquired in the last week for a maximum of a month, pending Luke's appointment of his own people. A meeting with the tenants was arranged for the following day.

Just as darkness descended early on this late winter's day, two visitors were announced by one of the temporary servants. Luke received the constable and rector in the presence of Peter Frost, Ogden, and Snigg.

Constable Dutton did not mince words. "Welcome to Abbey Dale! Ten years without a resident squire has not helped the social or economic development of the area. Bates's only remit was to exact the rents and fill the government coffers. Your reputation goes before you, sir. The previous landowners, the Leighs, were recusants, but this dale, probably because of that, was solidly for Parliament during the Civil War, excluding perhaps a few Catholics protected by the then squire. Your appointment as a magistrate will be a godsend to the restoration of law and order further up the dale and onto the moorlands. For the last two decades, the inhabitants of the dale have had to go to Whitby even for petty sessions. Consequently, most minor crimes were left unpunished. You can conduct your petty sessions here or in the village of Abbeythwaite just up the dale, where most of your tenants and potential workers live. There are several small hamlets farther north and isolated houses as you reach the moors. Most of us in the dale have grazing rights despite the efforts of some illegal settlers there to deny us access. In addition, the criminal landlord of the Pilgrim's Rest, Kit Jagger, a former Royalist, currently exacts the dues that rightfully belong to this manor."

The rector interrupted, "It will be a pleasant change to have a godly magistrate who will have the power to enforce God's Word and speed up

His return to rule us directly." Luke inwardly winced. His rector was a Fifth Monarchy Man determined to see the immediate creation of God's kingdom, a new Jerusalem ruled by the self-appointed saints.

Dutton addressed Snigg, saying, "So your friend Bates has run off before we can prove him to be a thief, if not worse?"

"Mr Bates has disappeared. Why would he run off? For ten years, the government was very happy with his administration of the manor of Abbey Grange. Despite the lies of the rector and yourself, there is not a shred of evidence that Mr Bates is guilty of anything."

Dutton continued his attack on the missing steward. "Now that the new owner is here, a thorough examination of the steward's books will confirm my suspicions. Sir Luke, with your permission, I would like Ogden to locate the books relevant to the management of the estate. You will undoubtedly have a bookkeeper examine them in detail, but even a cursory look will prove my point. Bates only passed on to the government a proportion of the income raised on the estate."

"What did he do with the rest?" asked Luke.

"He certainly did not spend it on improving the manor, assisting the tenants, or helping the church," answered an unnecessarily bitter Unsworth.

Ten minutes later, a chastened and shaking Ogden returned without the books and papers required. "Sir, all the relevant material was kept in a locked coffer in a small alcove. None of the papers or documents are there. The coffer is empty."

"The devious Bates has stolen them to cover up his decade-long theft," muttered Dutton.

"I'm afraid the news is worse than you think. A fire in the grate of an adjoining chamber was still smouldering. I sifted through the charred remains. Mr Bates has burnt all the estate's documents," admitted a chastened Ogden.

"The diabolic fiend!" uttered Unsworth.

Luke took a deep breath. He placed his head in his hands. He could not believe he had been injected into such an unreal world with a cast of flawed personalities—an obsequious reeve; a simpleton bailiff; an extremist, radical vicar; and a vindictive constable. He tried to restore a modicum of rationality and normality to the discussion. "Gentlemen, don't rush to any conclusion, especially one which convicts Bates of being a long-term thief when there is as yet not a shred of evidence against him. Over the years, was he or his wife outstanding in lavish expenditure? Was there the slightest hint that he was spending above the quite generous emoluments provided by the government for stewards caretaking sequestrated properties?"

"No! He probably converted his ill-gotten gain into gold and silver coin, which he concealed until the moment of flight," replied a relentless Dutton.

"Luke, you are not convinced that Bates has run away to conceal his about-to-be-revealed felonies?" asked Peter. "Why not?"

"The burnt documents!"

"What do they prove?"

"That Bates did not burn them."

"How so?"

"Bates as steward would know there is a copy of all the documents relevant to the operation of seized properties kept in York Castle, which last week were given to us. You have already given them a preliminary examination. Burning the copies of documents held here would be a useless exercise, if it was designed to conceal fraud and theft."

"So whoever burnt the documents was not aware of this legal situation and did so to incriminate a probably innocent man," Peter concluded.

Dutton turned to Luke, saying, "I can see why you developed the reputation that you have. If Bates has not run away to cover his misfeasance, why has he absconded from his position?"

"Could he have run away with another woman?" asked Peter.

"I don't know what went on within Abbey Grange. I was rarely invited," replied Dutton.

Ogden and Snigg sniggered. The former muttered loud enough for Luke to hear, "True, not when Mr Bates was at home, but as soon as he left, you visited the mistress."

"Someone had to. Most times, you two were too drunk to protect the then lady of the manor, Mistress Janet Bates," was Dutton's bland response.

"Was Bates involved with women other than his wife?" Luke asked.

"Not to my knowledge," answered Ogden unconvincingly.

Snigg was more believable.

"He had no extramarital relationships within Abbey Grange or in Abbeythwaite. How he related to women away from the manor, I do not know."

Luke once more cast a different perspective over the situation.

"Bates has not disappeared to prevent his arrest for alleged theft, nor do I believe he has disappeared to start a new life with a new partner."

"Then what is your explanation, Sir Luke?" asked Dutton.

"He has been murdered."

There was a stunned silence. Eventually, Unsworth asked, "Why would anyone murder the longtime steward of Abbey Grange, just as he was about to hand over his responsibilities to you?"

"To stop him revealing to me what has happened on this manor and in the dale as a whole over the last decade," answered Luke.

He continued. "Constable Dutton, first thing tomorrow, you will lead a party in search of a body. Take as many of my men that Ogden can free up. Captain Frost will accompany you. Over the next few days, I will question you and the rector and other members of the dale community on any events of the last decade that may have provoked Bates's possible murder."

Next day, Luke questioned Thomas Bates's wife after acquiring a few details about her from Charles Ogden. She was one of the younger daughters of a Border gentry family and spoke with a heavy Scots accent. She had been controller of the household but was not involved in her husband's overall management of the estate. Husband and wife led very separate lives.

The cottage was a misnomer for the steward's new premises. It was a large farmhouse that showed signs of recent renovation. As a maid led Luke to Janet Bates, he made a similar observation of the new fittings and furniture that dominated the rooms through which he was led. If Bates had been siphoning off some of the manorial rents for his own use, they had been well spent on the refurbishment of the cottage. It appeared to provide a more comfortable environment than the manor house itself. Bates would not have spent so much time and money on the cottage if he intended to disappear.

Janet surprised him. She did not resemble the picture that Luke had created in his own mind. She was a tall woman with flowing golden-brown hair, and her clothing was colourful and expensive. This was no conventional Puritan wife. She appeared a little older than Luke, perhaps in her early forties. Despite her current concerns, she was animated and gave Luke a warm welcome.

Luke was formally apologetic. "I imagine the transfer of Abbey Grange to me has caused your husband and yourself a considerable amount of extra work over the last few months. I hope you are happy with this house."

"When Thomas became steward ten years ago, we never expected to be here a decade later. Most confiscated properties were granted to new owners almost immediately."

"Why did the government keep direct control of Abbey Grange for so long?" asked Luke.

"Thomas did an excellent job for his masters. He actually increased the income from the manor, which was directly paid into government coffers."

"Which is why I am surprised that one of the greedy local parliamentary gentry did not obtain such a rich property for himself during that period."

"They were so divided that one faction made sure those of the other did not gain any advantage. And most would not want to confront some of the problems confronting any master of Abbey Grange. Abbey Dale is no heaven on earth."

"Problems such as?"

"There are few within the manor itself, but the farther you climb Abbey Dale to the north, you enter into an almost lawless land. I am not surprised that Cromwell allocated the manor to a leading soldier and also made you a magistrate. It is a pity he did not give you a regiment of troops to help you restore order and decency to the upper dale."

"I will discuss these problems with you later. Unfortunately, I am here about your husband's disappearance. I do not accept the view espoused by the constable and rector that Thomas has fled to escape punishment for defrauding the government of much of its income over the years."

"What is your explanation then of Tommy's disappearance?"

"I suspect your husband was murdered to ensure that some deep-seated secrets of Abbey Dale were never revealed to me."

Janet gasped and put her head in her hands.

Luke realised his insensitivity. "I am sorry for announcing my suspicions so bluntly, but are there any such secrets that could have led to your husband's possible murder?"

Janet remained silent for some time before announcing, to Luke's surprise, "Yes, many come to mind."

“UNTIL TWO YEARS AGO, Thomas was the only authority figure in the dale and, as such, drew to himself much antagonism.”

“What happened two years ago that changed the situation?”

“Two prodigal sons, who in their own way exuded authority, returned to the dale—the odious parson, Unsworth, and the new constable, Robbie Dutton.”

“What do you mean prodigal sons?”

“The Duttons have been farmers in the dale for centuries. Robbie’s father, Giles, was a good friend of Thomas and myself. Robbie left to fight in the parliamentary army in 1642. He spent fourteen years in the service. Perhaps we should address him as Captain Dutton, although he never discusses his time in the army. He only returned to take up the family property on the death of his father and was immediately made parish constable by the magistrates as the parish had failed to appoint any effective officer for several years. It was this tendency for the parish to elect disabled old men or callow youths to the position that forced Thomas to exercise extra-manorial jurisdiction. Robbie quickly proved to be an effective constable but blamed Thomas for the chaotic and anarchic situation he found in the upper dale.”

“And you have no time for Edward Unsworth?”

“A young upstart whose family farmed a small plot farther up the dale. His uncle Richard, a failed farmer but now cobbler to the dale and beyond, is, despite his reduced status, an influential figure. Our former rector who passed away at the ripe old age of eighty-five was tolerant and undemanding. He at the same time kept the significant portion of Catholics in the dale happy and also accepted the more extreme Puritans. Unsworth has a much narrower view of God's church. He reports the Catholics for nonattendance and has made it clear that Anglicans, Presbyterians like myself, and other Puritans, not holding his own dogmatic and narrow view of the world, are not welcomed."

"He is a Fifth Monarchy Man. I have had many a conflict with men of his ilk. Who appoints to the parish of Abbey Dale?"

"You do."

Luke smiled. "So I can dismiss him and appoint another rector?"

"Yes."

"We have strayed from my basic question. Who in the dale would have reason to murder Thomas?"

"Perhaps you should reframe your question? Tommy has had ten years of interaction with the inhabitants of the dale. Over that time, numerous people may have felt that to kill him would solve their personal problems. Your question should be, who had reason to murder Tommy now? He would have been much more vulnerable to attack before your arrival. If Tommy is dead, and I pray that that is not the case, why would he be murdered before he could talk to you? What is it that links Tommy's past with your arrival?"

"At the simplest level, the most obvious, Thomas could have told me something that the murderer could not allow to be passed on. Were there any events during Thomas's long stewardship that particularly troubled him?"

"Many, but the one that troubled him most was the abuse and apparent murder several years ago of a nine-year-old girl, Elizabeth Foxton."

"What happened?"

"Just after Thomas took up his position, Matthew Foxton sent his daughter to ride up the dale and collect a new saddle from a man who worked in a small hamlet on the edge of the moors. The horse returned alone to the Foxton residence in Abbeythwaite without the girl or the new saddle. Tommy organised a search, but her body was never found. The official explanation that emerged was that her horse had thrown her into the beck. The saddle was located farther down the beck by Elizabeth's cousin, Mark Foxton. Both murder and robbery were ruled out."

"Thomas was not happy with this conclusion?"

"Nor was Matthew Foxton, who claimed he had been told his daughter had been abused and then murdered by a group of young men."

"Did Thomas follow up these claims?"

"Yes, but he met a wall of silence. The person who had told Foxton that his daughter had been murdered denied she had done so."

"Did Thomas explain this lack of cooperation?"

"Yes, he believed that the girl had been killed deliberately or accidently by a group of males that included the sons of many of the prominent inhabitants of the dale, but he, as only a manorial steward, had no authority to probe more deeply."

"If the Foxton girl's disappearance is relevant, why would somebody wait almost ten years to silence Thomas?"

"Somebody might have panicked and thought Tommy may have kept notes of his abortive investigation and would hand them over to you, a magistrate with all the power of the law, to reopen the case."

"He kept notes?"

"On everything."

"So the documents burnt in the grate up at the manor may have been such notes, not only the legal papers pertaining to the manor?"

"Yes!"

"Was there any other incident that seriously troubled him?"

"The explosion in the hamlet of Nighby and resultant fire that destroyed all the houses and killed all the inhabitants. Tommy received no help at all from neighbouring hamlets or the people in Abbeythwaite. There was a general feeling that the inhabitants of that hamlet were devil worshipers and their houses had been struck by lightning, a punishment from God that did not need any investigation."

"Thomas suspected otherwise?"

"There is a lot of ill feeling in the upper dale and other hamlets such as Elderby had a long-standing feud with Nighby. Tommy thought that enemies of the hamlet had burnt it to the ground."

Janet's expression changed. She looked at Luke intently, and he felt her eyes eating into his head. She suddenly announced, "I don't think this discussion will get you far, my lord. There are so many people with secrets to hide within the dale that if Thomas has been killed, it could be by someone who believes their sexual indiscretions, or their record as a sheep stealer, or as a recipient of stolen goods might be revealed. North of us here, up the dale into the moors, is a lawless area where to a man, they would be very worried by the arrival of a resident magistrate with the authority and power to enforce order."

"I agree, but as a sign of my intentions to bring order to the dale, my reopening of the Foxton case might bring forth some useful evidence on other issues."

"It will certainly be an effective way for a new magistrate to understand the factions, feuds, and attitudes of those living in the dale and on the moors."

"Is Matthew Foxton still in Abbeythwaite?"

Janet reacted violently to the question, hitting her head with two hands and proclaiming, "I am a fool. The most pertinent fact relevant to what we have been discussing, and I did not mention it. After his neighbours refused to confirm their story of a murder to Tommy, Matthew left Abbeythwaite for Whitby, where he worked as a fisherman. He had a ninety-nine-year lease to work part of your estate and live in the house that came with it. His young nephew, Mark, maintained the lease and lived in the house until a month ago, when Matthew returned to resume his life here as a tenant farmer."

Luke had his first negative thought concerning Janet. Why had she not mentioned this key development when discussing Elizabeth Foxton's disappearance? It could be Matthew Foxton's return rather than his own arrival that provoked the suspected murder of Thomas Bates.

As he left the cottage, Luke encountered Robert Dutton, about to visit Janet. What was Dutton to her? This relationship required further investigation. Had a ruthless lover removed an unwanted husband? That would be a simple and not unusual explanation. And had wife and lover burnt documents in the grate to incriminate the unfortunate spouse?

Luke found Matthew Foxton and his nephew, Mark, digging drains on their leased land. He introduced himself as the new lord of the manor and enquired if Foxton's return was for the long term. Luke need not have worried about the man's sensitivity to him referring to the decade-old possible murder of his daughter. Matthew immediately raised it, citing Luke's appointment as magistrate as the reason for his return.

"Sir, my daughter was murdered ten years ago, and nobody lifted a finger to bring her killers to justice. There was no real law in the dale. My wife died giving birth to Elizabeth, and with the girl's death, I did not wish to remain here. My nephew, Mark Foxton, my brother's eldest son, maintained the lease in my name. When I heard that the new lord of the manor here was to be a magistrate, and had been one of Cromwell's generals, I return seeking justice."

"I shall do my best. I have already been informed of your daughter's case. At the time, did you blame Thomas Bates for the lack of action?"

"Tom Bates, not at all! He was one of few people in the village that believed that Elizabeth had been murdered, although I initially thought he might be protecting his younger brother, Stephen."

"I didn't know that Thomas had a brother."

"The Bates were and are yeomen farmers near where Abbey Dale joins Pickering Beck. They also had smaller portions of land adjacent to your manor. Thomas's father married a second time later in life and produced a nasty little piece of work, Stephen, who hates his elder half brother."

"Any clear reason?"

"Very simple, inheritance. Stephen received absolutely nothing from his father's estate. Thomas at the time, feeling sympathetic to his half brother's situation, used his influence with the county committee to find him as job as a government lawyer. If Thomas expected any thanks, he was disappointed. It only increased Stephen's resentment."

"Where is Stephen now?"

"I don't know," replied Matthew.

Another explanation entered Luke's head. Thomas's disappearance may be simply a family matter.

"You may not have heard, but Thomas Bates has disappeared. His enemies claim he has run off to avoid me arresting him for fraud and theft, but others like myself think he has been murdered to stop him revealing to me someone's deeply held secret. What do you think?"

"I know little of recent developments in the dale as I have just returned after nine years' absence, but Mark may know more."

He turned to his nephew. "Mark, if someone has murdered Thomas Bates, who would it be?"

Luke appreciated the direct approach. "A toss-up between Rector Unsworth and Constable Dutton."

"Why the rector and the constable?"

"Since their arrival, they had displayed open antagonism towards Thomas Bates, bad mouthing him at every opportunity."

"Why?"

"They blame Bates for all the problems of the dale, which they argue stems from his support of us Catholics. That is ridiculous! However, his recent behaviour in appointing the unfortunate Simon Snigg to replace his revered father is inexplicable. It fuels Dutton's antagonistic approach. Snigg is an incompetent that you must remove immediately."

"Could Bates have been blackmailed into making such an inappropriate appointment?" said Luke, probing asked.

"Maybe, but he has had a reputation of assisting the underdogs. In this dale, they are a group of Catholic families whom, throughout his tenure as steward of the manor, he has employed and protected, but such kindness does not excuse the appointment of idiots such as Simon."

Luke changed the subject. "Mark, what can you tell me about Janet Bates? Is she popular with the tenants and the workers on the manor?"

Mark laughed. "She was ignored by most, very popular with a few. Or rather, she ignored most of us and concentrated her attentions on a small group. She is certainly not the dour, moralistic Presbyterian everybody expected."

Matthew intervened, saying, "That is because she is not from the normal Scottish gentry. She is the daughter of the reiver raiders of the Borders, who knew no law or morals but engaged in the most violent solution of their problems. Reiver women were wild."

"Janet was wild?" queried Luke.

"For years, she had an affair with our constable's father, Giles Dutton, and more recently with the constable himself," claimed Mark.

Luke left the Foxtons with two lines of enquiry to follow should Thomas Bates's body be found. Was the murderer a jealous younger brother or his wife's lover?

A FORTNIGHT LATER, MATILDA had settled in. With no news of Thomas Bates, she invited Janet to return to the manor house as her companion. Matilda was anxious for mature female company, especially a woman who could update her with the gossip of the dale and with the issues involved in running the manor of Abbey Grange. Luke formally confirmed Peter Frost as steward and Henry Green as his valet and factotum. Charles Ogden would continue as deputy steward for the time being, and Simon Snigg would remain as bailiff but, given his limited abilities, with much reduced responsibilities.

After a discussion with Constable Dutton, it was agreed that any group he needed to assemble to enforce the law would include Frost and Green and that at any time Luke as magistrate could personally lead the law enforcement unit. Luke made it clear that he would to be a hands-on magistrate and his own men would play the major role in the law's day-to-day enforcement.

They then reviewed the disappearance of Thomas Bates. It was pointed out by Dutton that if Bates had been murdered as Luke thought, his body would probably never be found. There were so many places, especially on the moor, where a body might be concealed with no chance of ever being discovered. If he had absconded as advanced by others, the consensus was that he would have gone to Whitby and from thence anywhere in the known world. The more imaginative suggested he was starting a new life in the Americas, either with his ill-gotten gains or with a new woman.

Luke, against Dutton's advice, decided to concentrate on the old case of Elizabeth Foxton. He felt intuitively that it was relevant to Thomas's disappearance. He revisited Matthew Foxton to probe the issue further. "Matthew, who told you that your daughter had been murdered?"

"The current constable's late mother, Barbara Dutton."

"And she then refused to repeat the claim to Bates or any other authority?"

"Yes."

"Where did she hear such a story?"

"From a woman who had passed through Abbeythwaite from farther up the dale. She claimed she did not know the woman's name."

"That was unfortunate!"

"Yes, but I did my own sleuthing and know it was Grace Swan. She used to stay with the Duttons regularly when she travelled up and down the dale."

"Did you question her?"

"I tried, but she was murdered before I could meet her."

Luke began to wonder if Matthew might be obsessed but gently asked, "That is a serious accusation. What happened?"

"Swan lived in Nighby, and the day before I had arranged to visit her, the hamlet was blown up, and all of its inhabitants burnt to death."

"I have heard about that incident. Thomas Bates was very concerned by it."

"Yes, he thought it was suspicious but was unable to convince anybody in authority to investigate it. The dale preferred to believe that the hamlet had been hit by lightning and it was God's revenge for its past diabolic practises, which was absolute rubbish. Nighby was a godly, respectable hamlet unlike its rival, the accusing Elderby."

"This false idea was put forward by the inhabitants of Elderby?"

"Yes, Elderby has had a centuries-old feud with Nighby and was supported in this vendetta by a shadowy moorland figure who survives by sheep stealing, smuggling, and a host of other criminal activities. He is the local crime boss who has been allowed to operate unhindered for a decade or more. There were rumours that he set the hamlet alight."

"Kit Jagger?"

"Yes. He operates out of an isolated tavern well into the moors called ironically the Pilgrim's Rest. Centuries ago, it served as the last night's accommodation for pilgrims after crossing the moors from Whitby, who were visiting the great abbey that once was located in this dale."

Luke left Matthew and sought out the constable. "Robert, looking into the disappearance of Elizabeth Foxton, I have been told that your mother was a potential source of evidence, who, when pressed, refused to repeat her initial claim that Elizabeth had been murdered. Did she ever speak to you about the matter?"

"I was away with the army during that period."

"Did she not write to you?"

"Rarely! It was so long ago, but I do remember that her letters at that time were not her usual relaxed collection of local gossip. Now thinking about it for the first time in years, I should have seen that she was troubled by something, but she gave no details. You could ask her surviving sister, Margaret. When my father died, I was happy for Mother to stay on our farm, but she decided to move to York to live with her widowed sister, who had been married to a wealthy town merchant and alderman."

"Next time I am in York, I will question your aunt," Luke promised.

"Don't be too optimistic about the outcome. She is very old, and her mind is not what it used to be. What she tells you will be a mix of truth and fantasy."

"I understand your mother was a friend of Grace Swan, who was killed in the fire at Nighby several years ago."

"More than a friend! Auntie Grace was another of my mother's sisters."

"Did your mother write to you concerning your aunt's death?"

"Yes, I do remember that letter. My usually gentle and quiet mother was livid with rage."

"What angered her?"

"The opinion expressed by the superstitious inhabitants of the upper dale that the lightning strike was a judgement of God on a hamlet that practised diabolic arts. She felt this defamed her God-fearing sister."

"On an entirely different matter, I hear that Janet Bates is not the conventional middle-class wife but a little on the wild side."

"Absolute rubbish. I was not here during most of the last decade, but my father was a very close friend of both Thomas and Janet during all of that period. She was the perfect lady of the manor."

"Then how did this picture of her as an unconventional woman arise?"

"Pure ignorance. It was known that she was born on the Borders as part of a reiver family. The days when the reivers were an uncontrolled violent community that survived on mutual atrocities were ended when the late king's father became ruler of both England and Scotland over fifty years ago. He subdued the recalcitrant families and imposed the discipline of English law. As a boy, Janet's father may have experienced the wild life, but Janet was brought up in a God-fearing Presbyterian household."

Luke thought, *He defends Janet Bates a little too fervently. The rumours concerning an affair between the two of them are probably true.*

Three weeks later, Luke was in York and met Barbara Dutton's surviving sister, Margaret. He was received by an elderly but sprightly woman in a reception room that also reflected the immense wealth of the family. She immediately commented, "My nephew wrote to me saying that the new master of Abbey Grange in his role as local magistrate wished to talk to me about past events in the dale affecting my departed sisters Grace and Barbara."

"Yes, I am investigating the disappearance of a young girl, Elizabeth Foxton. Barbara passed on to the girl's father information she received from her sister Grace that the child had been murdered. Then she refused to repeat that claim before any authority." Luke turned to his hostess, saying, "Unfortunately, I don't expect you can help me much regarding events in Abbey Dale a decade ago as you were here in York?"

"Quite the opposite. I probably know more than most of the inhabitants of the dale. Both my sisters were prolific letter writers, especially Grace."

"So did Grace refer to the Elizabeth Foxton disappearance in any letters to you?"

"Yes. She was appalled. She said the little girl was set upon by four or five young men, physically abused, and ultimately thrown into the beck."

"How did she know this?"

"She saw it herself but was too far away to recognise the young males involved. She was on a ridge above the beck and, being on foot, could not reach the scene to help the girl, although she admitted she was too scared to go any closer to the scene. She wrote a similar letter to Barbara, who, in what proved to be an inappropriate act, told the girl's father and then refused to repeat it before any authority."

"Was Grace cross with Barbara over this?"

"Very!"

"Because she told Foxton or because she refused to testify?"

"Both, but she was primarily concerned that her name had been linked with a serious claim that had not been pursued by any authority and that this made her potentially vulnerable to the murderers."

"Did you really suspect that the youths who murdered Elizabeth or someone acting for them burnt your sister alive to stop her pursuing justice?"

"It was a possibility."

"Why did Barbara refused to testify?"

"She was frightened."

"Of whom? The alleged murderers?"

"No, her husband. Giles demanded that she retract her statement on the grounds that it created unnecessary angst for Matthew Foxton and upset many of the inhabitants of the dale and that as Grace could not recognise any of the men, there was no point to any investigation."

"Did Grace accept this interpretation of her brother-in-law?"

"In no way! She was blunt in her last letter to me. She felt that the leading citizens of the dale were involved in a cover-up."

"What sort of cover-up?"

"That the four or five young men involved were the sons of prominent dale families. Even if there was only a distant chance that your son was one of the men Grace had seen, you would not want the matter probed further."

"Why wasn't it followed up by the authorities?"

"Time and place. It was a critical time in the Civil War when far more important issues dominated the dales, and the nearest magistrates were in Malton to the south, or Whitby to the northeast, and there was no effective local constable."

"That was a pity."

"Don't despair, Sir Luke. If you want evidence of a cover-up, what happens next proves it."

"What happened?"

"Within a few weeks of Grace's claim, six or seven of the young men of the dale left the area. Barbara did not name them, but I know one of them was my nephew, Barbara's youngest son, Roger."

"I did not realise that Robert had a younger brother."

"There is no love lost between Robert and his sibling. Their father, imitating the gentry, left everything to Robert. He even left his own wife penniless. That is why she spent the last days of her life here."

Luke noted that this was not the picture that Robert had drawn.

"Is your nephew Roger still in the area?"

"At the other end of the county. He is a general merchant in Whitby."

"Good. I am holding petty sessions there in few weeks. I will seek him out. On another matter, I understand that your sister Barbara and her husband Giles were great friends of Thomas and Janet Bates. Did she ever make any comments regarding them that might explain Thomas's sudden disappearance?"

Lady Margaret screwed up her face and remained silent for some time.

Luke waited patiently for an answer.

"Sir, Barbara's mind had been failing for some months, and I do not know whether what she told me was true or a figment of her imagination. After Giles died, she asked me if she could come and live with me. When I asked her why she did not want to stay on the family property in Abbey Dale and live with her son, she bitterly exclaimed that it would constantly remind her of her husband's betrayal."

"Did she elaborate?"

"Not then, but months later, she made disparaging remarks about Janet Bates. It appears that Giles had a relationship with her. And now Robbie will also not hear a word against her. He has probably replaced his father as the lover of this disgusting woman."

"I have heard rumours along such lines," admitted Luke.

He returned to Abbey Grange and spent two delightful days alone with Matilda. Luke regretted that he had delayed marriage bliss for so long.

On the third day, he went to see Janet Bates again but was disinclined to raise matters of a personal nature. "Janet, I am probing the Elizabeth Foxton case. In the weeks immediately following her death, a large number of local youths left the dale. Do you remember who they were?"

"Too long ago! However, the manorial documents will help as many of the youths were employed by the manor before they moved. As Tommy was muster sergeant for the local militia, his muster book would detail who was here at various times of that year. Give me a few days, and I will bring you a list."

Janet was as good as her word. "Luke, six lads left in that period—some returned, others have never reappeared. They are an interesting lot, including my brother-in-law, Stephen, who left for York, and we have not seen him for four or five years. Simon Snigg went to Whitby but returned within a year, and Thomas allowed him to assist his father and then recently inexplicably appointed bailiff. Our not-so-loveable rector, Ted Unsworth, left for Cambridge. Mark Foxton disappeared at the same time but came back within a month or two to take over his uncle's tenure. Roger Dutton, the constable's brother, went to Whitby and is still there, and Arthur Swan also went to York and has not been seen since, although it is believed that he had the misfortune to visit his mother on the night of the fire and that he was incinerated in the blaze."

5

WITH THE ESTATE RUNNING smoothly under Peter's supervision; the household functioning effectively controlled by Matilda, advised by Janet; and minor local law-and-order issues effectively monitored by Robert, Luke concentrated on his magisterial role. In this, he faced a dilemma. Should he concentrate on the old case of Elizabeth Foxton or the immediate problem of lawlessness in the upper dale and on the moors?

The weight of recent cases forced him for the moment, against his own intuition, to give priority to the present. Sheep stealing, denial of access to the inhabitants of the lower dale, smuggling, illegal taverns and mines, assaults, murders, rapes, and diabolic practises were all attributed to Kit Jagger by the inhabitants of the lower dale. The Pilgrim's Rest, a few miles into the moors, was the den of iniquity spreading its poison throughout the area. According to Robert Dutton, Luke must confront Kit Jagger. He would do it immediately, but how many men should he take with him to the Pilgrim's Rest? He needed enough to protect himself but not enough to provoke the brigand into immediate conflict.

Two days later, ten heavily armed men, including Luke, Peter, Harry, Simon, and Robert, left Abbey Grange and made their way slowly up the dale. When they reached its head and began to cross the moor, Luke sent Simon, who said he knew Kit Jagger well, ahead of the main party. He was to inform the brigand that the new magistrate had come in peace to speak with him.

On either side of the slightly elevated road that led to the Pilgrim's Rest, the moorland was waterlogged. The two-storied tavern itself was visible for miles. It was an impressive edifice surrounded by several outbuildings, including surprisingly extensive stables. As they approached its main door, an incredibly tall man with flowing blond hair and a patch over one eye emerged. He was followed by Simon.

"Welcome, gentlemen! My men will house your horses in the stables. Tied to the hitching rail, they would be dead by morning due to the intense frost we have been experiencing. A roaring fire in the snug awaits you all as do lashings of lamb stew." Kit was the perfect host. His serving girls were buxom and inviting, his food and drink more than excellent, and the company of him and his men enjoyable. After an hour or so, Luke suggested to Kit that they adjoin to another room to discuss the matters that had brought him as magistrate to the moors.

Once alone, Kit was blunt. "Yes, why exactly are you here, general?"

"Simple! The dales men have indicated that all crimes in Upper Abbey Dale and on the adjacent moorlands stem from you. I am here to discover the truth for myself and, given my current position and experience, to vigorously enforce law and order. If needs be, I will commandeer a company of troops from York Castle and wipe you out. But I am hopeful that force will not be necessary."

"I will not deny much of what you imply. However, what civilized society might define as a crime, in this isolated and bleak environment, many such acts are necessary to survive. We could come to an arrangement. You have enough to do keeping law and order in the lower dale, especially as I hear from Snigg, you are reopening a number of old cases. Turn a blind eye to my moneymaking enterprises, and I will keep my people within the law," proposed Kit.

"I am not averse to your suggestion, at least until I am in a position to act against you, but I must convince myself that you are not responsible for the major crimes laid at your doorstep—numerous murders, disappearances, and rapes. In one cold case that I am examining, the disappearance of a young girl, Elizabeth Foxton, a key witness to her death, Grace Swan, was killed in the destruction of Nighby hamlet. You are universally blamed for this atrocity."

"Can I ask why, with so many current problems, you are wasting your time on old cases?"

"The former steward of Abbey Grange, Thomas Bates, went missing just before I arrived. I believe he has been murdered so that he could not tell me something. I thought one of these old cases might provide a motive for his demise."

"Tommy Bates is missing?"

"Yes. Why are you so interested?"

"Tommy and I were, and still are, great friends. We spent most of our childhood together roaming the moors and then were sent to the same school in Whitby. Tommy left for the Inns of Court in London, and I had various jobs until the outbreak of the war when I joined the Royalist army of the Earl of Newcastle."

"Did you last long in the Royalist camp?"

"No, I served for little more than a year, but I had no desire to be slaughtered by the invading Scottish army for a cause to which I had no loyalty. I escaped to the moors, where I began this lucrative career."

"If you knew Thomas Bates so well, is there anything that you can suggest that may have led to his disappearance or murder?"

"Thor's treasure!"

"What is that?"

"An old legend that obsessed us both as children. A thousand years ago, the Vikings looted Whitby Abbey of its gold and silver plate and bejewelled statues. A Saxon army cut them off before they could reach their ships, drove them onto the moors, and in a place still called Battle Moor, the Vikings were allegedly wiped out. Amazingly, none of the Abbey's stolen treasure was ever recovered."

"In the thousand years since, you would have thought someone would have found something?" remarked Luke.

"In the fifteen years I have lived and worked on the moors, I have probably entered every possible cave on these uplands and had my men dig extensively in the vicinity of Battle Moor, to no avail."

"So how does Thomas Bates fit into this treasure hunt?"

"Someone probably found the treasure centuries ago, but it is the type of discovery you would not broadcast. The only piece of the possible loot that has ever been brought to my attention was by Tommy only six months ago."

"Bates found some of the treasure? Where?"

"On your own estate, general. One of your tenants found in his pigpen a tiny gold candle extinguisher and a small statue of a Norse goddess that was all buttocks and breasts. Tommy, on his way to Whitby some time ago, showed me the objects and tried to convince me that we should both renew our search for the treasure's full recovery."

"How did he explain its discovery on Abbey Grange?"

"Not all the Vikings had been killed on Battle Moor, and one or more of them escaped down Abbey Dale, hiding the loot as they went."

"Which tenant found the gold object?"

"I don't know, but I am sure Tommy would have told his Scots wife, the formidable and alluring Janet."

"The discovery certainly creates a number of possibilities concerning Thomas's disappearance. Thomas was here on a more recent trip to Whitby. Did he drop in on his return trip?"

"Apparently, but I was not here. The girls tell me he was especially agitated or excited, depending on whom you believe."

"He was not his usual calm, sensible self?"

"Have a word with Elinor. She was always his favourite. I will fetch her."

Elinor was the most buxom of the servants and initially assumed that she had been offered by her employer to the visiting magistrate. The newly married Luke quickly explained the situation and began his questioning. "When Thomas Bates was here just before Easter, was he his normal self?"

"Sir, I don't know what you mean. Tommy was never the normal customer. We never had sex. He simply wanted to talk. He should have been a Catholic, always wanting to confess to me."

"Great! If he had confessed to priests, they would never tell me what was said. I am sure you will be more cooperative. How long has Thomas been confiding in you?"

"Five or six years."

"Did he tell you anything over that period that might explain his current disappearance?"

"Sleep with me all night, and I will reveal all," purred Elinor, still anxious to snare a customer.

"Relax, wench. I will pay you double your fee for a whole night, and we will just talk. What did he discuss on his last visit?"

"Going to or coming from Whitby?"

"Was there a difference?"

"Yes. On his way there, he talked mainly about his problems on the manor, getting it ready to hand over to you. On his way back, he was elated. He had discovered something at Whitby, which he claimed would explain a lot of the problems in Abbey Dale, and your imminent arrival would enable some action to be taken at last."

"Did anybody arrive from Whitby with or just after Thomas?"

"As I spent the night with Tommy, I do not know. You would have to ask the other girls."

Before he left in the morning, Luke ascertained that nobody had accompanied or followed Thomas from Whitby.

On his return to Abbey Grange, Luke immediately spoke to Janet. "I heard that some time ago, one of the tenant farmers discovered a small gold object in his pigpen. Who was that?"

"Tim Carver!"

"It must have excited Thomas?"

"He was beside himself. He has been obsessed with Thor's treasure since childhood. The gold candle extinguisher turned out to be brass and was probably stolen from our local parish church. There is no proof it was part of the Whitby loot. And the small statue may have been Celtic rather than Norse."

"Do you think the rumours that they were part of Thor's treasure in any way led to Tommy's disappearance?"

"Only if Tim talked and exaggerated."

"What do you mean?"

"The discovery of the apparent gold object was initially kept a secret. Only Tim, Tommy, and myself knew. Tim wanted to dig up his whole tenancy without the rest of the farmers knowing that he was looking for hidden treasure. If Tim thought Tommy had told anybody else, he may not have been happy."

"A possible murderer?" asked Luke.

"No, especially since the treasure proved to be brass rather than gold."

"I will talk to Tim. What can you tell me about him?"

"He is your youngest tenant, in his late twenties. He only took over the family's ninety-nine-year lease when his father died last year. His wife, Mary, is younger still, perhaps in her late teens."

Finding nobody working the Carver lease, Luke knocked on the door of their cottage in Abbeythwaite.

It was answered by a very young woman whom Luke assumed was Mary. She was a little flustered at seeing the squire at her door and, after a clumsy curtsy, asked, "What can I do for you, sir?"

"I came to see your husband."

"He is in Eskdale, buying sheep."

"Have you lived in Abbey Dale all your life?"

"Yes, I was born here on Abbey Grange and have never left it. My father is your deputy steward. My birth name was Mary Ogden."

"Did you know the young girl Elizabeth Foxton?"

"Yes, she was my best friend. If only I had stayed with her on that fateful day, she may still be alive."

"What happened?"

"When her father sent Elizabeth to collect the new saddle farther up the dale, I went with her . . . but only as far as Nighby, where I left her to visit a cousin. She asked me to stay with her, but I refused. I have had nightmares about it ever since."

"What do you think happened to her?" asked a probing Luke, probing.

"Her horse was spooked by something as it crossed the bridge and threw her into the stream, where she apparently drowned, although her body was never found. That's what Father and Mr Bates told all the manor children."

"Was there a different story circulating?"

"Some of the younger boys said their elder brothers told a different tale, and it so appalled their parents that they were all sent away from Abbeythwaite within weeks."

Luke smiled to himself. Mary's comments confirmed his suspicions. He changed the direction of his questioning. "On another matter, I have heard that your husband discovered some hidden treasure. Is that true?"

Mary, who had relaxed during Luke's earlier questioning, tensed and appeared quite disconcerted.

"I don't know where you heard such a ridiculous story."

"Has your husband really gone to buy sheep, or has he gone off with Mr Bates, looking for more treasure?"

"Mr Bates did fill Tim's head with silly stories about Viking loot, but they have not gone off together treasure hunting. Tim did find a small metallic object in the field, but it was only a brass candle extinguisher, probably stolen from the local parish church years ago. If there was treasure on our land, it would have been unearthed over previous centuries of ploughing and livestock ravaging."

"Do you have the brass object?"

"No, Tim handed it in to Mr Bates. It belongs to you as possessor of the manor."

"If it were gold, it rightfully belongs to the government. But I don't think any of us would report such a tiny object as you describe."

L UKE DISCUSSED HIS ONGOING enquiries with Matilda. He compared his list of suspects in the Elizabeth Foxton murder with the names provided by Kit Jagger, and allowing for those whose deaths could be verified, seven names remained—Stephen Bates, Simon Snigg, Edward Unsworth, Mark Foxton, Roger Dutton, Arthur Swan, and Timothy Carver. Only Snigg, Unsworth, Foxton, and Carver were currently in the dale. Swan was believed to have been burnt to death, but no remains were ever identified. Bates had left York, and his current whereabouts were unknown, and Dutton was in Whitby.

Matilda remained concerned by Luke's determination to concentrate on the Foxton case. "You began this investigation to help you understand Thomas Bates's disappearance. The link between the two cases, if any exists, is tenuous. Concentrate directly on finding Thomas! My conversations with Janet suggest that there were problems confronting him in the last few months that could have a more direct bearing on his disappearance."

"Such as?"

"Ask Janet for details, but he was struggling to counter deliberate economic sabotage in the months before we came—cattle and sheep driven into crops that were trampled into oblivion, savage dogs released from their chains that then killed lambs and calves."

Luke took Matilda's advice and questioned Janet. "In the months before we arrived, this manor was subjected to a series of attacks aimed at destroying its economic livelihood?"

"Yes. At least six tenant farmers and ourselves were subject to unexplained attacks. The most devastating was that just before last harvest, one small field of cereal crops was trampled into the ground by livestock driven through them. Two tenants had their cattle poisoned by someone who threw mercury-soaked feed into their stalls. Some had their dogs freed from their chains and let loose, slaughtering the poultry and young lambs of their neighbours."

"What possible motives could the perpetrator of these outrages have?"

"It could only be a personal vendetta by someone against the individuals whose property was attacked," replied Janet.

"Or part of an extortion racket! Did Thomas ever receive a threatening note indicating that if he did not hand over a certain sum, his crops and animals would be destroyed? It has happened elsewhere."

"He never mentioned it to me, if he did. If it was a major extortion racket, more damage would have been done. The attacks were sporadic and tapered off in the last few months before you arrived."

"That could be explained by Thomas paying off the extortioner after he experienced what they were willing to do. If there are discrepancies in the accounts, they may be explained by this development. Thomas had to siphon off some of the estates' profits to meet the extortion demands."

"No, these problems did not stem from organised crime. Many of the acts were very petty. They were designed to cause annoyance rather than serious economic loss—driving sheep and cattle to the pound, ripping up hedges that marked the boundaries between fields, or more common in this dale, smashing down stone fences and enclosures."

"Did anybody suffer more than the others?"

"Yes, but it was not one of your tenants. And that property did suffer substantial economic loss. It was the church. The cereal crops on the glebe, the church land, were completely burnt to the ground. The tithing young lambs, piglets, and calves, which the rector had just received, were slaughtered. Ted Unsworth put it down to the godless of the parish, which in his eyes were the Catholics, but others saw it as a family feud, Richard Unsworth getting his own back on the man who, as a boy, destroyed his property with similar acts of vandalism."

"Was it generally believed that Richard Unsworth was responsible for the other vandalism?"

"No, people split along the sectarian divide. Catholic families were convinced that it was Richard Unsworth, while most Protestants agreed with Ted Unsworth that it was probably a Papist plot."

"Who are these Catholic families?" Luke asked,. ing

"After ten years of Protestant dominance, only four of the Catholic families who faithfully served the Leighs, and were protected by them, remain. They include two of the leading servants of the manor—your deputy steward, Ogden, and your bailiff, Snigg. Ogden's daughter married into a third remaining Papist family, the Carvers. The fourth are the Foxtons."

Later that day, Luke spoke to Charles Ogden. "I understand from Janet Bates that your situation as Papists has deteriorated in recent years. As the new lord of the manor, I shall show no discrimination against you as long as you do not consort with Jesuit priests or Irish or Spanish agents. What has happened in recent years to upset your situation?"

"In a word, Edward Unsworth."

"He does appear an intolerable bigot."

"Sir, the Ogdens, Sniggs, Foxtons, and Carvers served the Leighs for a century and a quarter and throughout that period remained faithful to mother church. When the Leighs had the manor of Abbey Grange taken from them and a Protestant steward installed by the Parliament, I was retained as his deputy and Simon Snigg's father as bailiff, a position later given to Simon on his father's death. We all attended the parish church as required by law, and in return for our compliance, the old rector, Arthur Garnett, did not draw attention to the fact or ever indulge in a tirade against the papacy and our beliefs. Unsworth is the opposite. During the early days of his incumbency, we attended as usual, but after weeks of vicious personal attacks on us and our faith, we have refused to go to the parish church."

"And Unsworth has demanded that Dutton report your absence to the authorities?"

"Yes, but Mr Bates used his influence to prevent it from happening. You will no doubt receive a direct request from Unsworth to take the matter to the quarter sessions and have us heavily fined, such fines to revert to the parish church and Unsworth's pocket."

"Will you resume church attendance if I prevent Unsworth from attacking you or your faith?"

"I doubt whether Edward Unsworth would listen to such a blasphemous and diabolic suggestion," answered Charles with a knowing smile.

"He'll listen, or he will leave! This dale has enough problems without Unsworth creating additional and unnecessary friction."

"While you are here, my lord, I should inform you that the architecture of Abbey Grange reflects its Catholic origins. There is a hidden door concealed by the wall panels in your library that leads to a large priest's hole, which was used as a Catholic chapel under Mr Bates, and an escape tunnel that finishes up in one of the cottages in Abbeythwaite."

"Is this widely known?"

"No. The servants who were here in the days of the Leighs would know of it, but Mr Bates ordered that newcomers not be told."

"In whose cottage does the tunnel end?"

"That occupied for generations by the Carvers."

"Where exactly in that cottage does the tunnel emerge?"

"Not within the cottage itself but in one of the outhouses, which currently is used as a pigpen for pregnant sows but from time to time has also served as a hen coop.

Luke was very interested in this information. Next day, accompanied by Harry Green, he found the panels that concealed the hidden door. They descended a deep flight of stairs into the priest's hole. It was a large room that now contained a bed, a cupboard, a table, several chairs, and a box of large candles. Luke was amazed as he removed the top covers of the bed. Beneath were reasonably fresh, clean sheets. The bed had recently been used and remade.

Opening the cupboard proved the recent use of the room. There was a jug of stale ale and a loaf of bread that was still edible. They left the priest's hole and gradually made their way along the tunnel until they reached another small flight of stairs that led to a trapdoor, through which Luke could detect the smell of pigs. He decided not to terrify the sows and their piglets by suddenly appearing through their floor, but he would talk to the Carvers about their knowledge and use of the tunnel.

But first, he raised the matter with Janet. "Were you aware of the priest's hole and escape tunnel?"

Janet hesitated and then replied, "Tommy showed me the entrance from the library in case the manor was attacked by Royalist troops. We were to hide there until the threat passed."

"Did you ever use the tunnel?"

"No! The Royalists never came."

Luke thought the response was slightly misdirected. He repeated his question with a different emphasis. "So you have not been there in the last couple of weeks?"

"Of course not!"

"Someone has. Did Thomas use it in the days before he disappeared?"

"How would I know?"

"Maybe Thomas disappeared along it?"

"That is a possibility," Janet conceded.

"Come with me to the priest's hole. You may recognise some of the goods there, especially anything that may have belonged to Thomas."

Janet appeared reluctant, but Luke chose not to notice her hesitancy.

With Harry, they made their way to the clandestine room, where an excess of large candles soon lit up every corner and crevice. On viewing the bread, Janet appeared troubled, or was it feigned concern? "That loaf came from the manor's kitchen," she announced.

"Which means that any member of the household could have taken it?" asked Luke.

"Yes!"

"Sir, do not place too much reliance on it being brought here by one of your households. I have observed on two occasions kitchen staff giving or selling a loaf to one of the village lads," said Harry.

"That was a problem," confessed Janet. "Tommy long suspected that staff inflated their earnings by selling manorial goods to the villagers. He could never catch them at it."

"So for our purposes, the loaf could have been brought here by Abbey Grange servants or Abbeythwaite villagers?" concluded Luke. said, summarising

"Or even further afield. The bread could have been given or sold to an inhabitant of one of the hamlets where very few bake their own bread," added Janet.

"Do you recognise the sheets on this bed? They are much better quality than one would expect from any of the locals. Are they from the manor?"

"Yes, they are part of new batch of linen Tommy purchased two or three years ago. They have been brought here by someone in your household who must have had legitimate access to them," she replied.

"Not necessarily! They could have been stolen from the hedges and stone walls where they were placed to dry. I will ask the laundry maids if any of our sheets are missing," volunteered Harry. He then drew Luke's attention to a corner of room where the dust had not been disturbed. Clearly outlined was a boot print that contained horizontal lines across the sole and vertical lines on the heel, an unusual design.

"There cannot be many boots with such markings," said Luke. "I will check it out with the dale's cobbler, the rector's notorious uncle, Richard Unsworth."

"Look at this!" exclaimed Harry. Caught on a splinter on the edge of the wall panelling was a piece of light green fabric. "That material is from a petticoat. All you have to do, Luke, is to find the woman who has a light green petticoat with a fragment missing."

"How would a woman tear her petticoat on a wall?" asked Luke somewhat naively.

Harry bluntly answered, "She must have been partly dressed and probably thrown against the wall as part of a consensual or forced sexual encounter."

The discovery of the fabric fragment changed Janet's demeanour. Her bored disinterest transformed into stifled emotional involvement. She was perspiring and breathing heavily. Did she recognise the fragment, or even more intriguing, was it hers?

Suddenly, Harry held up his hands for silence. "Listen, somebody is coming along the tunnel from the village end."

Luke whispered, "Quickly extinguish all the candles, and move back through the door."

The trio waited in absolute silence. A male and female voice were heard, and a flicker of light was seen under the door. Within minutes, the room was bathed in light. At this point, Luke burst back through the door to confront the visitors.

OTH PARTIES REELED BACK in surprise. The newcomers were Tim and Mary Carver. Tim exclaimed, "We are too late!"

"What do you mean?" asked Luke apprehensively.

"Mary's father said he told you about this room and the tunnel leading from it. He asked us to clean it up before you inspected it."

"Not an issue! I am surprised how clean this room is despite its recent use."

"This upsets me, and Father will be truly astonished," said Mary, who had taken in the figuration of the room with some concern.

"You seem taken aback by what you see," remarked Harry.

"I am. The last time I was here was two years ago, when a visiting priest disguised as a pedlar came to the dale. Mr Bates was apprised of the situation, and this room, a hidden chapel since the days of the Leighs, was reopened for our use. Father only asked him a few days before he disappeared for permission for us to use it again, given the rector's nastiness towards us. I assumed it had remained a disused Catholic chapel, not converted into a bawdy house," lamented a now tearful Mary.

"There is no need for that extreme sort of comment, Mistress Carver. This was probably simply a hideaway for a respectable member of the household," Janet said, snarling.

Luke was surprised at the tone in her response and of her implied defence of its most recent use, probably by Dutton and herself.

"A perfect place to conceal a Royalist agent," added the ever-alert Harry.

"Tim, while you are here, could I question you about your teenage years in the dale around the time that young Elizabeth Foxton disappeared? Were you one of the local boys who moved up the dale onto the moors regularly to hunt and generally to play around?" asked Luke.

"I am sorry you have raised these issues now. It upsets Mary, who was Elizabeth's closest friend. I was particularly close to Mark Foxton, her cousin."

"Were you with him when he recovered the missing saddle?"

"No! I was the first to head back down the dale after Elizabeth's accident. Mark and some of the others stayed behind."

"Who was with you that day?"

"Roger Dutton, Simon Snigg, Ted Unsworth, Arthur Swan, Mark Foxton, and Stephen Bates."

"Why did all of them, except yourself, leave the dale shortly after Elizabeth's disappearance?"

"They were bad times. There was no work here, and they sought to increase the income for their families elsewhere or, were, in the case of Unsworth and Bates, sent away to get an education."

Luke suddenly turned to Mary and asked, "Have you recently seen on any drying hedge or wall a light green petticoat of fine fabric?"

Mary's face reddened as she vehemently denied any such knowledge, an overreaction to a simple question. Her husband, Tim, was also disconcerted. "Mary, you have such a green petticoat yourself? Sir, why do you ask?"

Luke lied, "Lady Matilda saw it and wanted to obtain one for herself."

Mary, quite angry with Tim, declared, "It shows how much you contemplate your wife's petticoats. None of mine are light green. They are emerald."

Tim, suitably chastened, did not reply, but he was not convinced. He turned to Janet, saying, "Mistress Bates, do you know where the precious plate, candlesticks, and other icons belonging to the chapel have been stored?"

"I have no idea" was the unhelpful response.

For whatever reason, Janet was becoming increasingly uncomfortable.

Luke answered Tim, "I will have the servants search the house for the missing items."

Over supper, Luke, as was becoming his routine, discussed developments with Matilda and Peter. Peter was convinced that the old priest's hole had been converted into a place where probably the Bates, Thomas or Janet, had indulged in illicit sexual activity without fear of being discovered. Luke intuitively freed Thomas from such activity but added other possibilities from within the household—Ogden or Snigg, husband or wife.

Matilda complicated the discussion by suggesting anybody from the village could have used the room by entering from the Carver's pigpen. "Your only bit of evidence that someone from the superior classes is involved is the torn piece of a high-quality petticoat."

"Not so, my dear. The sheets on the bed are part of the manor's linen."

"Which could have been stolen from a drying hedge," retorted Matilda. "I will ask the womenfolk," she added.

"This evidence creates two new possibilities to explain Bates's disappearance. He was having an affair, or he threatened to reveal the names of the parties that were," suggested Peter.

"What is your next move, Luke?" asked Matilda.

"Question our rector and bailiff over their memories of the day Elizabeth Foxton died."

An exasperated Matilda exploded. "Forget Elizabeth! Concentrate on Bates's disappearance, given your new leads."

An obstinate Luke visited Ted Unsworth in his manse. He decided to give no quarter to a man he had instantly disliked. "Reverend, you are the most hated man in the dale. As I am ultimately responsible for your continuance here, I want to hear your side of the story. How do you defend your offensive behaviour?"

Unsworth aggressively responded. "And what particular behaviour is that? Much of the local antagonism towards me stems from my days as a wayward youth, and does not fairly reflect the more favourable impression I am creating as a man of God."

"Tell me about this wayward youth!"

"There was a large gang of us dales boys. It was wartime and bad economic conditions, and we were to some extent out of control, although we limited our more outrageous acts usually to the upper dale and moors.

Life was so bad within our families that to go onto the moors with our friends was our one escape."

"What particular form did your outrageous acts take?"

"The usual assaults, theft, and vandalism, but at a critical stage, I was befriended by Mother Harland, the witch of Elderby, who gave my wilfulness and enthusiasm some direction."

"What did contact with her involve?"

"Running errands. Usually delivering potions to her customers and gathering the herbal ingredients that made up these mixtures."

"Were you paid?"

"No, but I learnt the importance of herbs and memorised a few spells."

"Was this time with Mother Harland at all frightening?"

"At first! That is why I took a friend with me, Mark Foxton at first and later Simon Snigg."

"Did they become equally involved?"

"Not Mark. As a Catholic, he believed that what Harland did was the work of the devil and ultimately refused to come with me. Simon did not understand much but enjoyed gathering the herbs when Mother Harland sent us on a gathering expedition on both the northern and western moors. Over time, she and I became close. She was the mother I never had."

"Your parents died when you were young?"

"Mother died giving birth to me, and Father was killed by a raiding Royalist cavalry troop retreating from Marston Moor. Our family tenancy reverted to my uncle, who never had any time for me. He still doesn't. Most of the bad mouthing I suffer in the dale today emanates from him."

"What sort of misfortune did Mother Harland's herbs and spells enable you to bring on others?"

"Sheep or cattle became ill, litters were aborted, and crops failed through deliberately introduced disease."

"Come, Edward, did you really believe that by incanting a few words, you could effect such fatal developments?"

"It was not the words. It was the potions. They certainly worked."

"Did you target particular people?"

"Yes, many, but I especially concentrated on my uncle's farm. His crops failed, and his animals died. So much so that he was forced to return to cobbling, which was his occupation before he inherited grandfather's estate. It was the only way he could pay his rent."

"Anyone else, your particular victim?"

"Given the killing of my father by Royalists, I hated the Catholics, whom I thought then and now are secret agents of the king. Although the Catholics Mark Foxton, Simon Snigg, and Tim Carver were members of our gang, we did considerable damage to their parents' farms, often with their eager participation. It was the difficulties all the boys faced at home that led to them being sent from the dale."

"So they were not sent away because of their role in the death of Elizabeth Foxton?" Luke asked., probing

"No. What lies have you heard about that incident?"

"Several. When Elizabeth attempted to cross the bridge on the upper reaches of Abbey Beck, your gang threw stones at the horse or made such a noise that it reared up and threw young Elizabeth and her new saddle into the stream."

"Not true. Those who were playing along the beck did nothing. The horse lost its footing on the bridge and threw Elizabeth into the stream, which was flowing so fast we had no time to rescue her. She was swept away. I alone searched for her body without success. The rest of the boys headed home."

"A lie! Your gang prevented the girl from emerging from the stream after her initial dunking. Every time she tried to climb the bank, one of you pushed her back into the water, time and time again. Her strength ebbed, and she was swept away to her death. Your gang murdered Elizabeth Foxton. Who was responsible?"

"Pure fiction. I never saw any such activity, so I cannot answer your question," Edward replied with obvious conviction.

Luke changed the subject. "So why then were you sent away to Cambridge, and who paid? You have confessed to ruining your uncle's finances. Did he force you out?"

"That's an interesting story. Mistress Swan, a widow who dominated Nighby hamlet, was a friend of Mother Harland. Apparently, the Harland family of witches had lived in Nighby for decades before the current witch, Tamsin Harland, moved to Elderby. Mistress Swan and the witch had been neighbours and schoolgirl friends. Between them, they forced my uncle to admit that my father had left me a considerable sum when I reached sixteen for my education. The whole dale was very pleased to see me leave."

"Did Cambridge change you from wild youth into the aggressive proclaimer of the Lord?"

"Quite the opposite. I was even wilder and uncontrolled at Cambridge than I was in the dales."

"What then turned your life around?"

"My theology tutor was convinced that he should do God's will and became a chaplain in the parliamentary army. He took me and his other students with him, claiming that in such a time of crisis, there was no place for idle students. I was sent to one of the regiments of Sir Thomas Fairfax, but instead of me preaching to the troops, one of the soldiers took over and delivered God-inspired sermons. They struck a chord with me, and within weeks, I became a devoted Christian determined to introduce God's kingdom here on earth as soon as possible. Removing corrupt civil government became both a religious passion and an immediate political aim."

"So you are a Fifth Monarchy Man, but of which faction? Some of you believed that the late protector was God's agent preparing the way for Christ's own kingdom and others that Oliver Cromwell had betrayed the godly cause and was now the anti-Christ."

"That division in our ranks is of no relevance now. His successor, the new protector, could not lead a platoon, let alone God's kingdom. All government is now corrupt."

"Be careful, Edward! If you preach that treason from the pulpit, I will not only sack you but also send you in irons to York Castle. Finally, our recusant brethren will return to the parish church next Sunday, and you will not attack them or their faith."

"You cannot order a man of God to sup with the devil" was Unsworth's truculent reply.

"No, but as lord of manor who has the advowson for the parish of Abbey Dale, I order you to modify your principles with regard to Papists or lose your living—a simple choice."

8

IF LUKE CONTINUED TO be obsessed by the old case of Elizabeth Foxton, Matilda would do her own sleuthing regarding the disappearance of the steward, Bates. And she would seek information from a quarter Luke would have been hesitant to use—the lower ranks of her servants.

In the washroom of the manor, she found two young laundresses, Phyllis and Abigail. From Janet, she ascertained that both girls loved Spanish, the roots of the Spanish liquorice, which was eaten raw in the dale and not confected with sugar and water as it was in the towns. Medieval monks had introduced the plant into Yorkshire, where it thrived in selected areas.

They girls were initially flustered by the lady of the manor's visit to their workplace. They curtsied, but Phyllis, so out of practise, tumbled forward, saving herself by grabbing the edge of a large boiler of bubbling suds. Her calloused hands did not appear to feel the heat.

The girls moved into the garden and were soon sitting on the grass in front of Matilda, who placed herself on an ornate stone bench. She handed the girls several sticks of Spanish.

"What does your ladyship wish to know?" asked Abigail as she began to chew the liquorice.

Phyllis knocked her hands away from her mouth and muttered, "Sister, do not eat in front of her ladyship."

Matilda ignored the sibling bickering and asked, "When you place the manor's washing on the surrounding hedges and walls to dry, the washing of the rest of the community is also displayed. Have you seen a pale green petticoat made of very fine material? I would like to have a similar one for myself and need to question the owner as to where it was purchased."

"There are several that are pale green, but most I have only seen from afar and cannot comment on the quality of the fabric. One of them, Abigail and I know very well. We washed it more than once in the weeks before your arrival. It belongs to Mistress Bates," replied Phyllis.

"Charlie Ogden occasionally slipped into the manorial wash another, which belonged to his daughter, Mary, but I have not seen it since she married," added Abigail.

"Any others?" asked Matilda.

"Unsworth's woman," Abigail replied.

"The rector has a woman?" asked an open mouthed Matilda.

The girls laughed.

"No, his uncle Dickie," they replied in unison.

"What do you mean woman—wife, mistress, servant?"

"Nell Briggs. She is now his housekeeper. She is only a little older than us. Before she moved in with Dickie, she was a servant at the Three Roses until our father was forced to sack her under pressure from our elder sisters. Even before her activities out of the tavern, she was well known up and down the dale as being very free with her favours for which she was well paid."

"Thank you, girls. That was very helpful. There is more Spanish here to take away with you, if you could spare me a few more minutes. I am trying to understand my new household, and perhaps you can help me. Mr Bates had disappeared before I met him. What was he like as the all-powerful steward of the manor?"

"He was too busy to notice us. Our paths never crossed, but we had only worked here a few weeks before you arrived," answered Phyllis.

"Surely, you heard the other servants talk about him?"

"Not in the manor. Mistress Janet kept the few servants she had apart doing their allotted tasks. There was no opportunity to chat until we left work and found themselves in the Three Roses." Phyllis continued.

"And what did you discover about Mr Bates from the assembled drinkers?"

"He was well liked. He was a dales man and often shared a drink with his male workers in the tavern. There, he lost his educated speech and spoke like a reight tyke, as do the rest of us. When he was not there, the only person who spoke badly of him was his deputy, Charlie Ogden, and more recently, the constable and the rector," said Abigail.

"What did Ogden have to complain about?"

"Mainly Mr Bates's constant absences, which forced poor Charlie to carry a heavier load than he thought reasonable, not that anyone believed that Ogden was overworked," added Phyllis.

"What did the rector and constable have to complain about?"

"The rector thought Bates was too easy on the Catholics, while the constable spread rumours that Bates was corrupt and lining his own pockets," said Abigail.

"Not that anybody believed Dutton. He was simply trying to undermine Mr Bates to justify his affair with Janet Bates."

Matilda decided not to probe such an affair with her servants. She backtracked. "Where did Mr Bates go on his frequent absences?"

"Mistress Janet always told the staff he had gone to London, York, or Whitby, but Snigg spread it around that he spent a lot of it on the moors," explained Phyllis.

"Doing what?"

"Everybody guessed something different. Some thought he had a woman on the moors, others that he was looking for the legendary Thor's treasure, others again that he ran an illicit coal mine or was a partner in Kit Jagger's criminal empire. They *were* boyhood friends," emphasised Abigail.

"A more serious explanation only surfaced after Robert Dutton returned to the dales. He suggested that Mr Bates was a Royalist agent, absent from Abbey Grange in order to organise Royalist plots and to meet other Royalist spies," explained Phyllis.

"I must persuade my husband to drop into the Three Roses. The landlord is your father?"

"Yes, James Harland!"

"You are sisters?"

"Twins but not identical," explained Phyllis.

"Why are you working here? I am sure your father could do with your help in the tavern."

"Eventually maybe. We have two elder sisters who work with Father in the tavern. As they marry, we will be needed to replace them but not at the moment," replied Abigail.

"The witch in Elderby is a Harland. Are you any relation?"

"She is our father's elder sister."

"Is that a burden to carry?"

"Not at all! Auntie Tamsin is a white witch. The farmers and graziers would be lost without her potions and balms to keep their livestock well. It has only been since the return of that obnoxious Teddy Unsworth that she has been accused of diabolic activity. And he once worked for her. The only diabolic agent in the dale is Ted himself. Even his uncle believes he is evil incarnate," explained Phyllis.

"Did Mistress Bates run an efficient household?"

"It was only a quarter of the size of that which you have created. We were not employed full time until just before you arrived. Mistress Janet did much of the work herself. She saw herself as a caretaker who would be replaced at any time. That the manor was left without a lord for nearly a decade surprised both the Bates and the dale in general," said Abigail.

"Did Mistress Bates have any particular friends?"

"Not in the dale! It is full of us common folk. There was no one of her status here other than the Duttons. Her regular trips to York or back to her home county on the Borders seemed to satisfy her. There was some tension with the women in the manor—with Charles Ogden's daughter, Mary, until she married and especially with Emma Snigg," added Abigail.

"Charles Ogden! I find it hard to believe that Mr Bates appointed him as his deputy."

"According to Father, so did the whole dale, although they thought it a kind gesture."

"Why was he appointed?"

"Charles Ogden was valet to Sir Peregrine Leigh, and when he was evicted, Charlie was jobless. Initially, he went into hiding as it was the time during the Civil War when Catholics were overtly persecuted. At the same time, his wife left him," explained Phyllis.

"Mr Bates took pity on him," added Abigail.

"His wife left him! Did he not try to prevent it or attempt to get her back?"

"No one tangles with Charlie's in-laws. His estranged wife, Agnes, was Kit Jagger's sister. Apparently, she met a sailor from Whitby at her brother's inn and disappeared with him."

"She never returned, not even for Mary's wedding?"

"From the day she left here nearly ten years ago to the present, she has not been seen in the dales," answered Abigail.

"If Charles Ogden, a Catholic, married a Jagger woman, does that mean that the Jaggers are also Catholic?"

"You would have to ask Father. We do not know," said the girls in unison.

"So when Mr Bates was appointed steward of the manor by the government, he selected as his deputy a local who was facing a number of problems?"

"Given that the manor was to run with reduced staff, and most of the land was to be utilised by tenants until a new lord was appointed, there was probably no need for a deputy steward," concluded Abigail.

"But there was a need for a bailiff! How does Simon Snigg relate to others?"

The girls laughed. "Simple Simon! He is strong but is not completely right in the head," explained Phyllis. "But he has only been bailiff for a few months. His father was bailiff for the Leighs and then for Mr Bates for over twenty years."

"If Simon is not right in the head, why did Mr Bates appoint him?"

"It was a stopgap solution pending your arrival, when it was assumed you would make your own appointment."

"If he is not right in the head, how can he do his job?"

"Mr Ogden and Simon's wife, Emma, make sure he did what Mr Bates wanted. Without his wife, the bailiff cannot do his job. When he was a boy, he was considered the village idiot."

"Emma Snigg?"

"A powerful member of the Catholic clique. She is Tim Carver's sister. The Ogdens, Sniggs, Foxtons, and Carvers are interrelated. I know little about her. A bailiff's wife or daughter-in-law is never popular, but we know nothing against her personally," admitted Phyllis.

"Why do Dick Unsworth and the rector hate each other?"

"In his youth, Edward poisoned his uncle's land and livestock, forcing him to rely on his trade as a cobbler. He has deliberately taken Nell Briggs as his housekeeper to annoy his nephew, the moralising rector."

"In what way?"

"Nell has always been free with her favours. Until the new rector arrived, Nell worked out of our father's tavern, satisfying the needs of many a male. Ted Unsworth threatened my father that if he did not remove Nell from his premises, he would take steps with the magistrates to close him down. At the same time, our elder sisters had the same approach and forced Father to forbid Nell access to the Three Roses. Dick, who was a regular customer of both Nell and the tavern, immediately offered her a position as his housekeeper," explained Phyllis.

"Nell is very popular amongst women as well as men. The old rector almost encouraged her activities, saying that they prevented much violence against the respectable women of the dales," said Abigail.

"Is violence against women a serious problem?" Matilda asked,. probing

"More serious than anybody admits. Most of us are too frightened to complain about it" was another joint response.

Matilda decided not to pursue the subject as both girls had tears running down their faces, and their jovial good humour had disappeared. She would alert Luke to the problem.

9

AFTER HER CHAT WITH the laundry maids, Matilda visited Emma Snigg, a petite, wiry brunette who immediately impressed Matilda with her confident, sensible answers.

"I hear that Abbey Dale is not a happy place, especially for women, and that a general malaise has taken over the valley in recent times. What is the problem?"

"The war disrupted the settled ways of the dale. The young men who would normally have stayed here and worked on their family farms went away either to fight or find employment elsewhere. With the removal of a Catholic lord of the manor whose family had dominated the dale for a hundred years, the non-Catholic majority asserted themselves against us Papists, which led to tension and, on occasions, violence. In our childhood, we Catholic girls were subject to physical and sexual abuse—Mary Ogden, Elizabeth Foxton, and myself. It would have been a lot worse for us as we entered our teens, if it had not been for Mr Bates. The death of Elizabeth alerted him to the sectarian tension building in the dale, and he took steps to stop it. He clamped down on any attacks on us and used his friend Kit Jagger to apply a little bit of force where words failed to be effective. He had the teenage boys that were terrorising even their own families leave the dale, including two Catholic lads, Mark Foxton and my now husband, Simon Snigg. Only my brother, Tim Carver, of his cohort of male friends never left the dale. Most of the exiles returned in a short time, but the major Protestant troublemakers, Stephen Bates and Roger Dutton, have never come back. Arthur Swan did but died in the fire at Nighby, and the worse of them all,

Edward Unsworth, has reappeared after a ten-year absence, unfortunately as the local rector."

"My husband has reopened the Elizabeth Foxton case. You grew up together. Was she a happy child?"

"My lady, I should not be saying this but we Catholic children suffer abuse not only from our Protestant neighbours but also from our own family members. Elizabeth often bore the marks of a regular beating, but she refused to say whether it was administered by her father, her uncle, or her cousin. Most of the girls and women in the dales—and it has continued into married life in a lot of families, Protestant or Catholic—are or have been beaten. This is certainly not a good place for women, but is it worse than anywhere else? The Bible instructs us to obey our menfolk. It has been so since time began."

"Was there nobody in the dale that tried to ease this violence?"

"Yes, Mr Bates, Kit Jagger, Mother Harland, and her friend and fellow midwife, Grace Swan. Most women in the dale have resorted to Mother Harland at one time or another for salves to cover their bruises and potions to moderate the violence of their menfolk. She has been their lifetime mentor. Some men fear her magic and have, as a result, modified their aggressive attitude towards their womenfolk."

"At the time, what were you told about Elizabeth's probable death?"

"Different stories circulated—a group of boys threw stones at Elizabeth and her horse, and it reared up, tossing her into the stream, which swept her away, never to be found, or that the horse lost its footing on the bridge, and Elizabeth was thrown off, unfortunately into the raging beck, and carried away before anyone could rescue her. It was suggested by some that Elizabeth was unhurt and tried to leave the stream but that she was pushed back by the boys or even that they held her head under the water till she died."

"Who did the children of the dale believe was responsible?"

"One or more of Teddy Unsworth, Stephen Bates, Roger Dutton, Mark Foxton, or Arthur Swan."

"Is the failure of the younger Bates and Dutton to return and the suspicious death of Swan related to this conviction? Only Unsworth has come back, and he claims he is a different person from the lout that left the dale at that time."

"Possibly."

"Almost ten years has passed. You are the sister of one of the lads that was present that day and the wife of another. Have either of them given a detailed account of what happened?"

"No. My brother claims he was separated from the group and was almost back to Abbeythwaite when the incident occurred, and my husband, who is often muddleheaded, does not have a clear recollection of anything."

"Let me change the subject of this discussion. What do you think has happened to Bates?"

"Over his ten years as steward of the manor, he would have discovered secrets about most people in the dale, one or more of whom did not want him passing that information on to your husband. I think he has been murdered, but by whom and why, I do not know."

"My husband has already had words with the rector about his attacks on Papists. As one of Cromwell's leading officers, Sir Luke has worked well with English Catholics during his career. It is the Irish variety that raised his ire. Although he will be quite tolerant of your religious beliefs, he will not be so easygoing on questions of loyalty to the government. Have any of you been tempted to participate in Royalist activity in recent years?"

"The Catholics of Abbey Dale are Catholics by conviction, but their support of the king in the early years of the war was a result of being loyal servants of the Leighs. For the last decade, we have readily accepted the changes of government as they occurred. Mr Bates came down heavily on any political thoughts or activities he considered potentially dangerous. Your husband will not discover any Royalist plots amongst the Catholics of the dale, although Kit Jagger retains some links with his former cavalier friends as part of his criminal network."

"Did anything happen on the manor in the months before we arrived that might explain Bates's disappearance?"

"Increased tension between him and his wife?"

"Over what issues?"

"Us. Thomas was furious with the new rector and his constant attacks on Catholics. Janet, given her Scottish Presbyterian background, sided with Unsworth. She ignored us for nearly a decade and drew her friends solely from the extreme Protestant inhabitants of the dale."

"So you are not a friend of Janet Bates, although you were for much of that period the bailiff's daughter-in-law and, more recently, the bailiff's wife?"

"Never once did I have a single conversation with her, such as we are having now."

"What was her relationship with her husband? Before the increased tension sparked by the new rector, were they close?"

"They have not been close since their daughter, Helen, disappeared just after Mr Bates was appointed steward."

"You are the first person to mention this disappearance. What happened?"

"Helen, a ten-year-old, was put to bed here in the manor one evening. Next morning, she was missing. Despite an intensive search and investigation, no trace of her was found. Mr Bates was so distraught, and receiving little help from the parliamentary authorities in York, he asked his boyhood friend Kit Jagger to help."

"The couple subsequently had no other children?"

"No, Janet was so upset by the loss of their daughter that it is rumoured that they never slept together again. You have not heard about little Helen's disappearance as both husband and wife made it clear to everybody that the issue must never be discussed."

"What did people think happened to the girl?"

"There were some ridiculous views that we Catholics had kidnapped her for some horrendous rituals or that the Witch of Elderby had taken her for equally nauseating sacrifices. There was a view that she had been raped and murdered. In the end, Kit Jagger's explanation that she had been kidnapped, taken across the moors, and sold into slavery or shipped to the Americas as an indentured servant became the accepted version. Jagger knows that numerous local children are shipped out of Whitby to this end. The majority of them have been sold by their parents to become indentured servants."

"How does Jagger know so much about this trade?"

"It depends on who you believe. His enemies claim he has and does play a major role in the purchase or abduction of young girls and boys for this lucrative business. His friends say he knows about the trade because he and his men have rescued a number of children being carried across the moors and returned them to their families."

"Did the loss of his daughter, apart from the rift it caused with his wife, have any other discernible effects on Bates?"

"His determination to get to the bottom of young Elizabeth Foxton's probable death stems from his personal loss a few years earlier."

"Is there any link between the two events?"

"Not that I know of."

"Given the rift between Bates and his wife that you referred to, did either seek solace in the arms of another friend or lover?"

"Mr Bates was the very model of respectability."

"Bates was not using the former priest's hole for such sexual adventures?"

"It is disgusting that someone used our old chapel for such a purpose, but Thomas Bates was not that sort of person."

"What about Janet? Did she have any lovers?"

"Once, she preferred younger men. When she went to York, she stayed with her much younger brother-in-law, Stephen Bates, until he left the city. Her Puritan morality is a charade. She is the daughter of a lawless reiver brigand from the Borders. For years, she had an affair with Giles Dutton, the current constable's father, while pretending to be a close friend of his wife. He was always at the manor. Since his death, his son, Robert, has shown a remarkable interest in poor Janet," Emma cattily recounted.

Matilda was cautious. These last comments could have been the resentment of a new bailiff's wife, who may have suffered humiliation no matter how slight from an imperious superior, who overtly had no time for Catholics.

She changed the subject. "I hear that your brother's mother-in-law walked out on Charles Ogden and has never been seen since. You have been close to Charles for over a decade. Why did nobody follow up her disappearance?"

"I was only a baby when it happened, but in recent years, I have been fobbed off with a simple explanation that she just left Charles, stayed with her brother, Kit Jagger, for a few months, fell in love with a sailor, and disappeared with him. Charles never talked about it, and most people, such as my own father who were close to him at the time, are now dead."

That evening, Luke was enthralled with the new information that Matilda had uncovered. It suggested several new leads that he must follow up.

10

LUKE AND HARRY IN Whitby on estate and magisterial business took time to seek out Roger Dutton. He was a junior partner in a firm of general merchants engaged in keeping London supplied with goods other than coal. The three men met in the snug of the Hind and Herring, where Luke explained he was investigating the Elizabeth Foxton case and the recent disappearance of the steward, Thomas Bates.

"Big brother, Robbie, as constable must be enjoying such a situation," commented Roger dryly.

"Not really. He does not approve of me opening old cases when there is, in his opinion, a glut of current crime to be investigated."

"And he could not help with the Foxton case as he was away with the army at the time."

"What actually happened to Elizabeth? I have heard several conflicting stories."

"I was someway farther down the dale when Elizabeth rode onto the bridge. Some of the lads shouted at her, and maybe a stone or two was thrown. The horse reared up, throwing Elizabeth into the beck. It was running so fast that nobody could rescue her."

"What about the witness who saw some of boys constantly pushing Elizabeth back into the water each time she struggled to get out?"

"A pack of lies that ruined many of our lives, mine included, over the short term. Too many people believed Goodwife Swan's falsehoods, and all the boys that were playing in the area of the tragic drowning, except for Tim

Carver, were exiled from the dale by their parents in case of any impending investigation."

"There was no such investigation, was there?"

"No, our parents and other vested interests in the dale put it about that Elizabeth accidently drowned as a result of a spooked horse."

"Why would a respected woman such as Goodwife Swan lie?"

"I do not know why, but she did. For most of the day, the upper dale was covered in fog. You could not see the bridge from fifty yards away. Grace Swan could see nothing from where she claims to have been except for a few minutes at a time. For some months before this several people had reported that Grace Swan had become a little strange."

"As a result of the lies, did any of the lads hate her and seek revenge? She died in a suspicious fire several months later. Did they light it?"

"No. We were just local lads enjoying ourselves in the upper dale. Such an idea would never have entered our heads. Maybe in retaliation throwing stones at her windows or stealing her chickens . . . but not murder."

"Not all the boys were as innocent as you make out?"

"Ted Unsworth had a vicious streak and had built up immense resentment against the older generation. He set out deliberately to destroy his own uncle who was bringing him up. He often persuaded or bullied the not-too-bright Simon Snigg to carry out some of his more outrageous pranks. He would never attack Swan for two reasons. She was Kit Jagger's lover at the time, and Jagger ruled the upper dale and moorlands with an iron fist. If the widow Swan had complained about any of us, Jagger would have acted decisively, and Elizabeth would not have been the only child to disappear from the area. Maybe this fear of retaliation from Jagger was another reason our parents sent us away, although sending me here to Whitby hardly removed me from his influence. Secondly, Grace Swan was a close friend of the woman who acted as a mother to Ted, Mother Harland."

"Is there anything else you can tell us about this episode?"

"Another reason none of us would have acted against widow Swan was that her son, Arthur, was the most popular member of our group. In fact, when Elizabeth's horse reared, he was the only one of us actually on the bridge. And if the fog had lifted temporarily, his mother would have known that the nearest boy to Elizabeth was her own son because he was wearing a bright yellow doublet, which would have been visible from a great distance."

"So you would vouch for all the boys with you at the time that they did not kill Elizabeth and later torch widow Swan, even Edward Unsworth."

"Yes, apart from my second exception, Stephen Bates. He was weird."

"In what way?"

"Because his much elder brother was the steward of the manor and the most important person in the dale, he thought he was a cut above the rest of us. He had an obsessive interest in girls, and he constantly picked on the Catholic members of our group who made up half our numbers—Mark Foxton, Tim Carver, and Simon Snigg. It split our group. Edward Unsworth, despite his other failings, was a strong defender of poor Simon Snigg, whom Stephen Bates particularly picked on."

"Things have changed a bit now. Unsworth is engaged in an anti-Papist campaign, although it may explain his antagonism to Stephen's brother, Thomas. Anything else you wish to add?"

"Not about young Elizabeth, but I may be able to help regarding Thomas Bates. When did you arrive at Abbey Grange?"

"The week after Easter. Why do you ask?"

"Just before Easter, I ran into Thomas Bates in this very tavern. I asked him why he looked like the cat that had swallowed the cream. He replied he had just unearthed some appalling information regarding Abbey Dale, information that the new lord of the manor and resident magistrate would have to act upon. It validated suspicions he had long held but could never prove."

"That confirms what I have been told about his last visit to Whitby and explains the timing of his murder must be. Now it appears he had just received information that one or more locals could not allow him to pass on to me. He didn't say whom he had spoken to here in Whitby or what the information was that he had uncovered?"

"No. At the time, I did not take much interest. It is only now that you tell me of his disappearance that it appears significant."

"On a related issue, the only two young men who left following Elizabeth's disappearance and have not returned to Abbey Dale are yourself and Stephen Bates."

"Stephen would never return while his brother was steward of the manor and the government's voice in the region. He hated his sibling. If Thomas has been murdered, my prime suspect would be his brother, Stephen."

"Why did you not return?" asked Luke.

"Why would I? Whoever bestowed on you the manor of Abbey Grange and exiled you to Abbey Dale has a warped sense of humour and must have been punishing you for past wrongs or had immense confidence in your ability to remove the malaise and reform an essentially evil place. Your current position as both manorial and magisterial leader will probably prove the greatest challenge of your illustrious career."

"I have not been there long enough to pick up on all this negativity, although my wife has heard a little concerning the abuse of women and children. Whether it is out of the ordinary, I have no way of knowing. What created your dark view of childhood and early adulthood in the dale?"

"As children, we were subjected to constant physical abuse, usually by our own families. Too many young girls had to visit Mother Harland for potions to abort their unwanted pregnancies. So many young people just disappeared, and our elders did not seem to care. Disappearances, unsolved murders, and constant violence dominated our life. In addition, we were forced to act against our friends because of a long-standing feud amongst various families. This was especially so at the time I left the dale. Very strong anti-Papist feelings emanated from most of the Protestant families."

"Why at that particular time?"

"For generations, the Protestant majority in the dale was subject to the Papist landlords, the Leighs, who favoured their coreligionists. When Leigh had his estates sequestrated by the Protestant parliament, and a Protestant steward appointed with most of the powers of the lord of the manor, we Protestants expected more of the benefits would flow in our direction. But Thomas Bates reappointed the Catholics, Ogden and the older Snigg, to key manorial positions and continued to protect the Papist families. Abbey Dale was and is a very unhappy place. Perhaps what Thomas Bates discovered here in Whitby might stimulate much-needed reformation."

"Did you see Thomas Bates here on a previous occasion?"

"Only once while sitting at this same bench. I saw him enter my place of employment just across the road. I questioned my business colleagues at the time, who said he had visited the company's lawyer."

"Great. I will speak to him."

"He died two or three years ago."

Luke's optimism was crushed.

"All is not lost. His son, Lancelot, succeeded him and may have some knowledge of relevant past events. Come back with me now, and I will introduce you!"

Luke explained that both as local lord of the manor and magistrate, he was looking into the disappearance of Thomas Bates.

Lancelot sent his clerk away to unearth documents that might be relevant. A small number of papers were presented, and after a careful perusal of them, Lancelot explained, "Thomas Bates was never a client of this firm. The only reference to him is that on several visits to Whitby, he asked my father questions about the ships we regularly use to transport our goods. He was particularly concerned to discover whether any of them sailed to the Americas. None of them did. Father noted Bates's initial disappointment at this news, but also his subsequent delight to discover that two of our ships sailed regularly to Bristol, from where much of the American trade originated. Those ships were the *Rose of Whitby* and the *Necklace*."

"Did Bates follow up this information?"

"The documents don't tell us."

"Bates was here just before Easter this year. Did he visit you?"

"No, I've never met him."

"If he wanted to follow up on those ships, would it be easy?"

"No. The *Necklace* was sunk off the coast of Norway last year. The *Rose of Whitby* was away for over two years but did dock here for a couple of weeks just before Easter. Whatever Bates was after, it is possible he talked to someone connected with the *Rose* during the short time she was in port and he in Whitby."

"Would the *Rose* have transported indentured children out of the area?"

"Yes, most ships that leave Whitby transport children or youths who have been indentured to labour in London or further afield. Most local indentures are open ended, which enables them to be transferred by the original owner to a third party. In times of economic crisis, many a family, especially in the dales, sold their older children into servitude."

"Many children are sold by their parents, but others have been abducted," commented Luke.

"Certainly but impossible to prove. Most contracts in this region are between two parties without the involvement of lawyers or the courts. The contract is written out twice on the same sheet of paper. It is cut or torn across the middle so that each party has an identical copy. The recruiting agent has the buyer's copy, but unless you could prove there is no seller's copy, abduction could not be proved."

"Are there regular recruiters in Whitby?"

"Not now. Most are aboard the ships that visit the port. The local suppliers would arrive with their indentured servants and transfer them to the ship-bound agent."

"Can you name a regular supplier, especially of dales children?" asked Luke, not expecting a meaningful reply.

"Definitely. No child comes out of the dales except through Kit Jagger."

ON HIS WAY BACK to Abbey Grange, Luke stayed as intended at the Pilgrim's Rest. He now had a series of specific questions for Kit. As they drank together in front of a blazing fire, Luke was blunt. "Are you engaged in the trade of freshly indentured servants to Whitby and beyond?"

"Yes, it's a legal trade, and you as magistrate, Luke, will have to enforce these contracts from time to time. There are always two or three boys who ignore this legal document and run away. They have to be drawn into line. Girls are much more amenable."

"Who is your agent in Abbey Dale for organising such contracts?"

"Nowadays, nobody. The system has been operating for so long that parents in the dale who want to sell their children into indentured servitude bring them here. I sign an open contract with them, which I sell on to the shipping agents. In good economic times such as now, there is very little activity. In bad times, almost every family in the dale is forced to sell one of their children into such servitude to make ends meet. It is not a life sentence and can be the beginning of a new and successful life, although sadly not always."

"In these reasonably good times, is there an increase in the illegal aspects of the trade, the kidnapping of children against their parents or their own desires? The demand of the labour market in London and the colonies seems insatiable."

"Yes, but I have never indulged in that activity. Quite the opposite, on several occasions, having been alerted by distraught families in Abbey Dale, my men have rescued several abducted children. I was so successful that today's kidnappers come nowhere near here."

"Where do they go?"

"Most are taken south or west to other ports."

"Was Thomas Bates's child abducted?"

"Almost certainly."

"You said you do not have an agent in the dale at present. Did you in the past?"

"Only in the sense that this person advised the parents that the placing their children into indentured servitude was a possible solution to their problems."

"What type of problems?"

"While some parents were desperate for the pittance of money paid, and only reluctantly moved their children away, others were anxious to rid themselves of troublesome offspring who were causing trouble, often daughters who had got themselves pregnant, usually after they gave birth or aborted the child. It was Tamsin Harland who initially suggested to some parents that selling their child into indentured labour would be better for all concerned. She did this in the interests of the child. She was well aware of family situations where the child was constantly abused. She was often helped in this work by her friend Grace Swan. Neither took any money for their efforts to help these troubled children."

Luke's intuitive revulsion to the idea of parents selling their troublesome children was moderated by the sudden thought that his own recruitment into the Dutch army in his teens at the behest of his father, who was responding to the young Luke's over attraction to the daughter of the local aristocrat, was not very different.

Kit was thinking along similar lines. "The removal of those lads suspected of involvement in the Elizabeth Foxton disappearance was a similar reaction of frightened or frustrated parents. If those lads had been lowered down the social scale, the parents would probably have sold them into indentured labour. The parents involved, being yeomen or above, instead found them employment or study out of the dale."

"How many children have disappeared over the last few years from Abbey Dale?" asked a concerned Luke.

"I can give you a list of the children that have officially passed through my hands, and Tamsin Harland may be able to add a few more. The best source for those children who simply disappeared without trace would be the former rector's widow, Mistress Garnett. She comforted the distraught parents."

"My friend, the governor of York Castle, has already interviewed her. I will question her on my next trip to York."

Elinor entered the room. "Sir, there is a gentleman from Abbeythwaite to see his lordship urgently."

Luke was surprised. It was Peter Frost. "What is so urgent that my steward has to personally deliver a message?"

"You must return with me immediately. My deputy, Charles Ogden, is dead, probably murdered."

"Interesting!" was Kit's enigmatic response.

"What do you mean by that?" asked Luke.

"Is it not odd that the former steward disappeared, and now his deputy is murdered? The heart of the problem lies within your manor rather than in the dale as a whole. Forget about the Foxton girl! You have a new murder to concentrate on. Solving it might help you find out what happened to Tommy."

"I am reluctant to close the Foxton case," admitted Luke. "Before I go, let me raise another old case with you, the destruction of the hamlet of Nighby. It is alleged that you burnt it to the ground, incinerating all the inhabitants, including Grace Swan, your supposed lover."

A tear ran down Jagger's face as he muttered, "Grace Swan was a beautiful and courageous woman. I loved her dearly. It is true. I destroyed Nighby."

"Why? Why fire the hamlet, incinerating the woman you loved?"

"I only acted after incessant pleading from Grace."

"Grace wanted you to destroy her and her hamlet in such a horrendous manner? I don't believe you."

"Let me explain. Her son, Arthur, left Nighby to gain a living in York. After only a few months, he returned with a friend. That friend brought with him another and fatal companion, the plague. It had been raging in York. Within days, it had spread through the whole of Nighby. Grace informed me, and in the absence of any legally constituted authority, I did as the law required. I sealed off the hamlet. It was a death sentence to those there, but the plague did not spread into the dale in general. Grace was the last to die. I placed all the corpses into one building, which I blew up. Rather than cause panic throughout the dale, it was put about that Nighby had been struck by lightning."

"Did Grace ever expand to you on what she saw the day Elizabeth Foxton was attacked?"

"Yes, but she regularly became distraught because she did not recognise any of the youths. I made it clear that if she did, I would make sure they received just punishment. Although she did not recognise any of them, she, as did I, had an idea of who they might have been. A group of youths from Abbeythwaite, Elderby, and Nighby frequently congregated together to catch rabbits in the upper dale or on the moors."

"Did she reveal anything else that might be helpful, especially after she knew her own days were numbered?"

"Yes, the last time I saw her, she wondered whether her own son, Arthur, may have been responsible and that the onslaught of the plague was divine retribution for his crime."

"What specific crime?"

"Holding Elizabeth's head under the water. Grace admitted that that day, the dale was covered in fog and she only had occasional glimpses of what was happening on the bridge. One such glimpse revealed a boy in a yellow doublet near to the girl struggling in the water. Arthur Swan was the only boy with a yellow doublet."

"Are you sure that Arthur Swan died in that inferno?"

"My men imposed a tight curtain around that hamlet for weeks. The corpses were all placed in one house and exploded into eternity. I never actually identified Arthur Swan's body. After the explosion, none of the remains could be identified."

"Was the belief that the murderer of young Elizabeth may have been your lover's son the reason you and others in the dale took no further action?"

"No, it was the realisation in those last few weeks that Grace's eyesight was so bad that her testimony could not be relied on. In addition I had noticed for some months she was becoming easily confused. Although she believed in what she claimed to have seen, her evidence was probably a mixture of fact and imagination."

Luke, Harry, and Peter reached Abbey Grange midmorning and were immediately briefed by the constable, Robert Dutton, in the presence of Matilda.

"Yesterday two lads who were fishing in one of the flatter parts of the beck, which resembled a deep pool rather than the usual raging torrent, found the body snagged against a protruding branch. It was brought back to his daughter's house to be prepared for burial. Initially, I believed it was an accidental drowning.

"What changed your mind?"

"Tim Carver, who was assisting his wife in preparing Charles's body, noticed a gash on the back of the head."

"Which may have been caused on falling into the beck," commented Peter.

"Not likely!" replied Robert. "The gash was caused by a sharp stone. Those in the beck have been rounded and smoothed over centuries of erosion by our fast-running stream."

"So Charles was hit on the head and then fell or was dumped into the beck? Is there a physician or surgeon in any of the surrounding villages that can look at the victim?" asked Luke.

"There is a physician in Pickering to the south. He would be the nearest. There are several in Whitby."

"What is usually done here when a suspicious death occurs?" asked Luke.

"After a superficial investigation, my predecessors for the last decade left it to the families of the victims to take matters further. It appears,,many consulted Mother Harland, who is very skilful in detecting poisons."

"Harry, ride to Elderby and ask Mother Harland to return with you! Robert, take me to the Carvers! I need to inspect the body!"

Matilda interrupted, "No, Luke! Wait until Mother Harland arrives! There is no need to upset the Carver family with two intrusive visits!"

Next afternoon, Luke and Mother Harland entered the small room in the Carvers' house where the body of Charles Ogden had been laid out.

Luke informed her that "Charles was hit on the head and then fell or was pushed into the stream. It is also possible that he was drugged or poisoned before the attack. Can you tell me if poisoning or drugging is a possibility?"

Mother Harland leant over the body and sniffed the mouth of the corpse and carefully examined every inch of his body. She then suggested that Luke examine the body for any signs that he might consider unusual. "You have seen a lot of bodies in your military career. Does anything strike you as odd with this body?"

"In solving a number of murders over the past decade, I have had the assistance of very clever physicians, army surgeons, and herbalists like yourself. They taught me to look for discolourations. I notice a bluish tinge around the lips that might suggest cyanide poisoning, white striations on the nails that give a hint of arsenic, and the ease in which the skin is shedding and the hair falling out, the effect of lead or mercury."

"You have observed well, but old Charlie was not poisoned. Or if so, it had nothing to do with his death. The bluish tinge on the lips was probably due to his immersion in near-freezing water, and the other signs you have picked up, at most, suggest slow and long-term exposure to dangerous substances. As to whether he was drugged before being attacked, I cannot tell. Any evidence has long disappeared."

"You believe Charles was hit on the head and, in that incapacitated state, thrown into the beck where he drowned," Luke asked.

"It was not that simple. Look at his wrists. They have been tied together. The rope marks are still there, although ever so faint. He was bound and gagged, placed in the stream, and his head held under until he drowned. His body was then swept away by the surging beck. You have a well-managed murder on your hands. Let me have another close inspection of the body."

After some time, she whispered to Luke, "Sir, this is indeed a murder, but I was wrong about the cause. At first, I missed the fatal incision. Charlie was not killed by poisoning, the blow to the back of the head, or drowning. Look carefully at his chest. There is a pinprick near his heart. Somebody rammed a large needle into his chest."

12

L UKE WAS IMPRESSED BY this short plump woman with a round face, tiny nose, red cheeks, and alert green eyes. She was far removed from the caricature of the witch that he had instilled into him as a child.

Unexpectedly, she suddenly changed the subject. "How well have your livestock survived the colder months? Your new steward, Captain Frost, has not called on me for help. Don't leave it too late! In the dales, diseases involving sheep and cattle spread very rapidly."

Luke wondered whether this was the animal healer appealing for business or a not-so-white witch warning what might happen to his animals if she was not more involved. Clearly, his childhood fears had not entirely disappeared. He acceded to her implicit suggestion.

Luke had Peter take Mother Harland on an inspection of the manor's livestock. He indicated that after this inspection, he would like to question her further on the history of the dale. As she left, she gave Luke a quizzical look and remarked, "Do not expect me to reveal the secrets of those I help. And I hear more confessions than any Papist priest."

Two hours later, she returned and reported to Luke. "Tommy Bates left you with stock in excellent condition, and your new man has so far been lucky. The chronic ailments that bedevil much of the livestock in the dales have not yet troubled your animals. Tommy knew his livestock. Captain Frost, from what he told me, has had no previous experience dealing with sheep and cattle. I suggest you employ the local publican, my younger brother, James, from time to time as stock master. Like me, he was well taught by our mother on the herbs and potions needed to keep animals healthy, and he has a natural ability with animals. Since he took over the local tavern, he misses his dealings with animals, and he would not cost you as much as I would. You already employ two of his daughters."

"I'll consider it. Both Peter and I have spent our whole adult life in the army, and I never expected to become a local landlord. The only animal I can claim empathy with is the horse. I had several great horses, to which I became closely attached during my life as a cavalry officer. It is because of this lack of experience that I need your help in understanding the history of the dale and the relationship between the families that make up its population."

"Sir, you spent much of your life in military intelligence where keeping secrets was paramount. In my role as herbalist and midwife to the dale, there is much that I too can never reveal. What specific problems do you think I can help you with?"

"In investigating the cold case of Elizabeth Foxton, and now the disappearance of Bates and the murder of Ogden, I have become aware that dozens of children have disappeared, been abducted, sold into servitude by their parents, or died as a result of abuse. Some of the inhabitants who have left refer to the dale as the dale of despair, especially for young people. As a midwife and herbalist, you must have been privy to many a distressful case."

"There is a lot of parental abuse of children, in addition to the sexual abuse of females by their masters. There are, and always have been, too many children in the dale created by the unrestrained lust of so many husbands producing children that the family cannot afford to keep. In addition, the impregnation of unmarried women by their employers, usually as a result of rape, adds to the problem."

"Kit Jagger speaks very highly of your efforts in placing some of these abused children in a better environment. What else have you done to ameliorate the situation?"

"I won't condemn myself by confessing that I prescribe potions and herbs to abort unwanted babies or prevent girls from becoming pregnant in the first place. One thing that I condemn is infanticide. When I was a girl, it was normal to leave an unwanted baby up on the moors to die. I, and Grace Swan before her death, and who was the midwife in Nighby, have successfully changed attitudes. Such babies are now

left with me, and I distribute them to families who want children."
"So there is a trade in newborn babies?"

"Yes, although in most cases, it is localised. As one woman has an unwanted baby, another loses a baby she desperately wanted. There are many people in the dale who are not who they think they are. They have no idea that they are not the children of those they believe are their parents. Those are the secrets I can never reveal."

"I can see that if those facts come out, it could destroy a family. Could such a revelation explain some adopted parents' brutal reaction to a child and vice versa?"

"Yes, unfortunately, it is revealed more often than you think by one of the adoptive parents, usually to attack the other. Drunken husbands tell the child that his wife is not the birth mother, while a woman often responds by calling the male's potency into question. You will find as magistrate that a large number of domestic violence cases that come before you arise out of a once-concealed adoption that is revealed when one of the parties is no longer happy with the arrangement."

"Do you have much to do with the Catholic families associated with this manor?"

"Yes, I do. They do not differ from the rest of the dale in their need for my services, with one exception. They are more inclined to adoption, and eschew abortion, and infanticide, more so than the Protestant majority."

"I am trying to discover what happened to the steward, Thomas Bates. Did he create many enemies during his ten-year tenure here?"

"Dozens of little issues over the decade upset a whole range of people but nothing that would provoke someone to kidnap or murder him. Tommy was well liked within the dale despite his surprise appointments to the staff of your manor."

"In what way surprise appointments?"

"When old Leigh was removed and an extreme Puritan administrator appointed, the Protestant families of the dale expected to benefit from the plumb positions and rich tenancies that were associated with them. Instead, Tommy appointed the Papist, Charlie Ogden, as his deputy and reaffirmed another Papist, Martin Snigg, as bailiff, on whose recent death was replaced by his son, Simon."

"Who were put out by those decisions?"

"The Duttons, the Unsworths, the Eades, my brother, James Harland, the Swans, and above all, his own wife, Janet Bates. Yet if their resentment led to action against Tommy, why would they wait ten years and after they had already reasserted their dominance within the dale with Robbie Dutton as constable, Ted Unsworth as rector, and yourself as lord of the manor and local magistrate? If you are trying to explain Tommy's disappearance, his past support of the Catholic families is irrelevant."

"What is relevant?"

"Since the disappearance of his daughter years ago, Tommy has become a loner, keeping very much to himself, despite his cordial relations with tenants and servants. Yet in the last few months, I did see a return of the spark that was there in the younger man. Maybe he saw your arrival as an opportunity for him to start a new life, well away from the dale that had caused him so much grief."

"What do you know about his daughter's abduction?"

"Very little. Tommy came to see me as soon as it happened, knowing that I dealt in the relocation of babies and unwanted children. I was aware that a gang of kidnappers operated throughout the dales. They were not locals but needed a local spotter who, for a fee, informed them of possible victims. I suggested if Tommy could isolate the spotter, he may be able to recover his daughter."

"Was the local spotter identified?"

"Nothing was ever proved, but Dickie Unsworth was widely suspected. Ted Unsworth certainly believed his uncle was responsible. It was one of the many areas of conflict between the two."

"I understand that the abduction of their daughter destroyed the Bates marriage?"

"Yes, but Tommy was not responsible. A year after the little girl disappeared, he came to see me about adopting one or more of the many babies that were passing through my hands. He could have created quite a large family in this way, which might have eased the pain of his loss. Janet absolutely refused to cooperate. Not only had she refused to sleep with him from the day their daughter disappeared, but she also ultimately refused to pretend to be pregnant so that one of my babies could be sent to the manor without loss of face by Tommy or herself."

"Do you give any credence to the rumour that he has gone off looking for Thor's treasure?"

"None at all. I heard that he was now convinced that bits of the treasure were as likely to found on this manor as anywhere else, but apart from the impressionable young Carver, none of the tenants seem greatly interested in digging up their land."

"I was told that the discovery of some treasure by Carver was a well-kept secret."

"Rubbish. To embarrass her husband and to reflect badly on his state of mind, Janet made it known that Tommy was in the grip of treasure fever, which was quite untrue."

"What are your views on the death of Elizabeth Foxton?"

Mother Harland's demeanour changed. She looked Luke directly in the eye and announced, "There are some issues best left alone after so much time. Grace Swan was sure she saw one of the local lads push the girl back into the beck, although her eyesight at this time was suspect as I think was her mind. Let's all accept that Elizabeth was the accidental victim of a spooked horse."

"Was it the general view that Grace's son, Arthur, was responsible?"

"No, it was not until after his death in the Nighby fire that Arthur was singled out. No, in truth, every parent of a teenage lad feared that their son was responsible."

"Why was Charles Ogden murdered?"

"Sir, you are the sleuth. Why do you think he was killed?"

"Two possibilities—sectarian tension or resentment against my reappointment of him as deputy steward. In essence, his position within the manor and his religion strike me as the most likely factors."

"My lord, don't underestimate the simple fact that Charlie Ogden was not a likeable character. His position within the Papist community and his role as husband and father might also be relevant. It would be hard for anyone to murder Tommy Bates because he was a likeable and good person. The opposite applies to Charlie. Many a time over the years, I could see myself concocting a poison to be rid of that parasite."

Luke noted Mother Harland's uncharacteristic venom.

13

"I NEED TO GET moving on the Ogden investigation," commented Luke over supper. "I should start with the murder weapon, the needle used in the fatal stabbing."

"The wound was so small it must have been a very fine needle such as we use in embroidery," suggested Matilda.

"Not likely. They would not be long enough to penetrate to the heart," said Peter.

Ignoring this comment, Matilda asked Emma, "Are there any embroiderers in Abbey Dale?"

"None now. There are no gentlewomen in the dale except yourself. Embroidery is a talent developed amongst the aristocratic and gentry women of the county but not amongst us yeomen wives."

"Janet Bates was of gentry lineage. Did she not embroider?" asked Peter.

"I never saw her at it, although I was rarely in the manor during her dominance," replied Emma.

"So you have no explanation of where the needle that killed Charles Ogden came from?" asked Luke.

"Incorrect. I know exactly where that needle may have come from if it was an embroidery needle," answered Emma. "The last lady of the manor, Lady Leigh, was a prolific embroiderer. Most of the wall and bed hangings and the curtains that adorn this manor were lovingly embroidered by her over several decades. When she died, and her husband was evicted for bearing arms a second time against the Parliament, her ladyship's needles were left behind. I saw the box as a young girl. Janet Bates must know what happened to it."

"Ten years ago, there was a box of Leigh needles stored somewhere in the manor?"

"Yes."

Janet no longer attended supper at the manor. Luke, after his recent interrogation, was reluctant to question her again. Matilda volunteered to do so the next morning.

She expected a cold welcome. As she waited in an antechamber, she glimpsed Robert Dutton leaving by a side door. The maid who had answered Matilda's knock claimed that her mistress was not yet dressed to receive visitors and suggested that Lady Matilda might wish to return later in the morning. Matilda's dislike of Janet intensified, and she informed the servant that she intended to stay put until Mistress Bates appeared.

When Janet finally appeared, the reception was even frostier than Matilda expected. "I thought his lordship had finished his distasteful questioning of me on a series of most personal matters," commented Janet.

"No need to distress yourself. My questions are of a trivial nature but may help find the murderer of Charles Ogden. Do you embroider?"

With this unexpected question, Janet relaxed. "As a girl, I was taught by my grandmother. I never really liked it. On the Borders, there were a lot of more exciting things to do."

"When you took over this manor and the boring routine you must have been subjected to, did you change your mind? I gather that the previous lady of the manor left behind a large box of needles and a range of coloured wools. It is so long ago you may not remember."

"I do remember that annoying set of embroidery needles and wools. It caused a major conflict with Tommy. When the box was discovered, he wanted me to teach some of the local girls the art. I was furious. What use is embroidery to common folk? It was a pastime invented for aristocratic women to keep them out of trouble until they were married off and then in their dotage to give them something to do. The girls in the dale lived in the real world and had no time for such fineries. They were needed by their parents to help make ends meet."

"Thomas was not happy with your decision?"

"No, he never accepted the argument that it would serve no good purpose and attributed my decision to an overinflated view of my own social superiority."

"What happened to the box?"

"He gave it to the only other gentlewoman in the dale at the time, the former rector's wife, Cecilia Garnett."

"Did she use it?"

"Yes, she improved the furnishings of the church with some exquisite embroidery."

"Did she teach any of the locals?" Matilda asked.

"Under great pressure from Tommy, she tried to interest a few girls, but few responded."

"Do you know what happened to the box?"

"I don't, but Cecilia is still alive in York and has her wits about her. She may be able to tell you what you want to know. Why the interest in an old box of embroidery needles?"

"Luke believes that Charles Ogden was stabbed with a needle, probably a crewel needle from that or a similar set."

Janet was cynical. "From my girlhood, I remember crewel needles, while incredibly sharp, were also very short. They would not reach, let alone penetrate, the heart."

"Very true of high-quality needles made on the continent, but I have seen several needles twice the length of my own made by local smiths," replied Matilda.

Peter, who had business in York, was asked to visit Mistress Garnett and discover the location of her embroidery box. Her answer gave Luke a reason to further interrogate the current rector, Edward Unsworth.

"Reverend, when your predecessor died, and his widow moved to York, did she leave many of their possessions behind?"

"Yes, Cecilia only took what she needed. Most of the family belongings are still here."

"Did you find a box that contained items she needed for her embroidery, or did she take that with her?"

"I remember a vague discussion about that. I thought she would be so bored in her new environment that her needlework would give her something to do. At that point, she admitted to me that her failing eyesight made it difficult for her to embroider and she would leave the box behind for me to dispose of, or should I marry a gentlewoman, it could be a gift for my wife."

"So you have kept the box in case you marry?" asked Luke with a smile.

"I still have the box because I have not got around to sorting through the Garnett possessions. I placed them all in a small storeroom where they remain untouched since the day they were placed there."

"Could you dig out the box and allow me to take it to the manor for Lady Matilda to examine?"

"No problem." Edward summoned a servant and explained what he had to look for and where it might be found. He continued. "If her ladyship is interested, I am quite happy to gift the box to her. Given her background, she must be a talented embroiderer."

"Thanks for the offer, but Matilda already has an extensive amount of embroidery tools and materials. I just need her to examine your box to help us solve the murder of Charles Ogden."

"Was he stabbed by a needle from my box?" exclaimed Unsworth with some alarm.

"Possibly. He was certainly stabbed by a very narrow needle-type blade."

Matilda arrived at supper after examining the embroidery casket. She informed Luke, Peter, and Emma that she may have identified but not found the weapon that killed Charles Ogden. "The box has an embroidered top and, within, an embroidered cushion that had been worked on in such a way as to create five depressions into which the five needles would have fitted. There were only four places occupied. After comparing it with my own set, the missing implement was the crewel needle, which is the longest, thinnest, and has the sharpest point. The only needle missing from this box, or one identical with it, is your murder weapon. In addition, to counter the point raised by both Peter and Janet, Mistress Garnett's needles are twice as long as mine and could penetrate deeply into a body."

Next morning, Luke returned the box to the rectory. He asked Edward, "Did you ever look into this box?"

"No. Why do you ask?"

"It is highly probable that the weapon that killed Ogden came from this box. The sharpest needle is missing. Where exactly did you store the box?"

Edward seemed relieved when he answered, "Not in the house. It was in one of the small outhouses between here and the barn. Any of my workers or even passersby have access to them." "These storerooms are not locked?"

"No, I keep nothing of value in them. It is mainly the Garnett leftovers, which I will sell or use as fuel."

"I must question your servants. They may have looked into the box or know of someone who showed an interest in it."

The house servant, apart from bringing the box to Edward at Luke's request the previous day, had never visited the storehouse. One of the labourers, quite unexpectedly, provided some relevant information.

"On Mother Harland's last visit about ten days ago to inspect the rector's cattle, she noticed that one of the cows was limping and had something stuck under its foot. She asked if we had any sharp implements that she could use to remove it. I said there were a lot of old boxes in the storehouse that may contain something useful. I went to look. I opened one box, and I found a lot of needles. I took it to the witch, who asked if there were any other needles with a blunted head or preferably a chisel that would provide a better scraper. I returned it to the box."

"Did she comment about the box and what it contained?"

"She joked that the aristocracy would be appalled if they knew their precious embroidery needles came close to being used on a cow."

"When you returned the box to the storehouse, were all five needles intact?"

"Yes."

Luke thanked the labourer and, on returning home, immediately told Peter and Harry, "The missing needle was still in its box a week before Charles was murdered."

Harry commented, "That needle could have been stolen by anybody. It would make a good concealed weapon, and I can see it being useful in picking food from a platter and taking it to your mouth. I will ask around at the tavern tonight if anybody was seen with such an object."

"It's a long shot, but I am beginning to learn that in this dale, everybody meddles in everybody else's business," remarked Luke hopefully.

Harry could not wait to inform Luke of his successful questioning of his fellow drinkers at the Three Roses. "There are a couple of troublemakers, casual workers, who are employed by the rector to clean up the drains on the glebe. They regularly confront some of their fellow drinkers. One of them, who was taller than most, used a needlelike implement to pick food from a communal platter and jokingly threatened to use it on another customer who annoyed him. However, he got his just reward before I arrived last night. A local gave him a good thrashing."

Luke was frustrated. "It looks like yet another visit to the rectory."

14

NEXT MORNING, LUKE AND Matilda were in their reception hall, bidding farewell to Mother Harland, who had stayed the night, when Emma burst through the door and announced, "Simon has disappeared. He did not return home, but I was not greatly concerned until I spoke to Mr Frost outside a few minutes ago. Two days ago, Simon told me that he would be absent over night because Mr Frost had sent him on an urgent mission to see Mother Harland at Elderby to lease a boar. Mr Frost says he gave no such instruction, and as I can see, Mother Harland is here."

Mother Harland commented, "Two days ago, I was still in Elderby, but until today, neither his lordship nor his steward was aware of my role in the sale and nurture of livestock."

Luke asked, "Does Simon have a history of returning late from assignments?"

"Simon gets muddled, but usually, others make sure he returns home. I should have known Mr Frost would not have sent him off alone."

"I'll get the constable to organise a search immediately," announced Luke.

Emma showed signs of distress. "No, I would prefer the search to be conducted by members of the manor and the Papist community. Constable Dutton has shown an intense dislike towards us since his elevation to that position."

"I'll get Peter and Harry to accompany Mother Harland home to Elderby, and in the process, they can ask questions along the way concerning sightings of Simon. He may have headed in that direction as he told Emma and become disoriented when he found Mother Harland was not at home" was Luke's optimistic response.

Mother Harland spoke quietly. "I have known Simon all his life. What he told you results from regressing to his childhood. From when he was little until well into his teens, whenever he became stressed, he would escape from the manor to visit me and play with the young kids, lambs, and calves that I happened to be looking after at the time. I agree with Sir Luke. Simon came to see me, found I wasn't home, and became confused. In the old days, he would probably have met Ted Unsworth there assisting me. They became the most unlikely of friends. How things have now changed! Nevertheless, I would talk to Ted."

Peter and Harry escorted Mother Harland to Elderby and questioned people along the path Simon may have followed. Later in the afternoon, Luke went to see Ted. He was not at home. Luke went on to the Three Roses.

The raucous din ceased as Luke entered the premises. He took advantage of silence to inform the drinkers that Simon had disappeared and asked if they could give him the details if any of them had seen the bailiff in the last two days. There was an overwhelming air of cooperation as most of the drinkers made the same point—Simon had been drinking with them the previous evening. If he had gone to Elderby, he had clearly returned.

Luke questioned the publican James Harland, who explained, "Simon arrived here early last night, completely exhausted. He had gone to Elderby to see my sister, unaware that she was here in Abbeythwaite, advising you on animal care."

"Did he stay here long?"

James began to fidget with the towel with which he was drying some pewter jugs. "Several hours!" was the terse response.

"And pardon, your lordship, as drunk as a lord," chimed in an eavesdropping female drinker.

"Did he cause any trouble?" asked Luke.

James answered as he glared at the interloper, "His behaviour led to a near riot."

"Not true, Your Honour!" countered the recipient of James's glare.

"And who are you?" asked Lukeasked,. ing

"I'm am Alice Eaves, sister of Emma Snigg. Simon is my brother-in-law. Poor Simon was deliberately provoked by the constable's cronies. He desperately tried to avoid confrontation until one of the riffraff threw a flagon of beer over him. Simon swung a few punches, and given his size and strength, several drinkers found themselves on the floor. The publican here sent for the constable, who arrived and immediately arrested Simon and ignored those that had provoked him."

"Is this true?" Luke asked of James.

"Simon's presence after a few drinks always creates a problem. None of his Papist friends did anything to control him. The constable was only doing his duty."

"Was Simon provoked as Alice claims?"

"Not that I saw! I was serving my customers and did not see or hear everything," admitted James.

Luke turned to the gathered throng and, after achieving silence, declared, "The last you all saw of Simon Snigg was here, last night, very late, very drunk, being led away by Constable Dutton?"

There was a mumble of agreement.

Peter and Harry returned next morning, confirming that Simon had been seen by countless people on his way to and from Elderby, and the last person they questioned saw him enter the Three Roses. Luke brought Peter up to date, and both headed to interview the constable.

Robert Dutton and his men were clearing the ditches to cope with the expected spring rains. The previous summer's uncontrolled growth of brambles had seriously dislocated the drainage system, a problem revealed during an unexpected unseasonable downpour.

Robert looked up from his work and asked, "To what do we owe the pleasure of his lordship's visit?"

"Simon Snigg!" answered Luke.

"That drunkard has had a good twenty-four hours to sober up. I feel sorry for him. Why Bates appointed him to succeed his father was unforgivable. It is unfair to Simon and to the whole of the dale. You must remove him. What has he done now?"

"Disappeared, and you may have been the last person to see him."

"Possibly. I was summoned to the Three Roses about eleven, well beyond the time they should have stopped serving drinks. Simon had caused an affray by flooring two other drinkers, and quickly, the tavern divided into supporters of Simon and those of his victims. I closed the drinking house immediately and, with the aid of a few members of the watch, escorted Simon out of the establishment and walked him through Abbeythwaite, almost to his old front door."

"Who were the watch members?" asked Peter.

"Billie Briggs, the miller, and Dick Unsworth, the cobbler," replied Robert.

"Why did you not deliver him to the redoubtable Emma at the manor?"

"He pleaded with us that he did not wish to be seen by Emma in his condition. He would sleep it off on the bank of the beck opposite his old house. That is where we left him, about midnight the night before last. He had forgotten that he now lived within the manor."

Later that morning, Luke informed Emma. "Simon did go to Elderby and returned the same day but spent too much time at the Three Roses and decided to sleep it off opposite your old house on the bank of the beck. Did you not completely move into the manor on your appointment as housekeeper?"

"Yes, but Simon gets confused. Did anybody see him come from the tavern to a spot opposite the old house?"

"Yes, he was personally escorted there by Constable Dutton and two of the watch, Billie Briggs and Dick Unsworth."

Emma glowered. "The extreme Protestants of the dale! In the past, they have hinted if they had their way, Simon would be put away and certainly not occupy any position in the manor. They would, if they have their way, remove all of us Papists from the manor, if not the dale itself. They started with Charlie Ogden, and now my Simon has gone. They probably pushed the poor drunken man into the raging beck. Mark my word, you will find his body farther down the stream!" she exclaimed with obvious anguish.

Luke had not realised that his Catholic employees were so fearful of the Protestant majority. Thomas Bates had done the right thing in trying to protect them. Accepting that Emma may be slightly hysterical given the situation, he was determined to examine the area where Simon was supposed to have settled down for the night.

The recent rain had softened the soil, enabling it to record a range of footprints. By their size, one set was clearly Simon's, and a small pile of vomit, which remained after the downpour, indicated a position where Simon must have been. Other footprints created more problems than they solved. After spending almost an hour in the area, he was unexpectedly accosted by Alice Eades, who asked, "Sir, have you found anything of interest? What is the latest on poor Simon?"

Luke carefully explained the substance of his investigation so far and received an unexpected response. "Sir, take what my sister, Emma, tells you with a grain of salt. From childhood, she has been obsessed by the belief that there is a Protestant conspiracy to murder every Catholic in the dale. And there was something strange regarding her marriage with Simon. I could never understand why such a bright girl married that simpleton."

"Surely, she or her father would have explained the situation?"

"No, I was never close to my birth siblings. The Carvers suffered more than most in the economic crisis of the last decade. They were not saved like the Ogdens, Sniggs, and Foxtons by support with employment and land by the then Catholic lord of Abbey Grange and later by the very tolerant Thomas Bates. Having had Tim and Emma, my parents could not afford to keep a third child, and as a baby, I was handed over to Michael Eades, whose wife discovered she could have no more children to accompany William, who was a surviving twin. I was brought up as his sister, but everybody knew I was a Carver, and when both of us reached adulthood, we married. The Eades were Protestants, as am I. While growing up, I spent some time with my birth family but did not revert to their religion or share my sister's obsessions concerning sectarian conflict."

"So Simon was not murdered by Constable Dutton and his men?"

"No. That is ridiculous. That is the sort of comment that brings onto the Catholics unnecessary antagonism. They cause a lot of trouble for themselves. They are so thin skinned."

"You are sure that Dutton is not responsible?"

"I am sure. Two nights ago, when the constable closed the tavern and evicted all of us and escorted Simon away, I dallied in the shadows. I was concerned for Simon's welfare. I saw the constable and his two cronies return from what I assumed was delivering Simon to his old house. I thought Simon had shown unexpected foresight in asking to be taken to his old house and not returned to Emma at the manor. Then I saw the two victims of Simon's punches head in the direction of the Sniggs's old house. I did not see if they reached the area where Simon was resting as my husband, hearing of the uproar at the tavern, met me and took me home."

"Who were these victims?"

"I don't know their names, but they work on the glebe land for the rector. A nasty couple!"

"Did they have any distinguishing features that would help me identify them?"

"They both lost a few teeth as a result of Simon's fists. One is lame, one leg shorter than the other, and the second man is exceptionally tall."

Luke was excited, saying, "That explains one set of footprints, one heavy and one lighter print." Then reality set in. Luke clarified the situation. He had nothing.

"What you say, Alice, is very important but inconclusive. You saw the constable and his men leaving the scene, but they may have already pushed Simon into the stream, and you saw his victims heading in the direction of his old house but did not see them confront Simon, although footprints suggest they were in the area."

15

L UKE AND MATILDA DISCUSSED events over supper. Luke was optimistic, believing that both the murder of Ogden and the disappearance of Snigg were probably the work of the casual labourers employed by Ted Unsworth. Matilda was more realistic. "You have nothing to connect those men with Ogden. As he lived within this house, our own servants should be able to give us the most useful information regarding his last hours, and they are probably the more likely suspects." It was decided that Luke would interview the Carver family while Matilda would speak with the manor's servants.

When Luke arrived at the Carver cottage next morning, only Mary was at home. She assumed Luke had come about the burial of her father. She immediately appealed to Luke. saying, "Please, sir, turn a blind eye and allow us to bury Father according to the rites of our church!"

"The law is clear, Mary. Catholics cannot be buried within the grounds of the parish church, although under the late king, most Anglican clergy did turn a blind eye and allow Papists to bury their loved ones at night in an unmarked grave. Unsworth would not allow you to do that here. What do you plan to do?"

"We are very fortunate in this dale. We can use the derelict but dedicated burial ground of the old abbey, which exists on the edge of your land."

"I will not prevent you from burying your father along the lines you suggest, but I will not tolerate the presence of any priest in the dale."

"I have not seen a priest in the dale for two years. Although Father will not receive the full rites of the church in the absence of a priest, we have laymen who can conduct most of the service."

"Will a local do this?"

"Not at the moment. Martin Snigg, the late bailiff of the manor, had such authorization, but with his death, we have to call on an outsider from York. We may need your help, my lord, in ensuring that the funeral is conducted with the dignity and tranquillity it deserves."

"Why? Have you received threats of disruption?"

"Not so much threats but objections. My husband's Protestant sister, Alice Eades, is causing trouble. She claims Father committed suicide because of his overwhelming sins and, as such, cannot be buried in any sacred ground, Protestant or Catholic. She horribly suggested that his body should simply be left on the moors for the crows and ravens."

"Rest assured I can officially confirm that your father did not commit suicide. He was murdered."

"Alice has also indicated that she will inform Constable Dutton and the rector that the layman coming to the dale to perform the ceremony is a Catholic priest in disguise."

"Why is she doing this?"

"She has always hated Father. He was not an angel and mistreated and abused me when I was a child, but that was his way. Whatever he did, he was my father, and with the flight of my mother when I was a baby, he brought me up. His lack of a wife made him over affectionate towards me. Alice sees this as an evil trait."

Luke stopped his line of questioning as tears began to flow freely down the cheeks of the bereaved young woman. He quickly changed the subject. "Mary, I did not come to discuss the funeral but to get your help in uncovering his murderer. When did you last see your father?"

"I did not see much of him in the last few months. When we were first married, he used to visit every day, but Tim was not happy with this. They had words. Since then, he only came on his way to or from the Three Roses when Tim was at home."

"Did you see him on the day before his body was found?"

"Yes, but only by chance. I was just entering my front door after visiting a neighbour, and he came past. As Tim was not at home, we simply nodded to each other."

Luke wondered what had turned Charles's son-in-law against him, although the refusal of many fathers to really let their daughters go, even after marriage, was not uncommon.

Luke gently asked, "Did your father seem agitated over your last few meetings?"

"Not at all. In fact, he appeared very relaxed after months of stress with the transfer of the manor to you. He said he found Captain Frost a very pleasant superior and yourself not the Protestant bigot that your past service with Oliver Cromwell might have suggested."

Luke smiled to himself. Sectarian antagonism was alive and well in the dale. Perhaps Alice Eades's vendetta against Ogden was so inspired.

Meanwhile, Matilda questioned the servants. She began with her most reliable source, the twins, Abigail and Phyllis Harland. "My husband is trying to discover what Mr Ogden did on the day that he was murdered."

"What day was that again?" asked Phyllis.

"Two days ago. Did you see Mr Ogden on that fatal day?"

Abigail ignored the question but confessed, "I never liked Mr Ogden. He was always ogling us and slapping us on the buttocks. He constantly invited one of us up to his rooms, but we never went. The very last time we saw him, he made a lewd remark, and I threatened him with the wringer handle."

"Was that wise?" asked an alarmed and surprised Matilda.

"He couldn't hurt us. We are two strong country girls, and he was a very puny little man. I don't know why he terrified so many of the girls in the dale."

"Had he always behaved like this?" asked Matilda, probing.

"We only came here just before you, but according to the gossip in the Three Roses, his interest in young women increased after the marriage of his daughter. She must have kept him in line. Mistress Bates would know if there was any trouble with him in the past."

Phyllis answered, "With regard to your question, I saw him late in the day heading off for what he claimed would be several hours of drinking that would combine work with pleasure."

"You saw him later that evening in the Three Roses?"

"Yes. By the time we arrived, he was very drunk."

"Was he talking with anyone in particular?"

"Not that we noticed. We were with our own friends, and old Charlie Ogden was not of any great interest to us."

"Did you see him in conversation with two newcomers, a tall man and his friend with a limp?"

"The two troublemakers that Simon Snigg flattened. No, we did not see Ogden and those two in any conversation," said Abigail.

"In answer to your earlier question, I did see Ogden have a few words with his son-in-law, Tim Carver, and a few minutes later, Tim's sister, Alice Eades, made a rude gesture in Charlie's direction," said Phyllis.

"You got a distinct impression that Tim and Alice were unhappy with Charlie?"

"Definitely," Phyllis confirmed.

That evening, Luke and Matilda updated each other in the presence of Peter, who immediately surprised them.

"If I had been here last night, I could have saved both of you the trouble of today's interrogations. Charles Ogden did have a link with the two casual workers as a result of my direct request. On the day he died, we reassessed our labour needs for the next month and agreed that an extra two or three casual labourers would be needed. Charlie offered to put out a few offers at the Three Roses that night as it was the drinking place of several casual workers, some of whose current employment would be coming to an end. It is more than likely he approached your two suspects with an offer of a job after their commitment to Unsworth ended in a day or two."

"If that be the case, why murder him?"

"Money. I gave Charlie a purse of silver coins to make an initial payment to any recruit," replied Peter.

"Was any money found on Charlie's body?" asked Matilda.

"No, but given his time in the raging beck, a purse could have been ripped off his body, or any loose change spread across the bottom of the stream by the forces of nature," replied Luke.

"However, if these two suspects have been spending more than their expected income, we have solved Charlie's murder," concluded Peter.

Emma arrived for supper late, having been detained searching for her missing husband. Matilda asked her a question that surprised everybody. "Why did your sister, Alice Eades, hate Charlie Ogden?"

Emma was flustered but quickly regained her composure and, in Luke's eyes, lied through her teeth. "I did not know that Alice held such a view. Given her upbringing outside our faith, she did display a coldness towards those who remained loyal to mother church, but hatred directed at one particular man is most unlikely."

Luke probed more deeply, asking, "Before we arrived here after Easter, were there any rumours that Ogden ill-treated young girls?"

"I was not closely associated with the manor until just before your arrival. My family, the Carvers, did not have positions here. It was only when my father-in-law died and his son, my husband, Simon, was named as bailiff in his place that I came here. Most of us as young girls faced constant harassment from males, whether they were strangers, fathers, or brothers. It is how things are. Charles Ogden was probably no worse or better than most of the males in the dale."

"One piece of evidence that Charles Ogden was not such a predator was that given his puny physique, any healthy country girl could physically stop any molestation," added Matilda.

"Yes, and it is a red herring that takes our main investigation away from the two casual labourers. I am anxious to uncover if they have unexplained silver coins on their person," Luke concluded.

Luke visited Ted Unsworth yet again. He was not in the rectory, and Luke was directed to the church. He saw the ideal opportunity to put this unlikeable cleric in his place. He walked to the front pew reserved for him as the lord of the manor, closed the gate, and called on Unsworth to approach him, ensuring he would stand like a penitent outside of it.

"Is this a formal visit of the holder of the advowson to his appointed rector?" asked a slightly disconcerted Edward.

"No, it is a visit by the local magistrate to interview a suspect in a murder and an even more recent disappearance."

"I have no information to offer regarding the disappearance of Simon Snigg. Why question me regarding the absence of your own bailiff, who, being a Papist, had no links with me at all?"

"Not true, as boys,you were very close, and as under stress Simon often reverts to his childhood, it is reasonable to assume that he may have visited you. But more relevant is that two of your workers were involved in a fight with Snigg in the Three Roses the night before last and were then seen near where Snigg disappeared. They are the prime suspects in his possible murder."

16

"**I** AM NOT RESPONSIBLE for the behaviour of my casual workers," Unsworth replied defensively.

"Maybe, but there is a fear that Protestant extremists of which you are one may have embarked on a systematic removal of all Papists and their sympathisers from the dale. First, Thomas Bates, and then Charlie Ogden, and now Simon Snigg. The murder weapon used on Ogden probably came from one of your outhouses, and the men who assaulted Snigg before he disappeared are employed by you. Some suggest that whoever actually did these dastardly deeds was acting on instructions from you or Robert Dutton. Of course, I do not accept such wild and scandalous assertions, but I must question your two workers. Who are they, and where would I find them?"

"I do not know their real names. I employed them casually to clean the drains and remove excess scrub from the glebe. I know them as Creepy Crawley and Tall Saul. The former was named Crawley and, given his gammy leg, obtained his nickname, while his companion was a Saul, who was exceptionally tall," explained the pedantic rector. Ted was determined to push Luke's patience to the extreme.

"I don't need a lecture in the origin of their names. Where are they now?"

"I don't know."

"How can that be? Masters have an exact picture of where their casual labour is every minute of the working day."

"True, but they are no longer employees of mine."

Luke waited with increasing impatience for Unsworth to explain. He did not. "Why are they no longer employed by you?" He was forced to ask.

"They both arrived at work yesterday morning drunk and with missing teeth. Their faces were smeared in blood. I sacked them on the spot."

"Where did they go?"

"North, up the dale."

Two hours later, Luke and Harry headed north in pursuit of the two itinerant workers. Peter, given the death of Charlie and the disappearance of Simon, remained at Abbey Grange to administer the manor and its associated farms.

The chase was not difficult. The quarry had started at the Three Roses, where they converted the pittance they had been paid by the rector into several pints of ale, which they consumed with relish. They clearly did not have a purse stuffed full of silver coins. They left after some hours stealing a large flagon of freshly brewed ale. Their path north was a litany of destruction and theft. One inhabitant complained of a broken hen coop with his poultry scattered across the dale and all the newly laid eggs taken. A passerby reported that the egg thieves had also stolen two hens, wrung their necks, and tied the bodies around their waists.

A group of Elderby women making their way to Abbeythwaite to sell their produce claimed that they were assaulted by two men who inappropriately fondled them. The complainants claimed that unless they kissed the smaller man, he said he would slash their faces. As there were six women adept at wielding their staves, and encouraged by their assessment that the two men were too drunk to cause any real problem, a united female attack drove them off. The only gain for thieves was a round of cheese that had been thrown at them during the fracas.

Farther up the dale, an irate farmer claimed that two men had stolen his shire horse and then acontinued in a northerly direction. His horse could easily carry the two men, but as it was part of a slow plough team, the magistrate and his assistant would have little trouble catching up with the pair. Such was not to be. On reaching the moors, there was no trace of the shire horse and its two riders. Luke assumed they had diverted into some small gully or cave to cook their chicken and eggs and eat their cheese. As it was getting dark, Luke decided to spend the night at the Pilgrim's Rest.

Kit welcomed Luke warmly and was interested in his mission. He was sorry to hear that Simon had disappeared and was presumed dead, at least by Luke. Creepy Crawley and Tall Saul were not unknown to Kit, being itinerant workers across the north,riding for several years. They were known to be violent and systematic thieves, but Kit did not think they were callous murderers.

"What if they were paid to kill?" asked Luke.

"I don't know. Tomorrow when you resume your search, take Elinor, my servant, with you."

"How can your admittedly attractive barmaid help?"

"Don't underestimate her, Luke! She has spent all her life on the moors and, with her father, was able to track man and beast across the landscape.

After our recent rains, a heavy shire horse should cause her no problems."

Next morning, Luke was concerned by the heavy fog, but Elinor claimed it would help her tracking by keeping any tracks moist. She suggested that they return to the head of Abbey Dale where it entered the moors. Travellers heading for Whitby would normally follow the track in a northerly direction until they reached the far side of the moors and then turned eastward along the Esk valley to their destination.

Those in a hurry or just foolhardy would attempt to cross the moors diagonally, directly from the head of the dale to Whitby itself, the whole journey spent on the changing conditions and landscape of the potentially treacherous moors.

It was not long before Elinor exclaimed, "Sir, this is where they left the main track! If there wasn't any fog, you would see in the distance a small hill known as Peter's Peak. The ignorant think that by keeping the peak in sight, they will have a reasonable journey across the moors. Unfortunately, this route crosses the most dangerous part of the moors with numerous sinkholes, concealed mine shafts, precipitous climbing over rocky terrain along barely defined paths, and wetlands that conceal deep ponds and even quicksand. The regular icing up of the rocky paths create a serious danger of slipping into oblivion."

Not far along the route taken by the two suspects, Luke's group passed an isolated hut. Elinor knew its inhabitant but suggested that as he did not talk to strangers, they remain out of sight, hidden by the fog. Ten minutes later, she returned. "Our quarry passed this way late yesterday and pleaded with Hairy Harry for some embers to light a fire. He obliged and sent them on their way, furious that in departing, they stole some of his dry wood."

The fog began to lift, and sometime later, they passed a small cave at the entrance of which were eggshells, feathers and chicken bones, and evidence of a fire. "At least they had a good meal," observed Harry.

Eventually, Luke's party reached a rocky outcrop, which they would have to cross. Elinor suggested they dismount and keep a tight grip of their horses' reins as they picked their way along what amounted to the edge of precipice. Having progressed only a few yards across these slippery rocks, she exclaimed, "My god, look below! It is a body!"

There at the foot of the precipice lay a body, which, given its length, was Tall Saul. Elinor pointed out scrape marks on the rocks where he had slipped and dislodged stones as he valiantly but unsuccessfully tried to hold on. She moved ahead a little and observed, "The man with the bad leg continued on despite the loss of his partner. He should have at least, according to custom, covered the body with rocks."

"If that is what goes for a Christian burial in this godforsaken place, let us give Saul such a resting place," observed Luke.

He and Harry carefully climbed down the cliff face and began to methodically cover Tall Saul's body to some depth with rocks. Harry suddenly exclaimed, "There is something metallic attached to his leather jacket!"

Both men were delighted. "It is a long needle that had been sharpened at the end," Harry announced.

Luke quietly commented, "We have found the murderer of Charles Ogden. There are too many coincidences. This is the only explanation that adds up."

As they returned to the excuse for a path, Elinor commented on the rock burial, "It has a practical reason. It stops the rats from eating the body." As if to underline Elinor's observation, within half an hour, they uncovered the work of rats. After leaving the rocky surface of the outcrops, they followed Creepy Crawley's path through the wetlands. Elinor warned that along this stretch of their route, there were a number of old mine shafts that had been filled in, but with the recent unusual rain, many had subsided. As they approached one, she warned the men to keep well away from the edge as it might crumble.

Harry, certain that his lighter weight would not cause any landslide, ignored the warning and, peering over the edge, shouted, "Stop! There's a skeleton down there, and it's wearing Mr Bates's doublet!"

Luke examined the relatively fresh body from which most of the flesh had been eaten away, leaving little more than a skeleton and some torn and ripped fabric. Luke turned to Harry.saying, "What makes you think that it is Mr Bates's doublet? You never met the man."

"No, but talking to our farmhands, they told me in passing that Bates always wore a bright red doublet."

"That's true," added Elinor. "Every time he stayed at the pPilgrim, he wore a red doublet."

Luke summed up the situation. "This discovery fits with what we can surmise. Thomas Bates finds out something in Whitby regarding his abducted daughter. With his marriage long over, and his job of a decade coming to an end, he probably decided it was his chance to start life anew in search of his child. He probably wished to avoid his friends at the Pilgrim's Rest and took this shortcut across the moors."

Elinor interjected, "No, no, no. Mr Bates knew these moors very well. As children, he and my master Kit spent most of their time discovering its secrets. There is no way he would have fallen into the mine shaft. He was attacked and his body thrown down the newly revealed shaft."

"A good point, which raises another more serious question. Was he the random victim of opportunistic moorland robbers, or did someone follow him from Abbey Grange and wait their chance to murder him?" asked Luke.

He remained silent for some time and finally decided on a course of action.

"Harry, continue across the moor and inform the constable at Whitby to put out a hue and cry for the apprehension of a cripple known as Creepy Crawley on the suspicion of murder. I will return to the Pilgrim's Rest to obtain men, ropes, and a wagon for the recovery of what is left of the body."

Elinor dissented, saying, "Sir, it will be dangerous for Harry to travel alone. I will lead him to Whitby and then back to the pPilgrim by this same shortcut."

Luke, and especially Harry, willingly accepted her offer.

17

HEAVY STORM CLOUDS GATHERED, and finally, the heavens opened with large hailstones and a downpour that continued relentlessly. Harry and Elinor sought shelter. Elinor found a dry, elevated cave that penetrated deep into a small hillock. No sooner had they entered the shelter than the silence was broken by a strange noise coming from deeper within the cave. Harry drew his sword, closely followed by a dagger-armed Elinor. The piglike snoring emanated from a human figure propped against the wall of the cave, perilously close to what appeared to be a fast-running underground stream.

It was a sleeping Creepy Crawley. Elinor took a rope from her saddlebag and tied his feet together. She was attempting to do the same to his hands when he awoke. Harry's sword was immediately at his throat. Creepy, who appeared to have sobered up, exclaimed, "Leave me alone! I have nothing to steal!"

Harry responded, "We are not robbers but officers of the law. I arrest you to appear before Magistrate Tremayne on suspicion of the murder of Simon Snigg. You and your late partner in crime were seen near the spot where Snigg was last seen alive," explained Harry.

Breathing heavily, Creepy explained, "When we heard that the constable had left Snigg beside the bank of the beck, Saul and I decided to get our revenge for the humiliation we suffered in the tavern. We were determined to give him the thrashing of his life. When we reached the spot where we thought Snigg was to be found sleeping off his overindulgence, the bank was deserted. Saul claimed the grass was depressed near the edge where

Snigg must have lain, but the area was completely deserted. We were about to look farther upstream, but I felt sick and vomited. We staggered back to our temporary quarters in the rectory barn."

"Did anybody see you come or go from the scene? Did you see anybody in the area?"

"I was obviously too drunk to take things in clearly, but I have a vague impression of a group of women in the middle of the road between Snigg's house and the stream."

"A group of women or a single woman?" asked Harry, seeking clarification.

Elinor, who, during this interrogation, had moved to the entrance of the cave to see if the rain had stopped, returned in state of alarm. "Harry, there is a large body of mounted horsemen heading this way. They are a military formation, but they are not government troops. Their leader is dressed in the most lavish fashion and wears his hair long, and several of the men are wearing white overcoats as did the Earl of Newcastle's troops early in the war. It is a unit of Royalist cavalry."

The recently retired parliamentary soldier reasserted itself in Harry. "We must hide. If this is a Royalist raid, they would not like their movements to be seen by a government supporter. They will probably need to kill us both to keep their whereabouts secret. Luke would want to know if they are a locally raised group coming out into the open as the republican government disintegrates or whether they are small invasion force landed from the continent."

"The rain has stopped. They might bypass this cave and miss us," whispered Elinor hopefully.

"To be sure, let's move our horses deeper into the cave and hope they do not probe its interior."

"What do we do with Creepy? Will I gag him as well?" asked Elinor.

"No, you lead the horses as far as you can into the cave. I will deal with Creepy."

Harry faced a dilemma. A quick shot to the head would be the simplest solution, but the sound of the shot might alert the approaching Royalists. What would Luke do? The answer was obvious. Creepy, with his hands and feet bound and sitting on the edge of the stream, was given a hefty push.

His scream was cut short as his body was immediately carried out of sight and, hearing, as the stream cascaded, deeper underground.

Harry rejoined Elinor, and both struggled to adjust to the darkness in the deep recesses of the cave. Luck was not with them as at least two men entered the cave. One was clearly the commanding officer, who complained, "These hand-drawn maps are almost useless. We need to find a local that can lead you to Sergeant Jagger and another that can take me to General Tremayne."

Suddenly, Harry's horse whinnied loudly. Both Royalist officers drew their swords. The commander shouted, "Come out of the darkness, whoever you are!"

Elinor ripped open her blouse. "Pretend to be lovers!" Elinor and Harry appeared before the two Royalist officers wrapped in each other's arms and kissing each other passionately. Elinor purred, "Please, sir, do us no harm. We are just a couple of lovers sheltering from the rain."

"No harm will befall you. Are you local to this area?" asked the Royalist commander.

Elinor immediately confessed, "Yes, I am a servant at the Pilgrim's Rest."

The commander's face lit up with delight. "Then, wench, you can lead my captain here and all his men to your master. What about you, lad?"

Harry thought carefully and responded, "I used to work at Abbey Grange, but since the Roundhead general took over, I have been seeking employment with Mr Jagger to be near my sweetheart." "This is my lucky day. You will take me to General Tremayne."

"Is that wise, your lordship? Travelling alone in the enemy heartland to visit a notorious Cromwellian general is not the wisest of moves," commented the Royalist captain.

"Tremayne is an honourable man and will see that I am treated appropriately. I carry a personal message from His Majesty to an enemy officer not as a spy but as an emissary of the king seeking to talk to various members of the current republican government."

Harry was troubled as he led the Royalist commander off the moors and down the dale towards Abbey Grange. Could his admired commander and stalwart of the Cromwellian regime and parliamentary army be contemplating desertion to the enemy? This angst was relieved by reliving the tingling feeling that his close proximity to the buxom Elinor had created.

The Royalist officer broke the silence. "I am not here to convert General Tremayne to the king's cause but hope to use his good offices to arrange a meeting between the leaders of the English republic and King Charles. As far as the rest of the world is concerned, I am Colonel Smith, a former comrade in arms of your general."

Harry relaxed. "I must confess that I lied to you on the moors. I am still Sir Luke's servant and was accompanying him on magisterial business. We separated after discovering what may be the body of a former steward of the manor. Luke is still on the moor. We will reach the manor before he returns."

They did. Harry left the Royalist officer in the reception hall while he reported developments to Lady Matilda. She returned with him to the hall to welcome her guest. She immediately recognised the visitor. "This is a surprise, Lord Ashcroft, commander of Charles Stuart's bodyguard no less."

"I too am surprised. I knew that Tremayne had married at last but not to the vivacious widow of my old friend Sir Nicholas Lynne."

"I hope, Ashcroft, that you are not here to subvert Luke to the Royalist cause. Although he is no longer in the army, which is in disarray, Luke will not transfer his allegiance unless he can be convinced that England would be better off by a return to the Stuarts."

"Not at all! I have a personal letter from the king to Tremayne, which I understand seeks his good offices to organise a meeting between representatives of the current English government and myself. As I told Luke's man, I am to be known as Colonel Smith, a former comrade in arms from Luke's days in Ireland."

Before Matilda could respond, Luke entered the room. He was flabbergasted. "Unbelievable! The commander of Charles Stuart's bodyguard in the North Yorkshire dales. Welcome, my lord, to Abbey Grange. My man tells me you have a letter for me from Charles Stuart himself."

Lord Ashcroft opened his doublet and withdrew an elaborately sealed letter and handed it to Luke. Matilda indicated that she would take Lord Ashcroft to his quarters within the manor and they would leave Luke alone to peruse the letter from the would-be king.

After reading the epistle twice over, Luke expressed a deep sigh of relief. Although the current state of the English republican government and its army was in disarray, Luke was hopeful that the situation would right itself and the army resume its mission of reform. He did not wish to be thrown prematurely into consideration of any change of allegiance in what might become another Civil War.

The letter was cleverly written. It did not in any way imply that its recipient was a clandestine Royalist. It simply asked Luke to use his standing to persuade Sir Thomas Fairfax, the former commander in chief of the parliamentary armies, to arrange a meeting between representatives of the republican government and Lord Ashcroft. It also contained another clause on local affairs that surprised Luke, but which for the present, he would keep to himself.

He put Peter and Harry partly in the picture, announcing, "Tomorrow I will take our visitor, Colonel Smith, across the county to the West Riding estate of Sir Thomas Fairfax."

Before he left with Colonel Smith, he had a solemn duty to perform. He had to inform Janet that her husband's body had been recovered.

Luke was direct. "There is no simple way of informing you, Janet, that a body has been found down a mine shaft, which could not be identified immediately as rats had eaten away most of the flesh. Harry and a servant girl both identified a bit of fabric at the scene as being of a similar colour to Thomas's array of red doublets." Luke produced the piece of fabric and asked, "Could you see if a red doublet is missing?"

"It won't help. Thomas had six or seven red doublets. I would not know if one of them was missing."

"You can at least ascertain whether this piece of cloth is or is not the same fabric as his other doublets."

Janet led Luke to Thomas's bedroom and to a gigantic wardrobe where he quickly established that the piece of fabric was identical to the fabric in all of Thomas's doublets.

Luke put his arm around Janet. "This is not definite proof that the body is Thomas's, but it strongly increases the probability."

"But I cannot see Tommy falling down a mine shaft. He knew the moors better than anyone. He must have been pushed or thrown in."

"Kit Jagger's servant, who was with us, made a similar comment. Kit will retrieve the body and bring it here, if we confirm the fabric could have been Tom's. Yes, I personally believe he was murdered, leaving the bigger question. Was it a random act committed by a passing traveller, or was he followed from here and killed by someone from the dale?"

18

S EVERAL DAYS LATER, LUKE and Colonel Smith were shown into Sir Thomas Fairfax's reception hall. The popular former commander was intrigued.

"Good god! My old adversary of a decade or more ago, Lord Ashcroft, and in the company of the late Oliver's most effective agent. Luke, you rose to influence after I retired, but I know Oliver entrusted you with many missions to the benefit of the country. Now the two of you together, an implausible combination? Explain!"

"His Majesty, requests that you and Tremayne use your good offices to arrange a meeting between me and a representative of the current government?"

"Waste of time, Ashcroft! Governments are changing by the week. The army is completely split. General Lambert is raising troops to fight the core of the army deployed around London. There is only one hope for order and the creation of a stable government with whom young Charles Stuart can negotiate—George Monk."

"What is Monk up to?" asked Luke with an innocent air but suspicious intent.

"At this very moment, his army of occupation in Scotland may have crossed the border and be marching south to restore order and enable a free Parliament to decide England's future. I have been asked to raise a West Riding force to take on Lambert. I will write you a letter of introduction to Monk. With luck, he will be in position within weeks to arrange a meeting along the lines Charles Stuart suggests."

He turned to Luke, saying, "If contacting Monk was not so important, I would offer you a position, Tremayne, as commander of my cavalry should we have to confront Lambert."

"It will be a sad day, Sir Thomas, when such eminent soldiers as yourself and John Lambert take the field against each other," commented a depressed Luke.

"Your late master, Oliver Cromwell, once told me that a united army removed the king and England would never again have a monarch unless an English army brought him back. Help that prediction occur. Join Monk!" Fairfax pleaded.

He continued. "These are dangerous times, gentlemen. I am in two minds about providing you with an escort. It might provoke the very attention you must avoid. At least change your appearance, Nicholas. Let my man cut your hair, and I will give you a new outfit of clothes that are not obviously French silks and lace. At the moment, you look like the Royalist courtier that every West Riding tyke has learnt to hate over the last two decades."

Ashcroft responded, "Thank you, Sir Thomas, but I am in the country openly as an emissary of the king, trying to make contact with the republican government. If I try to conceal my identity, I could be deemed a spy and executed on the spot."

"That still might happen. The locals do not have much understanding of the law in these matters," Fairfax confessed.

"How far towards Scotland will we need to go before contact can be made with Monk?" asked Luke.

"I have no idea. You know Monk. He was the most cautious of all Cromwell's generals. I expected him to move south weeks ago, but he did nothing. Contact with Lord Ashcroft might clarify his objectives and speed up his move towards London."

Luke was now very uneasy. He had no intention of being drawn back into high politics when he neither had the inclination nor strong conviction in choosing between the competing factions. He had enough problems as local magistrate and lord of the manor. He expressed these views to Fairfax and concluded, "I will take Lord Ashcroft to the northern border of the county but no further. I am urgently required at home."

"Your attitude is not uncommon amongst many senior officers following the death of Oliver. I disliked the man, but he certainly inspired loyalty and devotion. Lord Ashcroft, I will send my new deputy, Colonel James, to accompany you to Monk and give you a letter of safe conduct for what it will be worth in these lawless times," Sir Thomas announced.

Luke, prompted by a surprise revelation in the letter from Charles Stuart, changed the subject. "I have been the unfortunate recipient of an obnoxious cleric whom I believe you sacked, Edward Unsworth. Have you any information that might enable me to follow your example and be rid of him?"

"His public profession of extreme Fifth Monarchy views, preaching that secular government was evil and we should prepare for the coming of the Lord by tearing down existing figures of authority, was treasonous in itself. In addition, I had reports that he was fraternising with known Royalist sympathisers in Leeds. I suspected his overt religious extremism may have been a cover for a very different political and religious position. Do not trust him, lad!"

Ashcroft, James, and Luke were soon on the northern road, which was heavy with groups of men heading for the rival musters called by Sir Thomas and John Lambert. Others had the reverse intention—escaping involvement in any coming predicted conflict. Luke cynically reflected that this was his own position. Most travelling groups avoided each other until the trio rounded a corner to be confronted by a large contingent of armed cavalry that was clearly on a mission. Its commander confronted Luke. "Who are you, and where are you going?"

"On whose authority do you ask such questions?" was the unexpected response.

"That of the English republic as represented in these parts by General Lambert."

Luke answered with a mixture of truth and downright lies, "I am a retired general, Tremayne, and with the assistance of Colonel James, we are taking this Royalist prisoner, Colonel Smith, north to Scotland."

The commander turned to Colonel James, saying, "I know you. You are Sir Thomas Fairfax's deputy. You may well be telling the truth as this third gentleman certainly looks like a Royalist fop with his long hair and silken finery."

"May we proceed on our way?" asked Luke.

"By no means. My general would want to interrogate the three of you more thoroughly—a retired general, Fairfax's equerry, and a Royalist courtier. A strange mix in this troubled area at this critical time!"

The three men waited in the reception room of a large manor house. Eventually, they were ushered into an adjacent room, where Lambert sat at a large desk completely devoid of papers and ornaments. He turned to Luke. "General, I don't think we have ever met, but I was well aware of your work for the late protector as his head of military intelligence. I suspect you knew a lot more about me at that time than I about you. I thought in recent years, you were knighted, promoted to general, and sent on diplomatic missions to Southern Europe."

"We have met briefly. When you were in London some years ago, recommending some of your men for service in Flanders in the new army we had to create, I sat in on the interviews. You are quite right about my recent history, but on the death of Oliver, I resigned and took up a position as local landlord and magistrate in the North Riding of Yorkshire."

"What are you doing so far west and, according to my cavalry commander, Captain Welby, heading for Scotland?"

"I was a little loose with the truth with your man. I am actually heading home. It is Colonel James who is escorting our Royalist friend north to Scotland. He is not a prisoner but a high-powered emissary of the would-be king who wanted to use the good offices of myself and Sir Thomas to meet with representatives of the English republic. Sir Thomas and I agreed that such representatives could no longer be found in London and that any meaningful negotiations should wait until the matters clarified, but in the meantime, our Royalist Colonel Smith should talk to Monk."

Suddenly, Colonel Smith interrupted and addressed Lambert, "That was until I realised that the most important representative of the republican government could well be yourself. I make no apologies. Charles Stuart wishes to return to the throne of England, ideally at the head of an English army. Whether that army is commanded by John Lambert or George Monk is irrelevant to the king but could be critical for the future of the general concerned."

Lambert smiled. "A tempting offer, Colonel, but it is impossible for me to accept. I supported and continue to endorse the abolition of the English monarchy. Although Oliver made a few mistakes, the history of England under the republic, and even in its protectorate form, has been to the country's advantage. The men I am gathering around me are anti-Royalist to a man determined to save England from would-be traitors who would fall for your offer very quickly. If I declare for the king, I would have no army. But you are quite right about the generals around London and the constantly changing governments that they struggle to support. Put bluntly, England's future now rests with Monk, Charles Stuart, and myself."

Smith followed up with a risky question. "Would Monk have a similar negative response to my suggestion?"

Lambert laughed heartily. "No way! George has been a professional soldier all his life. He started the war as a Royalist, was imprisoned, and ultimately backed Cromwell, who made him military governor of Scotland. He has, in over half a decade, created an army there in his own image. He has removed the radical levellers and the religious fanatics. His men have no political or religious ideas. They will obey George no matter what he orders them to do. But don't think he will jump at your offer. He is so cautious that he will probably not act until it is too late to advance his or the king's cause."

Luke asked, "May we now proceed on our divergent ways?"

Lambert smiled. "If you were back as head of military intelligence, would you let the three of you go? Be honest, Tremayne! If you were attempting to seize control of the English government from the politicians and generals who are creating chaos out of London, you would not want any interference from Monk. Colonel Smith is out to encourage that interference. I cannot allow him to meet Monk for at least the next two weeks."

"You intend to hold us for that long?" asked Smith.

Lambert remained quiet for some while.

"Against my instincts, I will trust you, Tremayne. Colonel James, you may return to Sir Thomas and inform him that failing any objection on his part, I will call upon him at noon tomorrow. On your honour as a gentleman and officer, Tremayne, I expect you to escort Smith out of the county and hopefully out of the country. In effect, you will guarantee that he will not meet Monk within the next fourteen days. The two of you will stay overnight in the local tavern, the White Lion, and in the morning when you depart, you will be followed to the county border by my men."

The three soldiers were about to leave Lambert's presence when he announced, "Or you can accept an entirely different proposition."

"And what would that be?" asked Luke.

"You and James could join my army. Tremayne, I offer you command of my cavalry, and James, you could become my adjutant."

"And what becomes of me?" asked Ashcroft.

"You will remain under house arrest here until I successfully control the government, and then you can negotiate with me," answered Lambert.

"From what you said previously, there would be no place in that negotiation for the return of the king," said Ashcroft.

Both Luke and James declined the offers made to them.

19

COMFORTABLY SETTLED INTO A room at the White Lion, Ashcroft expressed his concern. "I am surprised that Lambert let us go. In the same situation, neither of us would have been so stupid."

"I agree. That decision is out of character. On the edge of seizing power within the republic, he allows two men who could undermine his chances of success to roam freely, content to accept the word of a former professional liar in military intelligence and a devoted servant of his sworn enemy. Lambert is not such a fool. I suspect we will be rearrested or, worse, murdered in our sleep," concluded Luke.

"More likely shot by unknown assailants as we cross some isolated area of the county. What should we do?" asked Ashcroft.

"There will be no point trying to escape during the night. Lambert will have his men watching our every move," replied Luke.

"I have an idea. Let's go down to the drinking chamber and find two persons of similar height and build to us, ply them with drink and money to join us in our room for a night of drinking, if they promise to carry out a small assignment for us in the morning."

"Which is to exchange clothes with us and leave the tavern, pretending to be us, and head north," surmised Luke.

"Precisely" was Ashcroft's reply. "And we will leave later as a couple of still intoxicated tavern frequenters and disappear into the countryside."

Luke and Ashcroft entered the drinking chamber and were stunned by their antagonistic reception. It was Ashcroft's appearance and clothes that aroused the ire of the drinkers. Someone shouted, "We don't drink with Royalists!" Someone else added, "Let's tar and feather them." A third was more direct. "No, hang them from the gibbet at the crossroads."

Luke acted quickly. He jumped onto a bench, drew his sword, and shouted, "You will answer to General Lambert if any harm befalls us! I am the late protector's head of military intelligence, and you quite rightly considered my companion Colonel Smith as a Royalist! He was, but now like me, he is here to join General Lambert as he attempts to save the republic from its enemies! It was the general himself who suggested we stay here, awaiting his decision on our future!"

A supportive voice from the back of room shouted, "Probably true! I saw them with the general earlier today!"

Luke took advantage of this positive remark. "Let's forget this unfortunate introduction. One of us may be your commanding officer when Lambert marches on London. The drinks are on me."

There was no shortage of volunteers to continue imbibing with the two officers in their room throughout the night. At first light, Luke and Ashcroft allowed the three most intoxicated drinking companions to remain asleep. The two more sober readily exchanged their rags for the clothes of their hosts and exited the front door of the White Lion. They soon disappeared into a light fog.

Soon after, Luke and Ashcroft left by a side door and were congratulating themselves on a well-executed plan as they staggered south. To the outside world, they were a couple of drunks who were forced to spend the night in the tavern until they sobered up. They had not progressed far when the clutter of horses' hooves could be heard thundering down the road from the direction of the White Lion. The pretend drunks were immediately surrounded, and Lambert's man, Captain Welby, was scathing in his verbal onslaught.

"Some might pretend that we have here a retired general and an active Royalist courtier, but that can't be true. Together, two such people would have had more sense than to time their escape from the White Lion only a few minutes after the decoys left out the front door. Any sensible person would have left an hour or so before or after sending out the decoys. No, what we have here, supported by the clothes that they are wearing, are two local thieves who left the White Lion without paying and who tried to discard this bag full of items stolen from the tavern. Ensign, arrest these destitute villains and proceed to the gibbet at the crossroads. Two early morning hangings will solve a lot of problems."

As Luke and Ashcroft drew their swords Welby continued his harangue. "Well, well, well! No common thief would own such expensive swords. Further proof of your thieving career. If you prefer to die resisting arrest, so be it." His men dismounted and approached their quarry. Back to back, Luke and Ashcroft, both expert swordsmen, would prove difficult to disarm or kill.

Captain Welby came to the same conclusion and carefully primed his carbine. The two defendants, completely unaware of Welby's activity, and continuing to hold their own against awkward and ill-trained opposition, were shocked by a sudden fusillade. Welby clasped his shoulder, and the two swordsmen nearest Luke and Ashcroft fell to the ground. Out of the fog Colonel James with half a company of dragoons emerged—their muskets still smoking.

As his men rounded up Welby's group, James explained, "Sir Thomas concluded that as Lambert was no fool, he would not allow Colonel Smith and yourself to leave the area. We thought his men might try to kill you in the tavern, so several of the drinkers were my men in disguise. Your simple plan to leave was soon common gossip, so I arranged to follow both the decoys and yourself. Sir Thomas, as the local magistrate, has issued a warrant to arrest Welby and his thugs as would be murderers at any time I thought appropriate. My men will now escort you both to the border of the West Riding. From there, you can call on your own resources, General."

Luke thanked Colonel James, who continued, saying, "Dressed as you are, you might be taken for vagrants by genuine parish constables." He threw a bundle of clothing at the men. "We recovered these from the decoys."

Back at Abbey Grange, Luke informed his household that Colonel Smith would be staying as a guest for ten days, after which he would rejoin his men at the Pilgrim's Rest. Later, alone with Luke, Ashcroft asked, "Surely, you are not going to keep me here under what amounts to house arrest for a fortnight? Your promise to General Lambert is now null and void given his attempt to have us killed."

"Lambert may not have been responsible. Welby may have acted on his own initiative, but my decision to keep you here is not based on that promise but on my assessment of the situation we find ourselves in. I am still a servant of the English republic, and I do not intend to take any step that will bring it down and lead to the restoration of the monarchy. If I release you now, you would meet your men at the Pilgrim's Rest and head for Scotland to negotiate with Monk. I prefer to wait until the warring generals solve their differences and can hopefully support a new effective and united republican government."

Ashcroft reluctantly nodded his acceptance of Luke's position. Luke asked, "Did the king reveal to you all the contents of his letter to me?"

"Not having read the letter, I cannot answer that question."

"Did he mention that he would reveal to me his sympathisers in this dale?"

"His Majesty would not betray his own people," answered Ashcroft with a wry smile.

An hour later, Peter, Matilda, and Luke discussed the developing situation. "Our guest's real identity as head of Charles Stuart's security and emissary at large to republican leaders in England and Scotland must be kept secret. The presence of such a powerful Royalist in the dale with an armed company of troops to call on, however, is not acceptable. Harry will be Colonel Smith's valet with the task of not letting the man out of his sight. I must know where Smith is every minute of the day and night. Given the existence of a Royalist force on the moors, as magistrate for the area, I must take immediate steps to capture them or at least move them on. Peter, ride to York Castle immediately and request a half company of cavalry or dragoons! I will explain the situation in a letter."

Luke changed the subject. "What has happened here in my absence?"

"Jagger's men brought the coffin containing the gnawed bones of Thomas Bates down from the moors several days ago, and it is resting in the parish church. Janet refuses to allow Edward Unsworth to conduct the service. She wants a retired Presbyterian cleric from Pickering to officiate. You will have to decide," replied Matilda.

"Any progress on the murder of Ogden or the disappearance of Snigg?"

"No!" answered Peter.

Luke asked him, "How is Jagger coping with the Royalist troops forced on him? Does his compliance suggest his allegiance is with the king?"

"I can't answer the second question, but the burden has been made lighter by the substantial financial contribution the Royalist troops have made. They are more than paying for their own food and accommodation. And Kit is selling a lot more ale than he normally would."

Peter left them to ride to York. Luke and Matilda, alone for the first time since Luke's return, embraced passionately. Within minutes, Matilda led Luke to their bedchamber from which they did not emerge until evening fell. Married bliss was a reality.

Before supper, Luke informed Janet that her request for a Presbyterian cleric was granted. Janet presented Luke with a bag of miscellaneous items. "Jagger's men brought this bag when they delivered the coffin. Apparently, they are items found around and in the mine shaft where Thomas's body was found. Their master said that maybe the military sleuth could find some valuable evidence amongst the items."

"Have you gone through them?" asked Luke.

"No," admitted Janet.

Whether this was because of some emotional baggage or plain disinterest, Luke could not assess. He decided to confront the issue. He upended the contents of the bag onto the table. "Is there anything here that you recognise?" he asked.

Again, Luke was confronted by an immediate no. He became cross. "Come, Janet, there may be something here that will help identify Thomas's murderer. You may have no interest as a long-estranged wife, but I, as a newly appointed magistrate, must do my duty. Let's go through these items one by one."

Neither of them expressed any interest as Luke examined and then passed each item to Janet until the second last object, a large mud-encrusted leather purse. Luke was impressed by its novelty, too large for a normal purse or wallet and too small for a satchel, perhaps an individual item designed for a person who wanted to carry papers on his person probably attached to his baldric. As he passed the item to Janet, the previously disinterested woman became animated. "I have seen this before."

"Good. Is it further proof that the bundle of bones found in the mine shaft was Thomas?"

"No, it did not belong to Thomas but to one of our neighbours. What would that neighbour be doing on the moors with Thomas?"

"Tell me more!"

"This belongs to Dick Unsworth. Although he is primarily a cobbler, he keeps the dale also supplied with all the leather goods it requires. He made this large purse for himself, which he always wore attached to his baldric to carry important papers."

"Would Thomas have seen it on Dick?"

"Most likely."

"Could he have ordered one for himself? As steward, he would need to carry papers up and down the dale."

"Not that I know of, but it is possible."

As Luke made his way to Dick Unsworth's cottage, he had already constructed an explanation for the discovered wallet. Dick had followed Thomas onto the moors, and a scuffle occurred near the mine shaft, during which the latter had grabbed at the former's baldric, dislodging the wallet that fell into the mine with the victim. It was Dick Unsworth who was progressively murdering the Catholics and their chief sympathiser. All Luke had to do was to prove it.

He would confront Dick with the wallet and seek his explanation for its discovery in a distant mine shaft, but an early clarification of the situation proved impossible. As Luke approached the cottage, he saw one of his tenants leaving, and after he knocked on the cottage door, it was opened by one of his labourers, who commented, "Sir, you will have to wait your turn. There are three of us ahead of you."

20

LUKE QUICKLY ASSESSED THE situation. In Dick's absence, Nell was plying her trade. He spoke to her imminent clientele. "I am here on magisterial business. After Nell's current customer leaves, I need to speak to her. I will not delay your enjoyment of her generosity for too long." There was a muttering of discontent.

Nell was visibly upset that Luke was not her next customer and immediately indicated that his lordship could have special privileges. Luke was not diverted from his quest. "Where is Dick, and when will he be back?"

"He is at the Pilgrim's Rest and could be away for over a week."

"What is he doing on the moors?"

"Kit Jagger has a large number of horsemen staying with him who need repairs to their bridles, straps, and saddles."

Luke accepted that Ashcroft's men may need such repairs and was about to leave without asking Nell any further questions when he jokingly quipped, "You are being kept busy in his absence?"

"My lord, I am Dick's housekeeper, not his mistress. He gave me a venue to carry out my trade after the local publican threw me out. He has no objection to what I do. He encourages it, but he does have one unusual condition. I am not to service any Catholics."

Luke was surprised. A random comment by the village whore advanced his investigation leaps and bounds. "Why does Dick so dislike Catholics?" he asked.

"His uncle, aunt, and numerous cousins moved to Ireland in the thirties and were all slaughtered in the Irish Catholic rebellion of 1641. That is one reason he hates his nephew, the current vicar. As a lad, Ted was too friendly with the Catholic boys of the dale. That is also why he had little time for the steward Bates. He thought him a clandestine Papist because of the way he pandered to the Catholic minority."

Luke could have kissed Nell. He did, to her delight and the consternation of the waiting clients.

Two days later, Peter returned from York, announcing that Sir Evan Williams would arrive with one hundred dragoons within three days. Luke and Peter discussed the developing military situation and agreed that Lord Ashcroft should leave Abbey Grange immediately and take control of his men stationed at the Pilgrim's Rest and hopefully lead them out of England. Otherwise, he faced being slaughtered by the approaching government dragoons. To this end, Harry would escort the Royalist emissary to the Pilgrim's Rest.

Before their discussion concluded, the door burst open, and Matilda entered. "Sorry to interrupt. Simon Snigg has been found."

"A body mashed into a waterwheel farther down the beck, I imagine," commented Luke.

"No, he is alive and is being cared for by Emma, who sent a maid to inform us. Apparently, he is not himself, but Emma will fill us in on the details later today."

True to her word, that evening, Emma came to the manor house. She explained to Luke, Peter, and Matilda that Simon had suffered no serious physical harm. "Apart from a wound to the back of his head, his body is reasonably well, but his mind, never the most alert, seems even more confused. He cannot resume his duties as your bailiff for some time, if at all."

"Where was he found?" asked Peter.

"On the moors to the west of Abbey Grange."

"Not the high moors at the head of the dale but the low moors that form the western boundary at the widest extent of the dale?" asked Luke, seeking clarification.

"Yes. One of your shepherds came across him, wandering aimlessly. At first, he had no memory of who or where he was. The shepherd recognised him and sent a message to me. My brother, Tim Carver, went and brought him home this morning."

"How did Simon finish up on the western moors when he was last seen precariously placed beside the raging beck in the middle of Abbeythwaite? Is he capable of being examined?" asked Luke.

"Not for a few days. After he is well fed and cared for, he may regain some memory of what has happened, although what he has told me so far seems sheer fantasy."

"In what way?"

"He claims he was held prisoner by hooded semi-naked women who danced around a cairn within a large cave in which he was confined. He fell asleep after drinking a magic potion. When he awoke in the cave, the women had gone. He wandered outside and was found by the shepherd, Johnny Harland."

Matilda led Emma from the room, offering assistance for the stricken Simon as they went.

As Evan's men had not arrived, Luke had time to visit Simon, who was resting on a heavily cushioned chair. Luke whispered to Emma, "Could you leave us? I want to question Simon alone without him reacting to any unconscious influence you might have on his replies." Luke was friendly and reassuring. "It is great to see you alive. Everybody thought you had drowned, either accidently or through foul play. What do you remember from the time you left the tavern after the fight?"

"I remember but not too clearly as I had drunk a considerable amount of ale. Given my condition, I decided not to go home but to sleep it off on the bank of the beck. I was half asleep when I heard a rustle behind me and turned just in time to see one of the combatants from the tavern about to smash a rock into my head. At the same time, they both rolled me into the stream. I remember nothing until I awoke in a large torch-lit cave in which a group of hooded women were dancing around and paying homage to a cairn of rocks. Almost as soon as I awoke, they gave me a drink that sent me back to sleep. When I awoke a second time, it was morning, and the cave was empty. I wandered outside and was met by Johnny Harland, the local shepherd who recognised me, and sent a message to Emma."

"You have no idea how you came to be found several miles west of here on the low moors after being pushed into the raging beck outside the front door of your old house?"

"No. Emma thinks the cold stream revived me and I struggled to the bank and, in a state of confusion, simply walked to the western moors."

"Do you know those moors well? Did you as a child and young man ever visit them with your friends?"

"Not with my friends. As youths, we always went up the dale to the high moors. In good times, there were too many shepherds and cowmen with their sheep and cattle on the lower moors. But I did go to the western moors with my father, the then bailiff, and then quite often to help Mother Harland and Ted Unsworth to gather herbs. I liked it there."

"Did you know about the caves?"

"No."

Luke called Emma back and agreed with her interpretation of what had happened. The icy beck revived Simon, and confused as a result on the knock on the head, he wandered across the dale and climbed onto the western moors, reliving his pleasant childhood experiences there with Mother Harland."

"Also, a hungry Simon could have helped himself to a hallucinogenic herb that convinced him that he had seen dancing women in various states of undress," she added.

"Have you heard of dancing witches on the moors?" asked Luke.

"No, most reports of witches on the moors involve individual women practicing their magic, not covens of dancing devil worshipers."

"Do you know the western moors well?"

"Yes, as a child, I went with my father when he drove his sheep from their wintering here up there for the summer. It was always good pasture, which led to many clashes between rival graziers, claiming they had exclusive rights to particular areas. My late father-in-law knew the area very well."

"Do you know the cave in which Simon claimed he was kept prisoner?"

"There are many caves in the area, several large enough to contain the dancing furies Simon thinks he saw."

At supper that night, Matilda asked Luke how his examination of Simon had gone. "Everything in his account seems explicable, and I am not convinced that his story of dancing women in a cave is a fantasy as Emma is very anxious for me to believe. We have never visited the western edges of our estate, let alone that moor. You have not done much riding since you have been here. Let's go exploring tomorrow, just the two of us."

Luke was most impressed with the fertile soils, lush crops, and fat livestock that he saw as he and Matilda travelled west. He now understood why his rental income was so high. The lower dale was very wide at this point and the lower moors simply a slightly elevated plateau that separated Abbey Dale from its western neighbour.

On climbing the slight incline that led onto the moor, Luke could see in the distance, sitting under the only tree in sight, a shepherd supervising a flock of fat lambs. Luke and Matilda introduced themselves and received a friendly reply. "You be the new master then. What brings you to these parts? I never saw Mr Bates up here, only the older Mr Snigg."

"Are you the shepherd who, a few days ago, found his son, Simon, wandering around?" asked Matilda.

"Yes, my lady. I knew Simon who, as a lad, used to come up here with his father and with my sister, Tamsin."

"You must know these moors in great detail. Are there caves such as Simon described?" She continued.

"I have been a shepherd here for several of your tenants for forty years. I know every cave there is. There are many large enough to house a group of dancing women. In bad weather, I drive my whole flock into the larger ones for shelter. But I prefer not to enter any cave too deeply after dark."

"Why not?" asked Luke,. probing.

"It is easier to supervise sheep at night that are neatly hurdled and protected by my dogs out here in the open. The caves can be home to snakes and foxes, and there are all those stories of the horrible black dog that lurks on the moors, ready to rip out the throats of man or beast."

Luke was not sure whether Johnny believed this legend or was simply trying to frighten the newcomers. He asked, "Have you seen at night any caves lit up with tapers similar to that which Simon claimed he saw?"

"Never, but that does not prove that such a well-lit cave does not exist. Many have very narrow entrances, some even concealed. Light from such caves would not be seen from outside."

"When you found Simon, had he been walking long since he emerged from his cave?" Luke continued.

"No, he was still adjusting his eyes to the daylight."

"Do you know which cave it might be?" asked an excited Matilda.

"Yes."

Luke and Matilda, who had dismounted, followed the shepherd to what looked at first like a hole in the ground. He pulled aside a small bush on the side of the depression that revealed a small entrance. Luke had difficulty entering the cave and almost immediately shouted in alarm as two terrified bats brushed past him and escaped into the unwelcome daylight.

Luke did not persist. "I could see absolutely nothing. I will return with tapers or candles and inspect it in detail. If Simon's story is true, and this is the cave, you think he would have mentioned the bats."

"Not necessarily, my lord. If the naked dancing was held in the middle of the night, the bats would have left the cave, and when Simon awoke midmorning, they would have been long back in their haunt, sound asleep. He would not have noticed them in the morning."

Matilda thanked the shepherd and commented, "You have been a faithful servant of our manor for decades, and if Tamsin Harland is your sister, then James, the publican, must be a brother and our two laundresses, Abigail and Phyllis, your nieces?"

"That is correct, my lady. James is much younger than Tamsin or myself."

Luke was thoughtful.

Simon claimed he saw women cavorting in a cave, and the possible protector of such activity in that cave was the brother of a known witch who herself knew the area very well. What if Johnny Harland was lying? On returning to the manor, Matilda expressed similar views.

"Luke, is there is a pagan cult of women within the dale? I know that you will be busy with the imminent arrival of Sir Evan and the pursuit of the Royalists. I would like to investigate the caves further."

"Great idea but wait until Harry returns from the Pilgrim's Rest. Take him with you and loads of torches and candles."

21

L UKE WAS DELIGHTED TO meet his former deputy, then successor as head of military intelligence, and friend, Sir Evan Williams. They chatted about Luke's last two missions to North Africa and to Portugal, and Evan brought Luke up to date on developments at the centre of power, just prior to and after Oliver Cromwell's death.

"The old protector must have had some hidden motive in sending both of us to Yorkshire. Perhaps he believed the future of the Protectorate depended on what happens here," mused Luke.

"Yes, it looks like whichever faction of the divided army comes out on top will determine our future. The generals in London are too divided and unpopular to succeed, and Monk in Scotland is too cautious to act. This might allow Lambert here in Yorkshire to emerge as the new leader. If that happens, it is hoped that both London and Monk would fall in behind him," commented the optimistic Evan.

"John Lambert was always the soldier's soldier. I never served under him, but he certainly created immense loyalty amongst his men. However, Sir Thomas Fairfax, the original commander of the New Model parliamentary army, might stymy his campaign. Sir Thomas believes George Monk is the man to save England and the army, even if it means putting Charles Stuart on the throne."

"George certainly has tighter control over his men than any other general. Discipline is disappearing elsewhere. Neither the London generals nor Lambert could raise enough troops and keep them in the field long enough to achieve anything without agreeing to extreme reforms demanded by the lower ranks. If that happens, every landowner and merchant in England would become a Royalist overnight. What's the true story regarding Ashcroft's visit to you?" asked Evan.

Luke explained his earlier dealings with Ashcroft and the royal court in exile some four or five years earlier and outlined their recent contact and his subsequent dealings with Lambert and Fairfax. "I gave Ashcroft two days start to rejoin his men at the Pilgrim's Rest and lead them out of the county and hopefully out of England. That why I sent for army assistance. We cannot have an active Royalist army unit operating in the county."

"I hear you are keeping your hand in at solving a few murders that have occurred since you arrived. Are you having your usual success?" asked Evan.

"Not really. At one point, I thought we had three murders—the previous steward, Thomas Bates, my deputy steward, Charles Ogden, and my bailiff, Simon Snigg. I initially assumed that it was an anti-Papist vendetta. Bates, a Protestant, continued to appoint local Papists to key positions, much against the feelings of the Protestant majority. Both Ogden and Snigg were Catholics. But now Snigg has been found, and his disappearance seems related to a bar brawl rather than any sectarian vendettas."

"And how is married life treating you? I always thought Matilda was the one woman who would settle you down. You are a very lucky man."

"I could not be happier, and Matilda is a great help in my work as manorial lord and magistrate. She is currently carrying out an investigation of her own into reported nocturnal activities by women on the low moors to the west of here. There is one witch in the dales, and her brother is a shepherd in the area where these women apparently meet. At the moment, those are the only facts I have. Deeper probing will have to wait until we deal with Ashcroft. We must ride north at first light tomorrow."

Around noon the next day, the government dragoons arrived at the Pilgrim's Rest. Kit Jagger welcomed them and indicated that the Royalists had departed less than two hours earlier.

Luke asked, "Were they from the continent or local lads raised by Ashcroft after he landed?"

"The officers came across with Ashcroft, but nearly all the troopers were locals. I served with a lot of them in Newcastle's army before it disbanded."

"So Ashcroft's task was easy. He disbanded his group here and let his men make their way to their homes."

Jagger hesitated. "No, and you are not going to like what I am about to tell you. A week ago, a Scots soldier arrived and said he would wait the return of Lord Ashcroft. I do not know if he was one of Monk's men or a Royalist. He said very little, and what he did say, I had trouble understanding. He refused to socialise with the Royalist troopers. But Ashcroft was delighted to see him, and I overheard his lordship confide in his deputy that he and the Scot would disappear and head north and that his deputy must keep the group together until they left Yorkshire."

"That is good news. We should be able to catch them before they disperse. We have more than double their number of men. When I return, I shall discuss your role in this incident Kit," warned Luke.

"Any aspects of my behaviour during the Royalist visit, or should I say occupation, that the government might find suspect would be forgotten because of my action in aiding you catch up with Ashcroft and his men. As you see, fog has descended, and without my tracking skills, you would have no idea where the enemy have gone" was Kit's appropriate response.

Luke and Evan had to concede that such help was needed as the fog became thicker.

After ten minutes of tracking, Kit announced, "They are heading due north. They are not going to Whitby." As the government troops reached the northern edge of the moors, the fog lifted, and as Luke looked down into the Esk valley, a group of thirty to forty stationary horsemen could be seen less than a mile ahead of them.

As the seasoned battlefield commander, Luke took control. "Evan, send one of your captains with fifty men to the west and descend into the valley of the Esk and then move along it to cut off the Royalist descent down the path they have obviously chosen. Once those men are in position, I will lead ten men in a traditional charge from here straight at them."

"Why only ten men? You have fifty available for the charge," asked Evan.

"If they see only ten men charging at them and there are over thirty of them, they will be inclined to stand and fight. Once the ten have engaged the enemy, you will lead the remaining forty men in a second wave. If I saw fifty men attacking me, I would give the order to disperse. If they did that, we would have difficulty in rounding them up, especially on these moors in intermittent fog."

Half an hour later, with Evan's deputy leading his men up the path by which the Royalists hoped to descend from the moors, Luke and nine others appeared from behind a boulder.,They made as much noise as possible, and charged the resting Royalists. As predicted, confronted by only ten men, the Royalists mounted their horses and took up their positions to confront the challenge., asAs soon as contact was made, Evan emerged on the scene with the remaining dragoons.

Twenty minutes later, the Royalists, completely surrounded and heavily outnumbered, surrendered. But it was a surrender executed by Ashcroft's deputy. There was no sign of Ashcroft or the unknown Scot. Evan ordered a complete count of his own men and his opponents. There were four dead, two from each side. Two of Evan's men were missing.

Kit, who had diplomatically taken no part in the skirmish, drew attention to a major problem. Luke had disappeared. Evan ordered an immediate search of the area. Luke's body was not found. Kit was pessimistic when he saw down a slight slope but pressed against a largish boulder a black stallion. Luke alone amongst the government forces rode a black horse. Evan and Kit clambered down the slope, expecting to find Luke's body under that of his horse. The horse was dead, shot during the charge that could have catapulted Luke in any direction, but there was no sign of him.

Evan acted. He ordered his deputy with most of the government troopers to escort the Royalist prisoners to Whitby as prisoners of war for immediate transport to the West Indies as indentured labourers. He and a small group would return to the Pilgrim's Rest as night was falling. The search for Luke would have to wait until morning.

Kit surprisingly intervened.

"Sir Evan, if Luke were here, he would show mercy to the Royalist troopers. They are all local lads who have families to support. I actually fought with some of them years ago. They have not been active against the government until recruited by Ashcroft for what was not really a military enterprise. They spent their whole period under arms staying at my inn, harming nobody. Release them to find their own way home!"

Evan thought for a while. "No, I cannot release men who have taken up arms against the government, but I can offer them a choice. They can change sides, a common practise during the wars, and join my men. If not, they will be sent to the Americas."

Kit spoke to the Royalist captain. Whatever was said was effective. The whole of the Royalist detachment volunteered to join the York garrison, and Evan's deputy with the majority of his troops and the new former Royalist recruits headed immediately back to York. By the time they reached the city late the next day, most of the new recruits had disappeared.

Back at the Pilgrim's Rest, Kit and Evan discussed Luke's possible fate. Kit was positive. "Luke is alive. After he was thrown from his horse as he lay on the ground, he saw Ashcroft and the Scot leave the site of the skirmish and decided to follow them. If Elinor, the best tracker on the moors, can pick up three tracks leading from that site in the morning, you will be well on the way to recover a live Luke."

Evan was more cautious but agreed. "Yes, if he were killed, his body would have been found during our search yesterday. It would be typical of Luke to do what you suggest. Let's drink to his safe recovery."

Not long after reaching the site of the previous day's skirmish, Elinor announced she had found three tracks leading away from the area in a westerly direction. The group made their way down into the valley of the Esk and then continued west up the valley, not east towards the coast. After some time, she spoke to Evan and revealed some potentially alarming news. "One of the three men we are following is wounded. There was a small trace of blood from the outset, but for the last half mile, it has increased. Whoever it is, his situation is getting worse. He could not continue for much longer."

"Let's hope it is not Luke," commented Evan as a tear ran down Elinor's face.

Twenty minutes later, their worst fears were realised. Lying beside the track, they came across Luke's body facedown in a considerable pool of blood. Elinor ran to the body, lifted her smock, and tore away much of her petticoat. By the time Evan reached the scene, she had stuffed much of it into wounds in Luke's chest, from which blood had been flowing freely. A couple of blood-soaked handkerchiefs were found with which he had unsuccessfully tried to stem the flow. After examining the body, Evan announced, "Luke's breathing normally, and if Elinor's petticoat can stop the flow of blood, there is every chance we can get him back to the Pilgrim's Rest alive."

Elinor suggested, "There are no surgeons or physicians close by. The white witch, Tamsin Harland, has saved many an animal that suffered severe blood loss. I will ride to Elderby and ask her to come to the Pilgrim's Rest to attend his lordship."

Before Evan could answer, she disappeared into the descending fog. The soldiers constructed a makeshift stretcher in which the front ends of the poles were attached to the leather straps of a horse while two men carried the rear ends of the pole. A third man walked beside the stretcher with his hand putting pressure on Elinor's petticoat against Luke's chest to stem the flow of blood.

On reaching the Pilgrim's Rest, Kit poured some Irish whiskey down Luke's throat and, before replacing Elinor's petticoat with pieces of bed linen, did the same to the wound.

Everybody awaited Tamsin's arrival.

22

MOTHER HARLAND CLEANED THE wound, and plastered the affected area with honey, and then administered various potions to the still-unconscious Luke. Evan, not convinced that this saviour of local livestock could work the same magic with humans, had one of his men ride posthaste to York to bring back an army surgeon to provide additional care. On his way, he was to inform Lady Matilda of her husband's situation.

Lady Matilda arrived at the Pilgrim's Rest the following day and arranged for Luke to be taken back to Abbey Grange. To limit the risk of the wounds reopening, Luke was placed in a heavily cushioned open coffin that was securely tied to a wagon. Elinor volunteered to sit next to the coffin to monitor Luke's condition, an offer that the perceptive Matilda declined. She would sit beside the open coffin and monitor his condition. Nevertheless, she thanked Elinor for her part in saving Luke's life. A few weeks later, the servant received three new petticoats.

Two weeks later, Luke's recovery was evident. The army surgeon was amazed at the effectiveness of Mother Harland's intervention, and his only contribution to the situation was to suture the wounds.

Luke had regained consciousness soon after his arrival back at Abbey Grange and, two days later, was able to recount what had happened to Matilda, Peter, and Evan.

"As I charged, all the old feelings of exhilaration came back to me. I remember two or more slight impacts in my chest, and then seconds later, my horse fell, throwing me down a slight incline. Luckily, I landed on soft moss and avoided the many stones and boulders that littered the area. As I took in the skirmishes around me, I saw Ashcroft and a companion leave the field of battle. I grabbed a riderless horse and followed them. I progressively became aware that I had been shot more than once in the chest and that I was losing a lot of blood. Gradually, I began to feel faint and eventually passed out. You know the rest."

Two Weeks Earlier

While Luke was tracking the Royalists with Evan and his men across the northern moors, Matilda decided to revisit the cave on the western moors. In addition to Harry, she would take a female companion with her.

This simple desire proved difficult to achieve. She first invited Janet Bates, but Matilda was surprised by her continued frosty reception. Initially, she thought she had interrupted a dalliance between Janet and Robert, but it quickly transpired that Janet assumed that Matilda had arrived to evict her from the cottage. As her late husband no longer held any position on the manor, his wife had no entitlement to the property. Matilda put her mind at rest and indicated that the issue of Janet's future could be discussed much later. There was no urgency. She could stay in the cottage until a mutually satisfying decision was reached. Janet calmed down but gently rejected Matilda's invitation on the grounds that she had long given up riding for pleasure.

Matilda then approached Emma Snigg, whom she had only recently appointed as housekeeper to assist her in the management of the household. With Simon incapable of carrying out the role of bailiff, and Harry appointed in his place, Emma was delighted with her new responsibility and the opportunity to maintain her manorial premises and property.

When Matilda elaborated on her planned excursion, Emma's initial enthusiasm suddenly changed. "My lady, could you delay your enterprise until tomorrow? I would love to accompany you, but unfortunately, there are problems associated with Simon that I must attend to today."

Matilda accepted Emma's excuse and was surprised when the latter continued, saying, "I would certainly enjoy ambling across the western moors, but you should not waste your time on the cave that was referred to by a delirious Simon. The area is full of caves, and no doubt, local shepherds and cowmen make up stories of witches' covens and pagan cults to keep people away from their favourite cavern."

"Although in this case, the local shepherd claims he had never seen any female nocturnal activity in his decades on those moors," Matilda gently countered.

Matilda next asked her two young washerwomen, Abigail and Phyllis, if they rode, and if so, would they like to take a ride onto the western moors, where they might visit their uncle Johnny. The girls could ride and were delighted to go with the lady of the manor and brought with them a flask of strong spirits from their father for his elder brother. Harry's presence was another incentive for Abigail, who was not an unwilling object of his fickle affections. As Harry attached a bag containing the candles and taper torches to his saddlebag, he mentioned to Matilda that there were not many of them left in the storeroom. He carefully filled a lidded ceramic container with embers from the fire burning in the reception hall to later light the candles he had so meticulously packed.

Departure was delayed as the three women readied themselves for the extensive ride and, with Emma's help, put together a basket of cold meats, bread, and cheese to consume after reaching their destination. Harry left five horses tethered to a rail in the courtyard while they all consumed some cold roasted chicken and a pint of ale. Any meal on the moor was several hours away.

As they made their way up the gentle slope to the western moor, Matilda noticed a woman riding down into the dale on a path that ran parallel to the one they had taken. Abigail informed the group. "That's Mary Carver. She is the only one in the dale who has a piebald horse."

Matilda immediately wondered, *Why is Mary on the western moor?* On eventually reaching the moor, she directed the group to head straight for the cave. On reaching it, she suggested to the girls, "I can see your uncle in the distance. Perhaps you would like to ride over to him and deliver your present."

They whispered to each other, and after an obvious disagreement, Phyllis announced with some irritation, "I will visit Uncle Johnny. Abigail prefers to stay here and help Harry."

She slapped her horse on its flanks and galloped off into the distance. Abigail blushed while Harry unloaded the container of embers, and with the aid of some dry grass and small twigs, he soon had a blaze going from which the candles and torches could be more effectively lit. Suddenly, he cried out in astonishment, "My lady, the bag of candles and torches is gone. I tied it onto my saddlebag most securely. I am very sorry. But I will be able to gather enough twigs and pieces of wood to get some light into the cave." Abigail could not resist teasing Harry about the lost candles.

Matilda came over and inspected Harry's horse. She was concerned. "It is not your fault, Harry, that the bag of candles has gone missing. Look at this piece of rope! The bag has been cut from the saddle to which it was attached."

"It must have happened while we were having a bite to eat. Someone at the manor did not want you to see what is in this cave," suggested Harry.

"I doubt it. Someone has simply taken a fancy to expensive beeswax candles compared with the smelly tallow variety. Common theft, not mysterious conspiracy," countered Matilda.

"His lordship may have a different interpretation when you tell him," added Harry with a devilish smile.

After ten minutes, Harry, who had entered the cave with his container of now burning twigs and lots of gathered sticks, soon had a blaze going within the cave that illuminated the cairn cum altar that had intrigued Matilda. She immediately inspected the flat top of the cairn and then asked Harry to help remove the top layer of flat stones. "What are we looking for?" he asked.

"Evidence that candles had been lit on this stone table as described by Simon Snigg. It will be proof that people were here, probably using this stone cairn as the centre of some ritual."

"Wouldn't the wax have spilled onto the top stones?"

"Exactly, but I suspect the top stones may have been replaced to conceal such activity since Simon Snigg's unexpected revelation."

"My lady, you are beginning to sound like your husband. The general sees conspiracies where no one else does."

"And he is nearly always right," answered Matilda proudly.

After a few minutes, Harry exclaimed, "You are also right! This stone has candle grease attached to it and so do a few others—expensive beeswax. This has come from candles stolen from the manor. My lady, I think

Sir Luke would conclude that there is a link between your manor and whatever happens here on two counts—beeswax candle grease, which of all households in the dale, you alone can afford, and the fact that Simon Snigg, your then bailiff, somehow finished up here."

"Let's question Johnny Harland. Where is Abigail?"

"I will look for her," replied Harry eagerly. When he had not returned after several minutes, Matilda went in search of them. As she approached some large boulders and small shrubs, she heard Harry cry out, "Tell Lady Matilda at once!"

Harry emerged from a smaller cave, the entrance largely concealed by a giant boulder, followed by Abigail, who was adjusting her clothing. "What must you tell me?" asked Matilda.

"Look into this small cave. There is a bag of candles, exactly like the ones at the manor, and three large candlesticks, and look at the hoof marks at the entrance. They are fresh, at least made after the early morning rain today. Someone carried candles here this morning, probably from the large cave."

Matilda declared, "Leave the bag where you found it!"

This small hole was hardly a cave. It was big enough for one person in a crouching position, but it did contain a number of naturally formed shelves. On one of them, wrapped in a protective leather sheath, was a small foot-high statue of a naked woman who was all buttocks and breasts. Matilda wondered if this "goddess" was the object of worship for what looked increasingly like a pagan cult. She rewrapped the statue and placed it back on the shelf.

"Let's question Johnny. He may be able to explain the fresh hoof marks outside the large cave."

The shepherd, who was still talking to his niece Phyllis, was not enthusiastic about his new visitors. Matilda explained, "We are on our way back to Abbey Grange and have come to collect Phyllis. Have you seen any other inhabitants of Abbey Dale on the moor this morning?"

"No, my lady" was the bland response.

Harry was about to probe further, recalling the sight of Mary Carver, when Matilda glared at him. She thanked Johnny for his help.

Why did he lie?

On returning to the manor, Matilda summoned Emma. "When Mr Bates handed over the manor to my husband, he left behind a detailed inventory. Would you obtain a copy of it from Peter and then check it against the goods supposedly in the storeroom next to the pantry? A number of goods have been stolen. Peter has the keys."

23

MATILDA WAS INTRIGUED BY the statue she had found in the tiny cave and went to visit the only person in the dale who might be able to help identify it—the rector, Edward Unsworth. She did not tell him she had seen it but pretended it had been described to her, and she wanted to know more. Edward was delighted that he could answer the lady of the manor's query factually and in detail.

"I know that statue well. It was stolen from the church just after I arrived. Apparently, Tom Bates and Tim Carver found what they believed to be part of Thor's treasure in Carver's back garden. There were two pieces—a golden candle snuffer, which eventually proved to a brass object stolen from this church decades ago, and the statue you describe. My predecessor sent the details of the statue to scholars at York, who were divided. Some claimed it was a Norse goddess, others that it was Celtic. However, they all agreed that this pagan deity was concerned with the protection and advancement of women. As nobody was certain as to which of two or three goddesses the statue represented, I simply refer to it as the goddess. If it is ever returned, I will smash it to pieces. Idolatry is anathema to the Lord Jesus."

"Did you suspect anybody of stealing it?"

"The obvious suspects were the aggressive women of the dale. Tamsin Harland comes to mind, but I have no evidence against her at all. It could have been stolen by devout Christians, who like me objected to a pagan idol resting in the parish church. That could involve most of the dale. The parish had enough problems without worrying about a stolen old piece of carved rock. How did it come to your attention?"

Matilda lied, "One of the village girls claimed that all the problems in the dale stemmed from the time that goddess was unearthed."

"Pure superstitious rubbish! I constantly hear that half the women of the parish are witches who meet secretly on the moors where they have intercourse with the devil. If any of them are on the moors having intercourse, it is most likely to be with Kit Jagger rather than Lucifer."

"You reject the idea of a cult of women?"

"Yes, simply on the practical point of opportunity. When could any large number of women absent themselves from their homes without their husbands or fathers knowing? Dales men are very, almost obsessively, protective of their women."

Matilda's intuitive response, which she did not utter, was that dales men were obsessively controlling rather than protecting.

Edward changed the topic. "I heard that Colonel Smith, who was staying at the manor until a day or so ago, was a Royalist spy whom Sir Luke had detained and that the contingent of government troops that arrived several days ago and left the following morning was to take the prisoner to York Castle. He must have been very important for the government to send so many men."

Matilda was interested that Unsworth's view of events was so wrong. She delighted in putting him right. Luke would be proud of her. "I know little of what you speak. Sir Luke and the York garrison troops are scouring the northern moors, looking for a Royalist detachment that apparently took over the Pilgrim's Rest." Unsworth was clearly surprised. Matilda diplomatically added, "Colonel Smith was a comrade of Luke from their days in Ireland."

On leaving the rectory, Matilda visited the Carvers. She asked Mary about her trip to the moors. "You were up early this morning. I saw you returning from the western moors just before noon."

"Yes, it was a little colder than usual last night, so I went to check on a half dozen lambs we had placed there for summer."

"You talked to the shepherd, Johnny?"

"Yes, I enquired about my lambs as I could not see them with the combined flock. He told me they were still in Aidan's cavern, a large cave where he had hurdled the lambs against the cold."

"You went to Aidan's cavern?"

"Yes, I rode there. My horse nearly slipped in the muddy entrance, and I released my sheep and drove them back to the rest of the flock."

Matilda returned to the manor confused. Mary had given a reasonable and plausible explanation of her presence on the moors, but why had the shepherd, Johnny, denied seeing her, let alone meeting her. But Matilda's conviction that there was a cult of local women meeting in Aidan's cavern had received a setback.

At supper that evening, she discussed what she had discovered with Peter, Harry, Janet, and Emma. As she spoke, the frown on Peter's face deepened. He interrupted Matilda's account. "My lady, you have been lied to. Only this morning, I was noting where each of our tenants was to pasture their livestock this summer. The Carvers have for decades, if not centuries, placed their flocks and herds on the northern moors, not the western."

Before Matilda could respond, Emma defended her sister-in-law. "Captain Frost is quite correct. My father and now my brother, Mary's husband, have always taken their livestock to the northern moors. However, if you look at your records, the Ogdens have always used the western moors. Since her father's death, his livestock have been looked after by Tim and Mary. Mary was on the western moors checking on the well-being of her late father's sheep."

Peter acknowledged the validity of Emma's comments.

Matilda turned to her and asked, "Did you check on our supply of candles and torches?"

Peter answered in her place, "Emma came to me with a list of goods contained in the storeroom. I have just completed comparing her list with the inventory that Mr Bates prepared before you took over. Even allowing that usage was high during these long winter nights, we have used almost twice as many candles as one would expect. A significant number have been stolen."

Emma was quick, perhaps too quick, thought Matilda in retrospect, to defend the household. "My lady, that storeroom is very close to where workers and traders deliver goods to the kitchen. The candles could have been stolen by itinerant workers or regular suppliers, not necessarily members of your household."

Matilda turned to Janet, saying, "During your decade or more as mistress of Abbey Grange, was theft a common problem?"

"Thomas was a miser and kept few supplies on the manor. The storerooms were controlled by Tommy himself, and he had the only keys. It would have been very difficult to steal anything when Tommy was in charge."

Matilda bristled at the suggestion that her supervision of the household was lax and that now theft was easy. Her anger was ameliorated by Janet's next comment. "However, just before your arrival, while compiling the inventory for your ladyship, Tommy did remark that of all the goods on the manor, the one area in which he could not balance his books was with candles and torches. Given what has just been said, it appears that candles may have been stolen over some time."

"It is not a surprise. Candles are a necessity of life in the dales, and most of us would prefer the sweet-smelling candles of the gentry such as we have here to our own creation from toxic, noxious-smelling tallow," remarked Emma.

"So you think that the theft of candles is related to the general need in the dales for better winter lighting rather than her ladyship's concern that they are used to service a cult of pagan-worshiping women in Aidan's cavern?" asked Peter.

"Yes" was the reply.

Matilda pursued her obsession. "Janet, during the last ten years, did you ever hear rumours that women of the dale met together in some strange cult?"

"No, but Mistress Snigg would know more about what the women of the dale did than I."

Emma, who interpreted this as thinly veiled attack on her, responded in kind, "That is probably true. Mistress Bates, during her ten years as lady of this manor, did not mix with many of us. If she had, she would have known that the witch of Elderby regularly retired to the moors to contemplate nature, and at times, others go with her. Talk to Mother Harland! These visits might be interpreted by the ill-informed as a cult of women meeting on the moors. Ignorant people of all classes will believe anything."

The tension between Janet and Emma escalated during the meal to the point that Matilda made a decision. When Luke returned, she would suggest that Janet be asked to leave. She would not have such a petty-minded, haughty woman creating an unnecessarily unpleasant atmosphere. And she liked Emma.

Four Weeks Later

Luke had sufficiently recovered to address the outstanding problems that continued to plague his lordship of Abbey Grange and his magisterial duties in North Yorkshire. Some problems such as the presence of Royalist troops in the area and the disappearance of Thomas Bates had been solved, and that of Simon Snigg was no longer an issue. However, serious issues remained—the death of Thomas was probably a homicide, and if so, was the perpetrator a dales man? Charles Ogden's murder needed to be solved. Were both a display of sectarian violence against the Papists and their sympathisers?

Was Matilda right in suggesting the existence of a pagan cult on the western moorlands? Who was responsible for the bout of vandalism that plagued Abbey Grange just before Luke's arrival? And what really happened to Elizabeth Foxton a decade ago?

Luke, still confined to the house, asked that Dickie Unsworth visit him.

He questioned the cobbler pleasantly, "I imagine you made a fortune out of reequipping that Royalist unit that took over the Pilgrim's Rest."

"Yes, they did pay well."

Luke produced the large wallet that had been found beside the body of Thomas Bates. It had been cleaned and repaired by an overzealous servant. "Is this yours?" Luke asked.

"In both senses" was the immediate response. "I made it, and for myself. It was stolen."

"Did you make a similar item for Mr Bates?"

"No, but he admired the craftsmanship and its functionality. He asked if I could make him one, but he disappeared before any transaction was finalised."

"Then how do you explain that this was found beside his body in a mine shaft on the northern moors?"

Dick Unsworth swore and commented, "You're not suggesting that it was the respectable Mr Bates who stole my wallet?"

Luke had never entertained such a thought. "I doubt it. Bates was an honourable man. I think whoever killed him had that wallet, and in a struggle, it was ripped from the murderer and fell into the mine shaft beside Bates's body."

"I can see where your questioning is leading, my lord. I disliked, even hated, Bates for his betrayal of our faith and his pandering to the Papist riffraff of the dale, but I did not kill him. In fact, apart from my visit to the Pilgrim's Rest a week or so ago, I have not been on the northern moors for several years. I frequent Pickering and Maldon for my needs rather than trek to Whitby."

"On a more general issue, are you and the Protestant extremists engaged in a campaign of harassment against the Catholics of the dale?"

"I am not confessing to anything, but I will not deny that I would like to see all Catholics gone from Abbey Dale, and I do encourage them to leave."

"Did you, your nephew, or Robert Dutton pay the rector's casual labourers to provoke and assault Simon Snigg and then push him in the beck?"

"Not that I know of, but Snigg, by his mannerisms, provoked a lot of people. At least that episode has ended happily in that you have appointed a good Protestant bailiff in his place. Bates must have taken leave of his senses to appoint Simon to replace his father."

24

L UKE HAD ANOTHER CONCERN that he had kept to himself. The letter from Charles Stuart had not only sought his help in arranging a meeting between Lord Ashcroft and republican leaders but also included a paragraph in which the would-be king named his supporters in Abbey Dale.

Charles explained this unusual act of betraying ardent Royalists to the republican administration represented by Luke. He argued it assisted both camps. Luke would know from where trouble might emerge and take steps to stop it, whereas the king would not be embarrassed by the premature uprising of overenthusiastic supporters, which had already seriously undermined his campaign to return.

The most disturbing aspect of the revelation was that the names on the list would never have been suspected of Royalist leanings. They were so unexpected that Luke doubted the veracity of the royal missive. Could it be a deliberate plan to undermine the republican government's authority in the dale by throwing some its most vociferous supporters under a cloud of suspicion?

He decided to confide in Peter concerning the import of the royal letter but to provide to his steward only one of the names listed. Peter listened, entranced as Luke explained his dilemma. Finally, Luke wrote the name he was about to reveal on a slip of paper and pushed it towards Peter. He was astounded. The name was Janet Bates.

Peter was silent for some time and then commented, "This puts a new complexion on what has happened in the dale over the last decade. It must raise questions about those close to her, such as her husband, Thomas, and the coterie of high-ranking Catholic servants. Thomas and the rest of them may have been clandestine Royalists all that time. He may have fled before your arrival as he feared you might discover his traitorous role and his death may be simply political. There are enough parliamentary extremists in the area who would murder a suspected Royalist on sight."

"And it does explain his appointment of the Catholic and presumably more Royalist families to key positions on the manor," admitted Luke.

"But to what end? Even if this manor was the home of a Royalist cell, what could it achieve? Abbey Dale is hardly the centre of political decision making, and there would be very little intelligence coming out of the area that would interest the Royalists on the continent. London and the seaports are another matter, but isolated rural settlements are of no interest" was Peter's response.

A pensive Luke commented, "There must be something. Cromwell chose this isolated dale to grant me a manor. There were plenty of other vacant estates in my beloved west country or in Matilda's Kent. Oliver must have had a reason to send his former head of military intelligence to this particular dale. Did he know something about Royalist activity here?"

"What is more worrying is given the difficult times in which we live, and with a possible Royalist invasion imminent, how far has Janet influenced her current friends towards the Royalist cause, people whose names do not appear on the king's list. On the other hand, how can you be sure that the list is valid? Charles Stuart would not hesitate to lie, if it suited his purpose."

"Yes, you may be right. It could be an attempt to subvert the republic's defences by sending its representatives here off on wild goose chases. Why did Ashcroft come here in the first place? He could have made his way to Fairfax without my help. He could have landed in the Medway and met with the London generals, which would appear a much more practical and effective approach," concluded Luke.

"What do you intend to do regarding Janet Bates?"

"Nothing, except keep an eye on her, which is exactly what the would-be king wants. We have absolutely no evidence against her other than her being named by Charles Stuart as one of his supporters in Abbey Dale."

"You could try to bluff her into a confession by a series of lies, a technique you perfected during your years in military intelligence," suggested Peter.

"Poor Janet! You want me to put her under pressure, and Matilda wants her evicted as she, with Thomas's death, no longer has any right to the cottage. His lands has already reverted to me."

Later that day, Luke arrived at Janet's cottage. She assumed he had come to discuss her vacating the cottage. Luke was agreeably diplomatic. "You are only partly right. I have come to discuss your future but not to effect any changes immediately. As neither Peter nor Emma need to move in here, there is no great urgency that you should move out. In fact, if you are in a position to lease these premises for a short term, I would consider it. Perhaps you have no desire to remain in the dale and will return to the Borders?"

"Her ladyship would not welcome me staying on the manor, but I hope to be remaining in the dale."

"With Robert Dutton?" Luke cheekily asked.

"Not as his wife" was the rapid reply.

"Why not? The rumours concerning your relationship appear widespread."

"Robert is already married."

Luke feigned complete ignorance of this fact. "I did not know that. She does not live with him in the dale?"

"No, there are problems that are personal to Robbie and his wife, which I will not reveal, that in time may clarify."

"If not as a wife, what other role could you play? I never considered you a person who would live with a man as his mistress, nor could I see Robert putting you in that position."

"As you know, Robbie is fast becoming one of the largest landowners in the dale, in addition to the several pieces of land he leases from you. I will live on one of his new acquisitions and manage it for him. If I were a male, I would undoubtedly be called his steward. My years with Thomas qualifies me for the job, even though my gender prevents me from formally exercising such a role."

"I wish you well. Although your future settlement needs to be clarified, it was not the prime reason I am here."

Luke was about to lie as was his technique in many an interrogation.

"Why then are you here?" asked Janet.

"You will not have any enjoyable future with Robert if you are locked up in York Castle."

"Why would I be locked up in York Castle?"

"Because you are a Royalist agent."

"Ridiculous! If I were a Royalist spy, what could I contribute to the king's cause locked away in this isolated dale?"

Luke inwardly had to concede the validity of this observation, but he continued his fabrication. "Military intelligence is aware of a Royalist cell centred on Abbey Dale. That is one of the reasons I was allocated Abbey Grange by the late protector, but I was surprised when your name was advanced as the leader of that cell."

"There is no cell, but I can understand how the government's agents were led to believe the contrary. Tommy's supportive attitude to the Catholic minority lies behind this false accusation."

"In what way?"

"The Protestants of the dale equate the Catholic servants of the Leigh family, which Tommy retained as clandestine Royalists, and probably in a fury with these appointments, complained to the government with lies about a Royalist cell."

"How would such lies be taken seriously when your strident Presbyterianism was well known? I understand you openly expressed disquiet about your husband's tolerance of the Catholic families."

"While it was well known that I am anti-Catholic, a few dales men knew that my family, like half of the Scottish Presbyterians, fought for the king. My personal sympathies remain with the king. No man can rightfully execute a God-appointed sovereign. I will certainly not be unhappy when the monarchy is restored, but that does not mean I have ever taken steps to bring it about."

"Are you suggesting that someone in the dale who knew of your family's position, and your own inclination, exaggerated your loyalty to the king and reported you to the authorities?"

"It appears the only explanation for the false views that apparently reached government intelligence. They were lied to."

"If this is what happened, why would somebody deliberately lie about you, in particular, to the authorities?"

"As the most senior woman in the dale, and the wife of a not-always-popular steward, you make many enemies. I was disliked by the Catholic families of the manor and never got close to the Protestant majority except for Robbie's parents. If you want me to name who I would suspect of spreading this false rumour, look no further than the late Charles Ogden, a mean, vindictive man."

"In my experience, the reporting of false information to bring someone down does not usually have a political or religious motive but is usually deeply personal, such as a rejected lover."

Janet blushed. Had Luke hit a nerve? Whose advances had Janet rejected? To Luke's surprise, the normally reticent Janet opened up. "When our Helen disappeared, Tommy and I quickly drifted apart. There were many men who sought to console me, and some of them wanted more. Over a ten-year period, I rejected these advances at their initial proposal, so no affair developed that had later to be terminated. This was my reaction to all but one of the advances. I had no desire for an affair, and to be blunt, most offers came from socially inferior males. Men may be able to sleep with socially inferior women, and it may even enhance their status. The opposite as you know is true of women."

"I am eager to know the exception in your list of rejected suitors, but first, I cannot discard those who may have made only a tentative advance towards you but could be cut to the quick and hate you forever. Men hate rejection."

"No, Luke, you do not need any of these personal details. I have said too much already."

"Janet, if I am to free you from the charge of being a Royalist agent, to uncover the person who reported you would be a major advance, and to explain it as a result of personal revenge on your rejection of him would be ideal."

"I will not name those who showed an interest in me but which I rejected on the spot. If you think such a cursory rejection is enough to create bitter hatred, then in one way or another, I may have offended all the males in the dale. The one affair I did have, and which I had to terminate in a quite bitter confrontation, was with my brother-in-law, Stephen Bates. I was flattered that a much younger male was interested in me. I brought it to an end when I realised that he was not interested in me at all and simply wanted to humiliate my husband, his own brother."

To Luke, it was more likely to be Stephen Bates who reported his sister-in-law as revenge for his rejection and hopefully as further angst for his brother.

Luke could hardly wait for Peter's return to bring him up to date. Peter was surprised at Luke's detailed report. He finally commented, "Luke, this is great detective work, but it is all based on a fiction. You have let your imagination run riot. As far as we know, nobody reported Janet to the authorities. Over the years, between you and Sir Evan, you would have received any such reports. You received none. But you have uncovered two aspects worth following up .First is the problem with Dutton's wife. Will it prove a permanent obstacle to Robert and Janet marrying? And secondly, did the aborted affair between Janet and Stephen lead the latter to murder Thomas? He may not have taken no for an answer."

Luke was content. Manorial management was running smoothly with Peter as steward and Harry as both his deputy and bailiff, Emma Snigg as housekeeper, and the regular employment of Mother Harland and her brother, James, to advise on the livestock.

His magisterial role was equally successful. Luke had removed a Royalist military unit from the area and was aware of a local Royalist cell; solved the disappearance of the steward, Bates, although the murderer remained unknown; explained the disappearance of Simon Snigg; and was convinced that he had unearthed the motives behind the murder of Charles Ogden.

He was not oblivious to the sectarian bitterness that enveloped the dale, including the extremism of his local rector and the perceived bias of the constable Dutton. The record of child abuse, their widespread sale into servitude, or clandestine adoption may have further increased tensions. The case of Elizabeth Foxton still troubled him. Matilda had become alarmed at the complaints of women about male predators, although Luke did not see it as an issue; such activities had always been the norm. She was also intrigued regarding a possible cult of pagan worshipers.

He was beginning to enjoy his life as a country squire.

25

A FEW DAYS LATER, THIS idyllic new world fell apart. The first blow to Luke's serenity was a surprise visit from Kit Jagger. "What brings you to Abbey Grange?" Luke asked.

"We both attended the funeral of my friend and the former steward of this manor, Tommy Bates, a week or so ago."

"An interesting gathering. All the Catholics attended, but many of the Protestant families were absent. What's the problem?"

"Tommy's body was only identified by his red doublet and a few possessions. One of my men who has been in London for months returned the day I came back from Tommy's funeral. He was perplexed when I explained where I had just been."

"Why?"

"He had travelled from Whitby by ship with Tommy about the time he disappeared from this manor."

"He must have been mistaken."

"No, he has known Tommy for years and often accompanied us on our youthful forays across the moors. Tommy told him he was no longer steward at Abbey Grange and was heading to London in search of a position and hopeful of tracing his long-lost daughter."

"Did your man remark on anything unusual or strange about Tom Bates?"

"Only that he was shabbily dressed."

"My god, who did we bury? Thomas must have changed clothes with a tramp to conceal his true identity until he was out of Yorkshire. The poor vagrant in Tom's finery was later set upon."

"We must tell Janet. She might receive an immense shock if he suddenly returned," said Kit.

"No, not yet, for two reasons. First, he is officially dead, and I don't know how you officially reverse that situation. I will have to seek legal advice. Secondly, I don't think Janet would want to know. She is about to leave here to live on one of Robert Dutton's properties. She would marry him, if he was not already married."

"Robbie took no time in replacing his late father in the affections of our lusty Scot" was Kit's surprising comment.

"What is the situation regarding his wife?" asked Luke.

"Now if you had nothing better to do, the case of Teresa Dutton is a real mystery. Teresa's origins were thought to be unknown except perhaps to Mother Harland. It was she who provided the sixteen-year-old servant for the Giles Dutton household. Within months, the girl was pregnant, according to local gossip, to her master, old Giles. However, within weeks, his teenage son, Robert, just before embarking on his military career, was married to her in the local church, suggesting to the dale that the real father was the then boy."

"So Robert has a child to inherit his growing domain?"

"No, a few months after Robert left for service with Parliament, Teresa had a miscarriage. A month after that, she disappeared."

"One of the many young people who disappear from Abbey Dale. Was there no follow-up, no attempt to find her?"

"No, old Giles Dutton had an explanation that convinced Tom Bates, who was now steward here, and others that there was no problem. The loss of the baby had so weakened the girl both physically and mentally that she needed to be looked after. With the help of the Catholic families in the dale, Giles managed to find a place for Teresa in a Catholic convent in the Spanish Netherlands."

"Who was the Catholic intermediary who assisted in finding a convent?"

"Charles Ogden. Giles Dutton was a great friend of Tommy and Janet, so I assume Tommy asked his deputy for help."

"Is there anything else of relevance?"

"Months after Teresa left, rumours began to circulate that although penniless, she was a legitimate descendant of the Leighs and could have a claim to what is now your manor."

"Well, I can't ask Ogden to confirm the story. I must try and locate the girl."

"Who will you ask?"

"Her husband, the constable."

Next morning, after bidding farewell to Kit, Luke rode to Dutton Hall. He did not waste words and started as was his technique with a lie. "Robert, someone has raised with me the question of your wife and her current status. Is she still alive?"

"No doubt the gossips of the dale have told you a pack of lies. Since I became constable, there have been the most outrageous stories circulating about Teresa and her current whereabouts."

"Where is she?"

"I don't know exactly."

"Surely, you have tried to find out?"

"Of course, and especially now given that I would wish to marry Janet."

"Which would only be possible if she were dead."

"Or mentally unstable. I could obtain an annulment."

"That seems a callous approach concerning a young girl you impregnated and then married."

"Let me explain. One rumour you would have heard that is absolutely true is that I hated my father. Teresa's situation is one of the reasons I could not stand this evil man, who ill-treated my mother, myself, and nearly all of his female servants. He slept with Teresa night after night. One evening, he thought I should learn to be a man, and he brought Teresa to my bedchamber, after he had already abused her several times that night. She was to initiate me into the world of sex. How my one single episode with Teresa made her pregnant and my father's hundreds of intrusions did not is a miracle. It was Father who got the girl pregnant, but I was to take the blame and marry the girl to maintain the family's honour. I ran off to join the army immediately after the ceremony. It was up to Father to solve the consequences of his own ill behaviour."

"Were you informed of what happened after you left?"

"Not by my father. Mother wrote telling me that Teresa had had a miscarriage and that she was seriously ill in both mind and body and Father had arranged with Charles Ogden, and with Mr Bates's approval, to have her taken to a convent on the continent to be cared for."

"Your mother never knew where?"

"No, and Ogden, when I questioned him, claimed he had handed the girl over in Ostend to a Royalist Catholic gentleman who was to take her to a convent. This gentleman had apparently been a friend of the Leighs and accepted her gentry lineage."

"Did you believe this story? Given your father's behaviour, could he have not simply had the girl murdered?"

"Quite possibly, and he may have tried even before she disappeared. Ask Mother Harland! She told me when I first returned to the dale after Father's death, when I questioned her on Teresa's miscarriage, that it was induced by herbs and potions that Father had obtained in massive quantities, well beyond what was needed for a simple abortion. She implied that Father had caused the miscarriage and possibly the subsequent deterioration in Teresa's physical and mental health."

As the two men talked, they were approached by one of Robert's servants. "Sir, as constable, you are required on the Foxton farm. Matthew has been found dead, smothered by bales of hay."

"I will come with you, but send one of your men to Mother Harland. We need her at Foxtons' to examine the body as soon as possible," said Luke.

On arriving at Foxton farm, the two law officers were led to the barn where Mark and three farm labourers stood around Matthew's body. Mark explained that a couple of bales had been removed from on top of his uncle, but nobody had touched the body in any way.

Dutton was sceptical. "There were only two bales covering his body?"

"Yes," replied Mark.

"Not enough to kill him. They could have knocked him out. Perhaps they pushed him into a sharp or blunt object that inflicted a more serious blow," commented Luke.

Dutton carefully examined the area. There was nothing that Foxton could have hit on falling that would have caused his death. In fact, the floor was covered in a substantial layer of soft hay. Luke agreed.

"Is he dead?" asked one of the labourers. "He may be simply knocked out."

Luke examined the body. "He is dead, and given how cold he is, he died some time ago. Mark, when did you last see your uncle alive?"

"Just after dawn this morning. Uncle Matt said he would spend the morning in the barn and sent me and the lads to a distant field with a wagon load of feed for the cattle."

"How did you come to find him?" asked Dutton.

"If we have had an early start such as this morning, we usually return to the house late morning for something to eat and drink. When Uncle did not join us, I sent one of the lads here to fetch him."

Dutton turned to the lad concerned, asking, "When you arrived, there were only two bales covering him?"

"Yes."

Luke intervened. "Mark, have the body taken to the house and stripped of all clothing! Mother Harland will make a thorough examination when she gets here."

Back at the house, Luke asked Mark and the labourers, "Did you see any strangers on the property this morning? Anybody near the barn?"

Mark replied, "Yes, a group of women who use our farm as a shortcut from the western moorlands to Abbeythwaite."

"They do it once or twice a week after they check on their livestock on the moors," added one of the labourers.

"Who are they?" asked Luke.

"A regular is Mary Carver, and sometimes I have also seen Nell Briggs and the blacksmith's wife, Alice Eades," he answered.

Mother Harland arrived midafternoon and made a detailed and extensive examination of the body. At one point, she exclaimed, "Sweet Jesus!" Then she whispered to Luke, "I need to talk to you alone. Clear the room apart from Dutton and yourself."

When that was accomplished, Luke asked, "What can be so important that you want to keep the initial news a secret?"

"Two reasons. Matthew Foxton was murdered."

"How can you be sure?" asked the sceptical Dutton.

"Gentlemen, look at his chest!"

"Good god!" exclaimed Luke. "The same mark that you found on Charles Ogden. Matthew was stabbed by a needlelike implement?"

"Yes, and you know what that means?" Mother Harland asked.

"That the casual workers from the rectory did not murder Charles Ogden and that there is a killer alive and well and making his way through the Catholic community of Abbey Dale," answered a deflated Luke.

"Don't be so pessimistic, Luke. It could be a copycat killing. There are hundreds of needles in the dale. The blacksmith turns out dozens at a time," replied a surprisingly comforting Robert Dutton. *Perhaps too supportive,* thought Luke. If this death was part of the anti-Catholic campaign, Robert would be a prime suspect.

Robert left to inform Mark and his men of the situation, while Luke questioned Mother Harland on an unrelated matter. "Tamsin, I have been alerted to another of the disappearing mysteries of the dale, our constable's wife. Can you help?"

"One of the biggest mistakes of my life. I should never have sent that poor girl to Dutton Hall, but at that time, Giles's predatory behaviour was not well known, and after that, I should never have sold Giles so much of my potions and herbal medicine. He misused them, not only to abort the baby but to incapacitate the mother. I saw Teresa before she was whisked away, allegedly to the continent for care. She was in a very bad way."

"Is she dead?"

"At the time, I was certain of it, but Tommy Bates, who was an honourable man, assured me that he had freed Charles Ogden from his responsibilities at Abbey Grange to take the stricken girl to the continent."

"Did Bates or Ogden ever tell you the exact location of the convent?"

"Both claimed they did not know. Ogden delivered the girl to a Royalist exile at Ostend who would take her to her final destination. To be honest, she was in such poor condition she could have easily died on the journey. I don't think you will ever find an answer."

"It is important for Robert Dutton that we do. He cannot marry Janet Bates until Teresa's death is verified."

That night, Luke confessed to Matilda that it had been a bad day. "Thomas Bates is alive, and the person buried in the churchyard is not Janet's husband. Robert Dutton's wife disappeared under strange circumstances, largely orchestrated by his father, and her current whereabouts are unknown, and Matthew Foxton has been murdered in an identical fashion to Charles Ogden. This suggests that the latter was not killed by Unsworth's casual labourers. And a large group of women continues to visit the western moorlands. For what purpose, I do not know."

26

N EXT MORNING, LUKE REVISITED Mark Foxton. He announced that he would turn a blind eye to Catholic interment at night in the old Cistercian Abbey graveyard, now part of a largely overgrown field on the edge of Luke's estate.

"Not necessary. I have arranged for Ted Unsworth to bury Uncle in the grounds of the parish church after a service conducted by him," Mark replied.

"Unsworth would never bury a Catholic in his parish cemetery. How did you persuade him?"

"Ted and I were close friends in our youth. I have been attending the parish church every Sunday. Several months ago, I secretly renounced my Catholicism and became a member of the Church of England. I told Ted that my uncle would do the same. As a member of his congregation, I had a right to ask that Uncle be buried according to rites he was about to accept. Ted saw my conversion as a major victory over the Catholics, and to bury Uncle added to this sense of success."

"Yes, I can see Unsworth rejoicing in such circumstances. But it does not stifle my immediate interpretation of the motives behind the killing, that it was a further attack on the Catholic community and their allies—Bates, Ogden, and now Foxton."

"Not necessarily. It may relate to what those men did individually or as a group years ago, unrelated to Uncle's intended conversion."

Luke was not convinced of Matthew's intended conversion. "Did your uncle intend to convert as you did, or was that a lie to convince the rector to bury him in the local churchyard?"

Mark simply smiled. "That will be forever a family secret."

Luke changed the subject. "Who do you think killed your uncle, and why?"

"As you know, he only returned to the dale a few months ago. He was away for almost ten years. In such a short time back, he could not have created such antagonism as to lead to his murder. Any motive must stem from something that happened a decade ago when I was only in my teens."

"Has he argued with anybody lately?"

"That was Uncle's problem. He argued with everybody over anything. His attacks on the government in the Three Roses did not endear him to the constable, Harland or Briggs, and he disputed every penny charged by William Eades for shoeing our horses. And closer to home, he refused to pay our labourers a fair wage, which they definitely deserved. I argued with him on that score many a time."

"Are you suggesting that the extreme supporters of the government, the blacksmith, or one of your own labourers could have committed the deed?"

Luke did not add "or yourself?"

"If disagreements lead to murders, who knows?" was Mark's meaningless reply.

This gave Luke a new line of enquiry. He would question the workers.

"Thanks, Mark. I will talk to your workers to see if they can add to the picture you have given. I will look for them on the farm. I don't want to interrupt their work too much."

Luke found one of the lads in a near field leading an ox that was pulling a largely ineffective plough across the still frozen field. He seemed flustered when approached by the local lord and magistrate. Luke put him at his ease, "Relax, lad. I only want to ask you a few questions. I am surprised that you are doing what you are at this time of year. It is still too cold to plough."

"So was Master Mark. He argued with his uncle only the day before the old tyrant died that ploughing this early was a waste of time and effort, our effort. It was Master Matthew's way of keeping us in our place."

"You did not like your late master?"

"Who did? He was a very bitter man, although given the murder of his daughter, and the lack of any finalization of what actually happened to her years ago, his behaviour is perhaps explicable."

"Did Mark and his uncle get on?"

"I do not want to get Master Mark into trouble. He is very kind to us, but he never fully adapted to his uncle's return. He ran this property for almost ten years beginning when he was only our age. Master Matthew went out of his way to humiliate his nephew by suggesting that many of the methods and procedures he used on the farm were ridiculous."

"How did Mark take this abuse?"

"He simply smiled."

Luke had just had a recent example of that smile. What did it conceal?

"Had the two had any serious arguments of late?"

"Yes, on two occasions this week, they had a major row. If Master Matthew had not been so drunk and almost incapable, they would have come to blows."

"What was the cause of these serious arguments, and how did you come to know about them?"

"We eat in the kitchen, which is next door to the family's dining room. You can hear everything in the kitchen, even whispers in the neighbouring room. The first argument was over religion. Master Matthew was furious that behind his back, Mark had ceased being a Papist and had become a member of the local parish. Our employer cursed his nephew with words I have never heard and condemned him to an eternity of hell's fires as a heretic."

"So clearly, Matthew was not going to follow Mark into the Protestant camp?"

"No. In fact, Master Matthew threatened to evict all Protestants from the property, although next morning, he did not seem to remember the threat."

"Was Mark distressed?"

"No, he assumed it as an idle threat, provoked by drink."

"And the second argument?"

"It was over the disappearance of Elizabeth Foxton. Master Matthew accused his nephew of not looking after his cousin and allowing the mob of youths then roaming the dale to murder the young girl. He kept emphasising that Mark did nothing to save her. He hurled Mark's alleged impotence at him over and over. Then he went a step further. He accused Mark of participating in his daughter's murder."

"How did Mark react?"

"He was very calm. All we heard was Mark saying he was innocent, and if anybody in that room was responsible for Elizabeth's death, it was Matthew himself."

"What did he mean?"

"I don't know. At that point, the three of us grabbed a jug of beer and a round of cheese and departed for the barn, where we sleep."

Luke did not conceal his disappointment. An answer to that question would have been very enlightening. He continued. "Did you see anyone else around the barn area the morning Master Matthew died?"

The answer to that question improved Luke's demeanour. "Yes. I was sent back by Master Mark from the western field to collect some scythes from the barn. Master Matthew was still with the troubled calf, but he was talking to James Harland, who was examining the beast."

"So James Harland was in the area around the time Matthew may have been murdered?"

"Yes, but he was not the only one. Although I did not see him, Matthew was expecting William Eades that morning to collect some monies owing to him."

"How do you know that?"

"While I was in the barn, Matthew called out to me, thinking I was Eades. I identified myself, and I heard Matthew say to James Harland, 'That jackanapes Eades is in for shock. He will only get half of what he claims. The man is a scoundrel.'"

"Did Eades actually come?"

"I never saw him."

Later that day, Luke visited the Eades. William was in his forge, fashioning a sword blade. Luke signalled for him to complete what he was doing. After hammering the hot red blade, he tempered it in cold water. Finally withdrawing it, he showed it to Luke, who was impressed. "You will have to make me one or two of these blades, William."

The blacksmith, who touched his cap in deference to the lord of the manor, humbly replied, "No, my lord, I will make you any implements you need to work the land, but these sword blades are largely for show or for those who have little need to use them. Gentlemen and soldiers would find my swords deficient in one essential. During intensive swordplay, any aggressive swing is most likely to shatter my blades."

"Why?"

"It's the iron I use. I cannot afford to buy the purest iron, nor have I the time to refine further the iron ore that I have. Nor do my skills allow me to compete with the specialised sword makers who have emerged during our two decades of conflict. And in reality, I have become a full-time farrier. Are your horses in need of new shoes?"

"When you are free, come and inspect them."

"Thank you, my lord, but your visit here is not related to your horses. Your steward would have sent one of the servants to make those arrangements. What is so important that you have come personally to my forge?"

Before Luke could answer, William's wife, Alice, entered the forge and was so surprised to see Luke that in her attempt to curtsy, she almost stumbled, saving herself by putting her hands on a bench top. "My lord, what brings you here? William has not been causing trouble, has he?" she joked with little enthusiasm.

Her husband replied, "Sir Luke was about to explain when you came through the door, my dear."

Luke accepted the cue. "Both of you would have heard that Matthew Foxton was murdered in his barn late yesterday morning."

"Yes," answered Alice, "but how does that affect either of us?"

"Witnesses place both of you in the vicinity of the murder about the time it happened. I am here to free you both from my list of possible suspects."

"I was nowhere near the Foxton farm yesterday morning. I was called to Elderby to help strengthen an iron-rimmed wheel on a farmer's wagon," replied William.

"Had you not arranged with Matthew to visit him at that time to collect monies owing to you?"

"Yes, I had, but given the urgent job in Elderby, I asked Alice on her way home from the western moors to obtain the money. Her feminine charms might have been able to wheedle out of him all the monies he owes. He is, sorry, was an obsessive skinflint."

"Alice, did you visit Matthew in his barn midmorning yesterday?"

"Yes and no," she replied.

"That's not helpful," commented Luke.

"Sorry. What I mean is that I travelled back from the western moors most of the way with Mary Carver. I told her as we crossed Foxton land that I had business with Matthew. She continued on their way with the others, and I went to the barn. I called out to Matthew several times, but assuming he was not there, I went to the house, where I again had no response. I caught up to Mary, and we came home together."

"You never went into the barn?"

"I went some way inside, far enough to ensure that I could be heard throughout the structure."

"How far in was that in relation to the stacked bales of hay?"

"They were at the opposite end of the barn and looked in disarray. They were not neatly stacked as I would expect from such a meticulously obsessive man as Matthew Foxton."

"So it is possible that Matthew was lying dead under those disarrayed bales at the time you visited the barn?"

"From what you say, it is most likely."

"Did you see anybody else in the vicinity of the barn?"

"Not while I was in the vicinity of the barn, but as we all approached it from the distance, I did see a horseman heading for the main entrance to the farm. From the distance, I did not recognise him or his horse."

Later, Luke confided in Matilda. "There are three possible suspects for Matthew's murder—Alice Eades, James Harland, and Mark Foxton with or without the help of his men."

"Come, Luke, you have had a busy day. Let me help you relax!" was her alluring reply.

LUKE AND MATILDA ROSE late. It was nearly midday before the married lovers untangled themselves from each other and emerged as lord and lady of the manor.

Peter immediately reported a serious disturbance at the Three Roses the previous night. "James Harland accused Alice Eades of murdering Matthew Foxton. She retaliated by saying the last person seen leaving Foxtons' barn before the body was found was James himself. The drinkers quickly formed into three groups—those who supported Alice, those who defended James, and interestingly, a majority who didn't care who had killed Matthew and thought it was a good thing. The killer, they believed, should be applauded and not handed over to the constable. The universal dislike of Matthew suggests the strong possibility that many more suspects might emerge."

Luke went to the Three Roses to speak to James. "You met Matthew the day he died?"

"Yes, since you employed me to keep an eye on your livestock, Matthew decided to follow suit, knowing that I did not charge as much as my sister for such services. I pointed out that while I could probably diagnose the problem, I did not have my sister's expertise in prescribing herbs and potions to effect a cure."

"Foxton was a man who did not readily pay his bills?"

"Decidedly, that is why I took my sister's advice to obtain payment before I delivered any service. He was livid when I refused to look at his calf until I was paid. He shouted at me, delivering such a torrent of abuse that I walked away. As I did, the calf went into convulsions. Matthew called me back, threw a few coins at me, more than I asked for. He claimed I was lucky that he had money on him as he was expecting William Eades at any moment to collect his debts."

"Did you see Alice Eades while you were there?"

"Not while I was in the barn. I discovered the calf's problem was minor. It had some fabric stuck in its throat. Once removed, the animal was fit as a fiddle. As I left the property, I saw a group of local women crossing the field, with one of them, Alice Eades, lagging behind, therefore my claim that she was the last person to see Matthew alive. Her counter claim that the murderer was me lacks credibility. What would be my motive?"

"That is the problem I face as a newcomer to the dale. I do not know enough of family interactions over the past decade to isolate possible motives. Did the Harlands have much to do with the Foxtons? Have you had any recent clashes with Matthew?"

"Matthew only returned to the dale a few months before your arrival, and since then, until he asked me to look at his calf, I have had no contact with him."

"Not even as publican of the Three Roses?"

"I have not seen him there, although the girls tell me he sometimes came with Mark around sunset but rarely stayed beyond one drink compared with his nephew, who is often here until we close."

"Did any of your girls have any problems with Matthew?"

"Not that I know of. My girls, from an early age, learnt to deal effectively with predatory males."

"What about your sister?"

"On his return, he no longer sought my sister's help with his livestock as Mark had done on a very regular basis. I doubt if Tamsin would have noticed the loss of the Foxton business. She has more work than she can cover in livestock care alone."

"Why did you name Alice Eades as the killer?"

"Simply a diversion tactic. The two obvious suspects, given our presence at the farm around the time of the murder, are Alice and myself. She is trying to divert attention from herself onto me, so I returned the favour."

"Have you and Alice clashed in the past?"

"As the publican of the Three Roses, I have had to ask Alice to leave on numerous occasions. She gets fired up over issues and, with a few drinks, can be confrontational to other drinkers. The most recent was when Simon Snigg clashed with the rector's two casual labourers. She was aggressively supportive of Simon and thought I had been very unfair in summoning the constable to remove him."

"What is behind this apparent zeal?"

"Perhaps her unusual upbringing. She was a Carver by birth, but her parents gave her away to the Eades, who brought her up beside their son, William, who then surprised everybody by marrying her. The experts declared that as they were not blood relations, it would be legal and cause no problems with their offspring. The fact that her adoption involved a change of religion may have been a factor. Whatever the cause, she has emerged as the conscience of the dale. She was the only person I heard in the tavern praising your efforts to reopen the Elizabeth Foxton case."

Luke was delighted. "James, it has taken all this conversation to come up with a fact that may have a direct bearing on the case. Alice Eades is one of the few people still interested in the Elizabeth Foxton case, and she is one of the last people seen near the scene of the death of Elizabeth's father. That is an interesting fact. Did Alice know Elizabeth?"

"Yes, but I don't think they were ever close. Elizabeth's best friend was the then Mary Ogden, now Mary Carver. Alice was a few years older than those two, but at times, she did visit the Foxtons. It was discouraged on both sides, the Foxtons and the Eades, because of the religious difference. Protestant girls should not play with Catholics. Strangely, that rule did not apply to the boys who were friends across sectarian lines, although this friendship did not continue beyond their youth."

"What are the current views in the dale regarding Matthew's murder? Who do your customers think did the deed?"

"The amateur sleuths have a simple criterion—motive. Who gains by the murder? Only one person stands out—his nephew, Mark. He ran that farm effectively for nearly ten years, and with his uncle's return, he lost control. Matthew was old fashioned and reversed a lot of positive changes Mark had made. It must have been humiliating. What made it even worse was that Matthew was not a pleasant man, and his treatment of Mark may have provoked the younger man to act. Their property involved a ninety-nine-year lease, and Mark is named as Matthew's successor in the revised document drawn up by Mr Bates just before Matthew left the dale after his daughter's disappearance."

Luke decided to leave further questioning of Mark until after the funeral, which in itself raised further interesting questions. It was sparsely attended. Only two Catholics attended, the others unhappy about Mark's decision to have the service in the parish church. While Mark may have become a Protestant, Matthew, in their eyes, remained faithful to the church of Rome. Mark, a few of his drinking friends, and his current workers were the main mourners. Luke and Matilda as lord and lady of the manor and Robert Dutton, who combined with his role as constable with that of church warden, made up the official guests. In addition to Matilda, three women were in attendance.

This troubled Luke. The only two Catholics present were Mary Carver and his own housekeeper, Emma Snigg. The third woman and, given the circumstances, the most surprising was Emma's somewhat estranged birth sister, and Luke's prime suspect, Alice Eades.

Why those three women? pondered Luke. He mentioned his concern to Matilda, who offered to raise it with the women informally. An interrogation by magistrate Tremayne might be counterproductive.

Next morning, Matilda casually asked Emma why she had attended Matthew Foxton's funeral.

"To support my sister-in-law who was defying the Catholic community's refusal to attend because a Protestant burial was clearly against the wishes of the deceased."

"Why would the normally timid Mary take such a step? Was she particularly close to Matthew Foxton?"

"Not in recent years. After all, Matthew was absent for nearly a decade. No, in her mind, this was a way of finally farewelling her close childhood friend, Elizabeth. There was no funeral of Elizabeth, but in Mary's mind, to attend the funeral of her father was a way of bringing closure."

"What about your sister Alice's attendance?"

"You would need to ask her. It may have been for the same reason as Mary. She did know Elizabeth, although she was quite a bit older. On the other hand, since Matthew's return from Whitby, she has gone out of her way to blacken his name. She hated him, but I do not know why."

Matilda took it upon herself to visit the Eades on the excuse that she wanted a pair of scissors sharpened as William was cutler, as well as blacksmith, to the dale.

While she waited for the scissors, Matilda was entertained by Alice with a range of cakes and biscuits and several cups of mead. Matilda asked, "I was surprised to see you at Foxton's funeral yesterday. Very few women attended."

"That is the very reason I went. Why don't more women attend such major events? Death is not a male preserve."

"Was that the only reason?"

"No. Foxton was not a nice man. He treated his nephew, Mark, horribly since his return to the dale. We will all be better off with him gone. I had great satisfaction in seeing him put to rest."

"Making sure he was really dead?"

"Something like that. But I also rejoiced in Mark's success in having the old Papist scoundrel buried as a Protestant. With Mark about to become only the second Papist after myself in the dale to convert, I thought my presence would be a sign of support for him."

"So you really attended as a manifestation of women's rights, Protestantism, and justice," commented Matilda, wondering if this peasant girl would properly understand such concepts.

Matilda informed Luke of what she had discovered, and he decided to follow up her impressions with Mother Harland. She would be able to add to the picture of the three women who, for the moment, intrigued him.

Mother Harland was also intrigued. "My lord, they are a strange trio. Mary is timid, shy, and the most put upon of the three, being completely dominated by her late father, Charlie Ogden, and now submissive to her husband. Emma is the most practical and well-organised woman in the dale, full of common sense. And Alice Eades is a very special young woman. If she had been born into your class and a man, she would be the local magistrate and member of Parliament. For a girl with such a poor education, although she rapidly learnt to read and write under old Garnett's tuition, she has an overdeveloped sense of injustice. There is hardly a cause of which she is aware that she does not want to put things right."

"I know about her adoption by the Eades. Was there anything else in his upbringing that might help explain her current attitudes?"

"Yes, she was my most effective assistant during her teenage years. So much so that I decided, given the lack of interest of my four nieces, that I would pass my secrets on to her. She might succeed me as the white witch of Abbey Dale."

"She rejected your offer?"

"No, she soaked up everything I could tell her. She has a remarkable knowledge of herbs and their healing properties, and she would know much of the history of the dale involving its womenfolk as she assisted me in my role as midwife. Why has God wasted such ability on a woman who, given the attitudes of society, is in no position to use her talents to any great extent? She still helps me, and is well equipped to succeed me, but she has not told me that that is what she wants. Not many people are aware of her abilities and knowledge."

Luke began to consider Alice Eades in a new light. Could she be the mastermind behind the problems that had beset the dale? Or was she the person who could help him solve them?

28

NEXT MORNING, LUKE'S ATTENTION was diverted from the key issues by several cases of economic vandalism. Peter reported that for three nights in a row, the manor's poultry had been freed from their overnight coops and found the next morning scavenging across several fields. Some were dead or badly injured, savaged by dogs, cats, or foxes.

"Did you place a man in the area after the first intrusion?" asked Luke.

"Yes, I had a man hidden in one of the outbuildings. We have several housing chickens. The vandal attacked the one farthest away from our watchman, who heard nothing."

"Sounds like an inside job. Do we have any workers so alienated that they would do this?"

"It is unlikely as you pay illegally above the stipulated rate. Why would they risk what is a well-paid position?"

"Be careful with your use of words, Peter. As a magistrate, I do not break the law or pay above the maximum rate. I just provide a little extra that is not part of their wages."

"It gets worse, Luke. Releasing the chickens is hardly likely to decrease our income substantially, but destroying part of our barley crop, if continued, would. Last night, someone took a scythe and cut a path a yard wide across our barley field. I can only see that as a warning of further destruction."

"We can only be grateful that most of our livestock, the basis of this manor's wealth, has already been transferred to the moors—the sheep to the western and the cattle to the northern," commented Luke.

"But we do have a considerable number of young calves and lambs that are still here being hand-fed because they were considered by James Harland to be still too weak to face the colder nights on the moors."

"Peter, send Harry immediately north to check on whether there has been any trouble on the northern moors. I will ride up to the western moors myself. Tonight we will place as many people as we have in key places. We do not want our wheat and barley crops further subjected to the mystery destroyer. Use the in-house staff. The washerwomen twins, Abigail and Phyllis, can sleep with the calves and lambs. Give them a bell that they can ring if trouble starts! You and I will take turns on watch in what could be a growing emergency. What could possibly be the motive other than a disgruntled worker?"

Next morning, Luke had a pleasant ride across the dale and enjoyed the gentle climb onto the western moor. It was covered with sheep. He finally located Johnny Harland, who, with the growing number of animals under his care, was now assisted by three young lads.

Luke was impressed with the frolicking lambs and the quietly grazing mature sheep. They covered the entire landscape. He could not help calculating that every one of these animals added substantially to his income either directly through the sale of their wool or for the older animals as meat or indirectly through the rents paid by his tenants who owned three quarters of the animals he could see.

He asked Johnny, "Whose sheep dominate the moors?"

"Many belong to the late Charlie Ogden, which will be the Carvers, and the Sniggs, which are now yours. A few each from the smaller farmers, such as my brother, James, the Eades, and the rector. The biggest groups are yours and constable Dutton's. You will, as lord of manor, need to sort out a developing problem. Over the last two years, people who used to send their sheep to the northern moors are placing them here. This is all right in a good season, but when fodder becomes limited, there will be serious trouble."

"Hasn't this change been balanced out by the fact that the cattle that used to graze here have now been sent north?" asked the less-than-expert Luke.

"No, my lord, sheep are more intensive grazers than cattle. One sheep will do more damage than three cows. What brings you onto the moor this fine morning?"

Luke explained the situation and asked whether there had been any attempt to take or disperse his sheep overnight. Johnny explained that with the arrival of the young assistants, all the sheep were either hurdled or placed in one or two of the large caves and watched over all night. Apart from the need to frighten away a few foxes, there had been no trouble.

Johnny's next comment startled Luke. "My lord, don't you talk to your constable? An hour ago, Dutton was here complaining about a similar outrage and asking the same questions as you have."

"No, I have not spoken to Dutton, but what was his problem?"

"Three of his hand-fed calves were stolen."

"That seems simple theft. They would fetch a good price or provide several good meals."

"No, my lord, that is the mystery. The calves were simply moved to the rector's barn, who immediately recognised them as Dutton's. It is a dangerous prank in this changeable weather."

On his way back to Abbey Grange, Luke dropped in on Dutton.

A servant informed him that he had been summoned to Abbeythwaite as everybody was up in arms as their gardens were being destroyed.

Luke trotted into Abbeythwaite to find most of the village running hither and thither in pursuit of dozens of pigs that were rooting up every vegetable they could find. He found Dutton supervising the roundup. "Where have the pigs come from?" he asked of the constable.

"Throughout the village and probably your manor as well. Someone broke into several pigpens overnight and drove the pigs out. It was not until midmorning that people realised that these were not a few pigs from one of their neighbours that may have escaped. Most of the men had already gone to the fields, and the women did not realise what was happening. This is the second strange act last night. My calves were stolen and put into Ted's barn."

"I know. I was up on the western moor, checking on the safety of my livestock as we have had two strange incidents over recent nights. Our poultry have been driven out of their coops, and someone cut a swathe through my barley field. All so senseless!"

"It is the behaviour of a child," said Robert.

"Yes, you could be right," answered Luke. "That might explain why he or she has not been seen. Most adults in the dale are easily accounted for, but children are not always where their parents think they are."

Over the following days, the situation worsened. The more suspicious of the villagers began to talk about poltergeist and other supernatural or magical beings. This pagan view was given credence when Dickie Unsworth reported that half a dozen shoes that he was working on disappeared and were later found placed very carefully around the edge of his well.

The experience of William Eades, the blacksmith, was even more convincing. All the tools that he had carefully hung from hooks in his forge were found in the morning lying on the floor but arranged in some sort of diagrammatic pattern. Luke visited the Eades to find out more details of the pattern that the intruder had made. William dismissed the arrangement as simply a random placement of his tools, but Alice thought they reminded her of the runes that Mr Garnett had shown her years ago, which intensified the feeling that the village was under attack by some pagan spirit.

According to the dale, only one person could save them—Mother Harland. Secretly, however, a small group of women were not satisfied even with this response. Christian ritual and the magic of the wise woman were not enough. If the village was being attacked by some alien spirit, then the old gods might be the best protection.

They would call upon the goddess to save the village, but this necessitated a trip to the western moors at night during a period in which villagers were acutely alert to any nocturnal movements.

Two of the women believed it could be done as their husbands would be busy elsewhere, having been summoned to join the watch for the next three evenings. The third was more cautious. Instead of one shepherd to avoid on the moors, there were now four or five, and given the increase in sheep numbers, the goddess's sacred cave could be full of sheep overnighting there with their carers.

The cult leader acted. She openly visited the area next morning, secretly retrieved the goddess, and brought it back to the village. They could now hold their ritual of prayer, praise, and sacrifice in a safe place within the village or even the manor itself.

The mayhem continued. While the inhabitants of the dale lay in wait to protect their animals and crops, the vandal demolished a stone wall and used the rocks to block a ditch that drained most of the manor fields into the beck. If heavy rain occurred, many of the lower fields would be inundated and the crops destroyed.

The three worshipers of the goddess found an ideal secret place—the tunnel leading from the manor library to the Carvers' pigpen. The leader wanted to use the room near the manor end of the priest's escape route, but the others thought that to use what had been used first as a Catholic chapel and then for the sexual adventures of an unknown couple was not appropriate. They would turn the slightly enlarged tunnel near the Carver end of the outlet into their shrine.

The ritual consisted of pleading with the deity and praising her, asking her for help to save the village from this relentless vandal and remove the alarm and almost hysteria that had enveloped parts of the dale. Unsworth did not help calm the situation by preaching that it was God's punishment for their sins and that until they repented, the devil would continue to destroy the dale.

The goddess was placed in a niche in the wall and candles put in other niches that the women had enlarged. A young pullet had been carried there in a basket by the leader, who, on her knees, cut its throat and drained the blood into a bowl. Eventually, the blood was spread over each of the women. The bird should then have been plucked and boiled and flesh eaten as a celebration to the goddess, but in the circumstances, the bird was taken with them and would be eaten in more secular surroundings in the kitchen of one of the participants. The leader was totally convinced that these enforced changes in ritual would not negate the positive effects of their prayers and sacrifice. One of the other women promised to protect their new sanctuary by ensuring that entry from the manor end would be rendered impossible.

After three days, the women were convinced that their activities had saved the dale. The acts of vandalism had ceased.

The dale had no rational explanation for what had occurred or who the destructive agent might be. On the following Sunday, after morning prayer, the answer was delivered to Luke on a plate and confirmed by another that afternoon.

As he and Matilda were leaving the church, the rector caught up with them. "Sir, will you accompany me into the vestry? I know the identity of the mysterious vandal."

Matilda made her way back to the manor.

Ted Unsworth, as he removed his ecclesiastical garments, informed Luke. "It is Simon Snigg."

"And how do you know that?" asked an incredulous Luke.

"A decade ago, I did every one of things this modern-day vandal has done as part of my youthful rampage against my uncle and his generation."

"How does Snigg relate to that?"

"My enthusiastic childlike accomplice at the time was Simon. The buffeting that the beck gave him has made his mental condition even worse, and he has reverted to childlike behaviour. He clearly remembers in detail what we did a decade ago."

Later that afternoon, Mother Harland dropped into the manor and sought a private audience with Luke in which she revealed that the pattern of vandalism was identical with an attack on the dale almost ten years earlier. She affirmed that the earlier episodes were enacted by Ted Unsworth and Simon Snigg, and as now, Ted was the respectable rector, Tthe current perpetrator must be Simon.

LUKE RELATED THE NEWS to Matilda and Peter. "It is a huge embarrassment that the perpetrator of activities that have placed the dale in a state of panic is the husband of our housekeeper and an inhabitant of this house."

"Does Emma know what her husband is doing?" asked Peter.

"That is what I need to establish," replied Luke.

"I will speak to Emma quietly. Your interrogation might frighten the young woman. Is she aware that you suspect her husband?" asked Matilda.

"No, I asked both Ted Unsworth and Mother Harland not to tell others of their suspicions, but undoubtedly, many an older inhabitant will reach similar conclusions at any time."

Matilda spoke to Emma. "How is Simon progressing? Is he more lucid than he was?"

"No, he seems to have regressed further back into his childhood. He does not recognise me as his wife."

"That is very sad. What about sleep? Does he sleep a lot?"

"Yes, but that is largely induced. Mother Harland gave me a potion to give him each night. It knocks him out until midmorning the next day. That is why I can enjoy a long supper with you or escape to the Three Roses without worrying about Simon."

"Do you give him the potion yourself?"

"No, when he retires early each night, I place a cup of the potion on the table beside the bed and a half pint of the locally brewed ale, which he loves. He takes the potion and has the half pint as a chaser."

"How do you know he takes the sleeping potion?"

"Every night between half and a full hour after I have farewelled him for the evening, I look in on him and remove the empty cup and half-pint mug."

As Matilda later told Luke, "Simon could easily have poured out the potion, and knowing that after her visit to remove the utensils, he would not be disturbed until midmorning, he could spend the whole night vandalising the village."

They disagreed as to whether Emma should be told immediately that Simon was the prime suspect. Luke believed she should not be told but eventually conceded to Matilda's argument that Emma must know now in case Simon attempted it again.

The sudden cessation of his activities had yet to be explained.

Emma's reaction was mixed. She conceded that the spate of attacks was childlike and fitted Simon's current level of understanding and behaviour, but she refused to concede that he was able to escape his room at night and carry out such activities.

"Since we moved from the cottage in Abbeythwaite to rooms here in the manor, he would need to unlock several doors to get to the outside world at night. He does not have the keys to do this."

"That is a very valid point. The outer doors are locked every evening. None of our servants would allow Simon, whom they know is convalescing, out of doors without informing us," commented Luke.

After supper that evening, Luke retired to his library. This was his new obsession. He had quickly adopted the fad of many landed gentry—build up a library and bar everybody from such a room, which would become your private retreat. Even Matilda accepted this new idiosyncrasy.

He worked quietly for some time on magisterial papers that pertained to a meeting of the quarter sessions in Maldon, which would take him south for the next three days. Before he retired for the night, for the first time, given his reasonably long absence over the ensuing days, he locked the door of his library and pocketed the key.

Luke left for Maldon at dawn. Midmorning, an anxious Emma approached Matilda. "My lady, I am worried. Simon has disappeared again. When he did not arise an hour ago, which is now a well-ingrained habit, I went to his bedroom. He was not there. The bed was cold, which suggests that he had been long gone."

Matilda told Peter, who organised the manor staff to search its many rooms and outhouses. Harry informed the constable, who, in turn, organised a search of the village and surrounding areas. As the day wore on with no sightings of the missing man, Emma visited her fellow goddess worshiper, her birth sister, Alice Eades.

"No sign of Simon yet?" asked Alice.

"No, but I am here to discuss the recent burst of vandalism and our apparently successful appeal to the goddess to bring it to an end."

"What is there to discuss?"

"It was not the goddess's intervention that brought the spate of destruction to an end. It was an act of mine," said Emma quietly but firmly.

Alice was alarmed. "Be careful, Emma! It is dangerous for a mortal to claim greater power than a deity. A jealous goddess could bring misfortune to us all. What makes you think you are responsible?"

"My Simon is his lordship's main suspect as the vandal. He is apparently repeating a sequence of destructive acts he carried out with Ted Unsworth a decade ago."

"Why has Sir Luke not acted against Simon?"

"Because he can't explain how Simon left the manor to carry out the rampage. All our outer doors are locked, and neither Simon nor I have the relevant keys."

"But now you know how Simon did it?"

"Yes. All he had to do was to get into Sir Luke's library and enter through the wall panel into the old priest's hole, which had been for years our Catholic chapel, and then continue along the priest's escape route that took him to Mary Carver's pigpen from where he could emerge and do his damage. After our last meeting, I entered the priest's hole and locked the door that led to the tunnel. I did this to prevent our new sanctuary for the goddess from being discovered by anybody entering from the manor end."

"So you believe that Simon may have begun his nocturnal adventures to find he could not progress down the tunnel, thus stopping his series of destruction?"

"It fits the facts."

"Does it also relate to Simon's current disappearance?"

Emma suddenly appeared dazed.

"By the goddess, it does! I know where poor Simon is. He is trapped. Until you asked that question, I had missed the obvious. Simon set out on his well-worn path to wreak destruction and was stopped by the locked chapel door. Maybe he fell asleep on the bed that is still there, and when he awoke, he attempted to return to his room through his lordship's library, but as of last night, the outer door of the library has also been locked. Simon is either in the old chapel or in Sir Luke's library and is unable to escape."

"Have you got the key that you used to lock the chapel door to the tunnel on you?"

"No, it is back at the manor."

Alice thought for a while. "Emma, return to the manor and retrieve that key. I will meet you in half an hour at Mary's place. We can enter the tunnel from that end, and if the door opens with your key, we can enter the old chapel and then through the wall panel into his lordship's library and rescue Simon, if he is there. Wouldn't his lordship have heard Simon in the chapel?"

"No, his lordship is in Maldon for a few days, and I do not think even Lady Matilda knows where he keeps the key to his library door."

"Nevertheless, if Simon is locked in the library, you would have thought he would bang on the walls, and someone in the manor would have heard him."

"Not necessarily! Since his brain received such a pummelling as he was pushed along the raging beck, he has regressed into childhood in so many ways. Probably he is sitting on the floor, sucking his thumb, and crying quietly."

"How very sad!" whispered Alice, who, to Emma's surprise, put her arms around her and gave her a firm yet gentle almost sisterly hug.

Half an hour later, Alice, Emma, and Mary entered the tunnel and, with two large candles, made their way towards the chapel room. Their expedition almost came to end when Emma had trouble opening the door. The key that had worked without trouble from the chapel side seemed unable to engage from the tunnel approach.

Alice looked into the keyhole and, with a thin stick, began to push and pull and gradually removed tiny pieces of paper that had been pushed in from the other side. Then she set the thin stick alight and thrust its flame into the keyhole to burn out the more recalcitrant bits of paper.

Emma's next attempt to open the door worked. The three young women were soon in the old chapel. Emma's suspicion was validated. The bed had clearly been slept in very recently, and the pillow was soddened by what Emma declared was Simon's dribbling, which had become part of his reversion to childhood.

She turned to her friends. "Simon could easily be frightened. Stay here! I will go through the wall panel alone and try to calm him before he sees anybody else."

Alice was practical. "If we hear you talking to Simon and hear him responding, we will disappear back down the tunnel so that he is not frightened by two shadowy figures in the candlelight."

Emma carefully pushed the wall panel apart. She was devastated. There was no one in the room. She placed the candle on the desk and sat in Luke's chair while she recovered her equilibrium. Despair permeated her whole body.

Where could Simon be? In his current state, it was impossible to predict his movements. She began to sob.

Then she heard it.

The absolute quiet was broken by the sound of very gentle breathing. Emma pushed her feet further under the desk and came in contact with a body. She pulled the chair away and knelt on the floor. Curled up within the desk's leg cavity was Simon, sound asleep.

Emma returned to the chapel room. Her cheerful appearance answered their obvious question. Alice asked, "Is he well?"

"As far as I can tell. He is sound asleep. I will stay here until he wakes and then bring him home. Alice, if you could tell the constable that Simon has been found. He can call off the search. Mary, visit Lady Matilda, inform her of the good news but that I will be absent from duty for a few hours while I care for Simon. For the moment, we should conceal the facts. Simon wandered away from the manor and fell asleep in your pigpen, Mary."

The women nodded agreement and disappeared down the tunnel. Emma returned to the library. As Alice walked down the tunnel, resentment began to build. In her mind, there was a new injustice that must be fought. Did she have the strength to rectify the situation? Should she face it alone? Could she discuss it with anybody? A long session of meditation and prayer in the presence of the goddess was essential.

MATILDA WAS DELIGHTED THAT Simon had been found but remained cynical of Emma's eventual explanation that he had wandered out of the manor house and fallen asleep in Mary Carver's pigpen. There was no way he could have just wandered out of the house unless he had an accomplice. Matilda's imagination as to whom that might be threatened to get out of hand.

Against Emma's obvious wishes, she visited Simon to assess for herself his allegedly deteriorating condition and the possibility that he had not acted alone. It was immediately clear to her that Simon had reverted almost completely to childhood. Now when he referred to Emma, he called her mother.

Matilda felt an immediate surge of sympathy for her. Sadly, the care of Simon was regarded as a domestic matter. There was the struggling Bethlem Hospital in London and, to Matilda's knowledge, only few small charities set up by the gentry to look after such people elsewhere, but none as far as she knew in Yorkshire.

With Emma and Simon being Catholics, Matilda broached another possibility. "Emma, would you consider having Simon moved to a monastery on the continent where the monks are expert at dealing with such cases? Sir Luke would meet the costs of any such move."

Emma burst into tears, and Matilda had enough sensitivity to let her sob for a considerable period. Eventually, Emma spoke. "In the eyes of the church, I am still his wife. For years, Simon, although not the brightest man in the dale, was a loving and caring husband, and I was very happy as his wife despite initially resisting my father's inexplicable command that I marry him. Until his immersion in the beck, and the bashing its rocks gave to his head, Simon was a normal person, if a little slow. Since that episode, he has regressed into childhood, a regression that has speeded up in the last few weeks. I am now convinced that his lordship was correct in assuming that the child Simon was responsible for the outburst of vandalism. I will nevertheless be able to carry out my responsibilities as your housekeeper and still look after him."

Matilda returned to a reception room in the manor where Peter sought her out. "I have just received a message from Kit Jagger. A gang of marauders are sweeping across the dale, creating chaos. They appear to be a gang of ex-soldiers who have been expelled from the army in Scotland for their religious beliefs, and are making a living by ravaging the countryside from the Scottish border through Cumbria and Northumberland, and are now entering Yorkshire. I have informed Sir Evan Williams in York that Abbey Dale is vulnerable to attack and asked that he send a detachment of troops as soon as possible and another to inform Luke and the other magistrates of the North Riding at their general sessions of the situation."

Peter and Robert Dutton had a serious discussion on how many armed men could be put into the field against these marauders, pending the arrival of the government troops. They could raise only twelve, all former soldiers, who, given the assumed nature of the marauders' intrusion, might to able to divert or delay but not stop their activities.

The two former officers hoped that Abbey Dale might be seen as providing less lucrative rewards than the dales to the west and those that led to Whitby. The latest news Kit Jagger had of their whereabouts was that they were in the upper reaches of Eskdale and making forays onto the moors to both the north and south. Kit assumed they would either continue along the Esk towards Whitby or move into one of the dales that led to the more lucrative south.

Cold comfort for the inhabitants of Abbey Dale, which provided one such corridor from the Esk valley to the richer valley of the Derwent. The inhabitants were in a state of despair. Still recovering from the spate of vandalism, the source of which had not been revealed to them, they were now confronted by the threat of armed men intent on rape, looting, and general mayhem.

Midmorning of the next day, Matilda was in one of the large reception halls of the manor, discussing household management with some of the servants, when they all heard a loud scream. Abigail commented, "That's Emma Snigg. I would know her voice anywhere." Matilda indicated that the group, apart from Abigail, stay where they were. The two women ran to the Sniggs' section of the house.

They could hear weeping and what appeared to be slapping emanating from Simon's bedroom. As they entered the room, a crying Emma was shaking Simon and hitting him across the face in an attempt to waken him. Young Abigail dragged Emma away from the bed, and Matilda examined Simon. He was not asleep.

He was dead.

She acted quickly. She sent for Emma's friend Mary Carver to come to the manor and stay with the bereaved widow for the time being. She sent for Peter and the constable to examine the body, and remembering Luke's approach to previous deaths in the area, she sent a servant to Elderby to fetch Mother Harland. She gave Emma a large drink of Scotch whisky from a supply that Janet Bates had accumulated over her years at the manor.

Peter and Robert, after examining the body and the room, concluded that Simon probably received an overdose of the potion that Emma had prepared for him every night since his accident. They asked Emma before Mary took her to the Carver home in the village, "Did you give Simon anything different last night from his usual sleeping potion?"

"No."

"What exactly did you give him?" asked Robert.

"Mother Harland gave me a container of dried and powered herbs, mainly valerian. Each night, I infuse a tablespoon in warm water. Simon would drink the potion and follow it down with a half pint of ale. Last night, I did exactly what I have done every night since his accident."

"Where do you keep the container of herbs?" Robert continued.

"In her ladyship's kitchen. It was there also that I obtained the heated water in which to dissolve the ingredients. I took the prepared potion back to my apartment, where it cooled and remained until I gave it to Simon."

"Did anyone come to your apartment since you had the infused potion resting there?" asked Peter,. probing

"Yes, my friends—Mary Carver, my sister-in-law, and my blood sister, Alice Eades—dropped in to see how I was coping with Simon after his latest short disappearance."

Emma left with Mary, and Peter closed off the room, awaiting Mother Harland's arrival, much to Robert's annoyance. He could see no role for a dithering witch. And he was very ready to accept the simplest and least controversial explanation. "It is easier for everybody to accept that there has been an accidental overdose. Matter closed."

Peter was surprised at such an assumption. Did Robert have something to hide? He simply commented, "We have no evidence that an overdose of that potion could even prove fatal."

Mother Harland arrived and was shown into Simon's bedchamber by Matilda. The wise woman picked the cup that had contained the potion. She sniffed deeply into it, rubbed her hands around its inside, and then licked her fingers. She appeared alarmed and, turning to Matilda, asked, "When will his lordship be back?"

"Late tonight or tomorrow, but he could be delayed with these rumours of marauding hordes on the moors. He might wait the despatch of a unit of troops from York Castle and return with them."

Mother Harland opened Simon's mouth and looked at his tongue as well as smelleding the orifice. She recoiled not in disgust but with deep concern.

"What is the problem, my good woman?" asked Matilda.

"I was about to hold back my findings until his lordship arrived as I did not want to worry you with the bad news. The potion that Simon drank last night has been tampered with. The cup and his mouth smelt of herbs that I did not prescribe."

"Would these additional herbs have killed him?"

"Even though they are powerful, death would be unusual. They would simply give Simon a deeper sleep and the inability to wake up for half a day. Where did Emma keep the container of herbs?"

"In the main kitchen."

Matilda led Mother Harland to the kitchen, where she took down the container of powered herbs she had prescribed. She smelt the ingredients and rubbed them through her hands. "My lady, this jar has not been contaminated. It is the valerian I prescribed. Consequently, a stronger herb must have been added in Emma's room after the initial infusion of Simon's medicine here in the kitchen."

Both women looked at each other in disbelief.

Matilda broke the silence. "Given all this, you do not know what killed Simon?"

"Not yet, but thinking of the deaths of Charles Ogden and Matthew Foxton, I have a simple examination to complete."

The two women returned to Simon's room. Mother Harland carefully examined the body of the dead man as it lay on its back. Eventually, she informed Matilda. "My lady, this is another murder, achieved in the same way as that of Ogden and Foxton. The victim was incapacitated in this case by medication and then stabbed through the heart by a needle or very thin blade."

Earlier that day, Peter received a message from Kit Jagger that his men had confronted some of the marauders at the head of Abbey Dale and assessing Kit's strength, they had withdrawn. However, he believed they would probably head south down a neighbouring dale and then confront the wealthier landowners at the confluence of Abbey beck and the Pickering.

Peter decided to take a posse of eight men to meet Luke on his way home from Maldon in case he was set upon by these brigands. Hopefully, he would already be protected by a unit of cavalry from the castle.

Not far from the confluence of the two streams, Peter met Luke and the troops from York Castle. Luke explained that Sir Evan had sent several troops of cavalry to Maldon to escort the various magistrates back to their homes. After some discussion, the two men and the commander of the soldiers became agitated.

It dawned on all three simultaneously that their assumptions about the marauders may have been wrong. Peter expressed it succinctly. "They may not have travelled down a neighbouring dale to attack Abbey Dale at its southern end. Halfway down the adjacent dale, they may have climbed onto the moors and found themselves on our western boundary from where they could attack Abbeythwaite, Abbey Grange, and much of Abbey Dale at their leisure."

"Good god, our people are completely unprotected. We have no time to spare. At a gallop, gentlemen," ordered Luke.

On reaching Abbeythwaite, Luke and Peter were seriously alarmed. It was deserted. They moved on to the manor and were met with absolute silence. Yet there was no damage. Looting and arson, the trademark of these men was not evident. What had happened in Abbey Dale?

31

WHILE THE UNIT COMMANDER stationed his troops in appropriate places, Luke and Peter led six men into the manor house. They progressed silently. It appeared completely deserted. The first sign of trouble was Luke's library. His brand-new lock had obviously been removed. These were indeed strange marauders, selecting a library as their object of attack. Luke signalled for his men to prime their weapons—Luke and Peter their pistols, the soldiers their carbines.

Luke pushed open the door, and they all rushed into the room. Then they stopped in their tracks. Sitting in Luke's chair, facing the door with a primed musket resting on the desk, was Harry Green.

"Good god, Harry, what is going on?" asked a relieved Luke.

"Am I glad to see you all. For some time, I was the only defence against the expected attack."

"Where is everybody?"

"Safe. Johnny Harland sent one of his assistants to warn us that a gang of marauders were on the western moor and presumably headed this way. Lady Matilda took control and sent a message to those in the northern half of the dale to move immediately to the Pilgrim's Rest and inform Kit Jagger of developments. Those in the central and southern part of the dale were brought to the manor and are still hiding in the old priest's hole and along the extensive tunnel. They will be glad to escape their by-now-stifling conditions."

"I see you had to destroy my new lock?" bemoaned Luke.

"Yes, and I had to smash the door from the old chapel to the tunnel. It was locked, and nobody seemed to have the key. Quite a few people—the

Eades, Carvers, and Emma Snigg—entered the tunnel from the Carvers' pigpen. Have the marauders done much damage outside?"

"None that we can see. Peter and I will head towards the moor to ascertain what has happened there. Evan has sent enough troops to protect Abbeythwaite. Allow the people to return to their homes, but forbid anyone to work on distant fields until we discover where the brigands have gone."

It was dark when Luke and Peter reached the western moors. Luckily, a cloudless sky allowed a full moon to light up the landscape. Luke's heart sank. He could not see a single sheep or shepherd.

Peter was less alarmed. The shepherds may have led the sheep to safety.

As they approached a flat table like rock near one the caves, their worst fears were realised. It was covered in blood. Numerous sheep had been slaughtered and their carcasses allowed to drain. One could almost talk of rivers of blood now congealed. A couple of rats were enjoying a good meal.

Luke followed several trails of dripping blood leading away from the rock. The marauders had killed their sheep there but had long departed. Luke approached one of the caves and called out. "This is Luke Tremayne. The brigands have gone." Eventually, a bush that covered most of the entrance was moved aside, and Johnny Harland emerged.

Luke immediately thanked Johnny for getting a message to the village and then asked what exactly had happened on the moor. "The brigands completely ignored us, but I told the lads to conceal themselves in one of the more secretive caves and take as many sheep as they could muster. The gang simply rode into one of the flocks and cut the throat of as many animals as their horses could carry. They allowed the carcasses to drain for some time and then attached them to their saddlebags. They will have plenty of mutton and lamb for some time."

"Did you see which way they headed?"

"No, but I followed the blood trails until they ceased. They were heading north and would eventually enter the northern moors, which they have apparently made their temporary home."

"A goodly supply of meat was probably a more valuable seizure than they could have expected from the other property of the dale community. Your sacrificial sheep probably saved the village and the dale."

"But not without loss. We will muster all the sheep in the morning and give you an account of the missing sheep and their owners. I suspect most of them belonged to the late Charles Ogden."

Luke and Peter arrived back at the manor in the early hours of the morning. Matilda awoke as he joined her in bed, and she foreshadowed that there had been another murder, and Mother Harland wished to see him before she returned to Elderby. When both of them finally awoke, Matilda outlined the events that led up to Simon Snigg's disappearance and then, according to Mother Harland, his murder.

Later in the morning after she had visited the animals on a number of neighbouring properties, Mother Harland returned to the manor. Luke listened intently to her professional report on the death of Simon. She concluded, "Now I have to agree with what your lordship said weeks ago. There is a serial killer in the dale who has so far successfully murdered three men, and you are no closer to solving any of their deaths."

"True. My basic problem is motive. What did the victims—Charlie, Matthew, and Simon—have in common?" pleaded Luke.

"Two obvious links—they were all Papists, and they were all associated with your manor. Two of them were manorial officials and the other a tenant who had just resumed his lease," replied a not-too-helpful Mother Harland.

"I need to understand the Catholic community before it is completely wiped out. Three of the four families have been destroyed—Ogdens, Sniggs, and Foxtons. The only one remaining are the Carvers, and Tim has married the only heir of the Ogdens, and his sister had been married to the last Snigg."

"Talk to Tim Carver! He is the remaining sensible voice of Abbey Dale Catholicism," advised Mother Harland.

Later that day, Luke approached Tim in his meadow field. "Tim, with the murder of Ogden, Foxton, and Snigg, do you feel any apprehension that you, as the last Catholic head of household in the dale, will be targeted next?"

Tim appeared genuinely surprised. "No, not all! I can think of several reasons why those men were murdered other than their faith. Ogden and Foxton were both unpleasant men. At least a dozen men or women in the dale would want them dead. And poor Simon had deteriorated so badly that there would be some who would have put him out of his misery to give my sister a chance to enjoy a normal life. From time to time, I even entertained such a thought myself."

This last comment forced Luke to focus on the family. When one considered the major investigative tool next to motive, opportunity, it did appear that Mark Foxton was in the right position to murder his uncle and Emma Snigg to kill her husband. Family was nearly always central in such situations.

"Tim, what is the state of the Catholic community given these recent deaths?"

"It is not so much the recent deaths, but your arrival as lord of the manor and the pressure you put on the rector for us to worship in the parish church have changed things. We are reduced to myself, my wife, and my sister. Emma will want to bury Simon in the old Catholic cemetery up near the abbey, but apart from that, we will outwardly conform to the religious practises of the rest of the dale. Twelve years ago, the lord of the manor was Catholic, all the manorial officials were Catholic as was the constable, and we were paid regular visits by our priest, and the chapel in your manor was used regularly. Those days are gone. Failing the return of the Leighs, I cannot see a reversion to those happier days for my community. I regret the lack of instruction and ritual because my wife and sister appear to be accepting views that the church would frown upon. And I can't ask the Protestant rector to drag them into line."

"If they are not tending to Protestantism like the younger Foxton, what appears to be their problem?" asked Luke, half suspecting the answer.

"It is my fault, helped a little by Mr Bates. I found some treasure on my plot that Mr Bates thought might be a missing Norse hoard. One piece appeared at first to be a gold candle snuffer that could have been stolen from Whitby Abbey. The other was a pre-Christian statue of a voluptuous woman, which later disappeared from the parish church where it had been placed by Mr Garnett. Then to my surprise, I saw it near the exit of the tunnel from the manor when we entered it yesterday to escape the marauders. Mary quickly removed it, but I did not comment, pretending I did not see it."

"At least none of the deaths reflect a pagan element," uttered Luke sympathetically. He changed the topic. "Did the Leighs leave an heir who might at any time should the king return emerge and claim the manor of Abbey Grange?"

"The lawyers would have a field day. The last three generations of Leighs had only one child, a son. Peregrine's only boy was killed in an early encounter of the war. There are therefore only very distant cousins who would have inherited through the female line. You should be worried about your neighbour, the parish constable Robert Dutton. He could mount an admittedly distant claim."

"On what grounds?"

"His missing wife carries Leigh blood."

"Until recently, I thought she was a lowly servant seduced by Robert's father, who attributed her pregnancy to his son."

"That was the story put about and is substantially true. It was not revealed that the girl was a great granddaughter of an earlier Leigh. She had fallen on hard times. Do you think Dutton senior would have bothered to send his son's wife to a convent on the continent if she was the run-of-the-mill servant? And the ease in which the convent accepted her suggests that her gentry forbears and religious affiliations were well known to the religious authorities."

Luke returned to his original argument.

"Is there anyone in the village with a vendetta against Catholics?"

"One man remains obsessed with us—Richard Unsworth. His parents were massacred in Ireland."

"What about his nephew, the rector?"

"The man who returned to the dale spouts anti-Catholicism, but I remember him as a boy. As youths, he was the friendliest of the Protestant lads towards us Catholics. He took the unfortunate Simon Snigg under his wing. He was very kind to my late brother-in-law."

"Where do Kit Jagger and Mother Harland stand in this sectarian divide?"

"Over the years, Kit had mistresses who were Catholic, and his sister married a Catholic, Charlie Ogden, but I doubt if Kit adheres to any particular view. Mother Harland, given her occupation, was more sympathetic to the Catholic view of magic than the complete renunciation of all magic by most Protestants. The rest of the Harland family are strong, if not extreme, Protestants. The group who openly expound anti-Catholic views include Dutton, Richard Unsworth, James Harland, William Eades and his wife, my blood sister, Alice, and maybe Billie Briggs, but only the older Unsworth would I consider thatcapable of murder."

Luke thanked Tim for his forthright and useful commentary.

32

LUKE WAS HAPPY FOLLOWING his talk with Tim Carver. The remnant of the once-dominant Catholic families was now content to live beside their Protestant neighbours with the minimum of trouble. Luke still felt that there was a fervent Catholic killer within the dale community, although Matilda, Peter, and Mother Harland were more inclined to find personal antagonism rather than religious conflict the probable motive behind the murders. He had to admit that close relatives, a nephew in Foxton's case and a wife in Snigg, had the best opportunity.

Johnny Harland eventually reported that three sheep and six lambs had been taken by the marauding band and all belonged to the Ogden flock, which was now the Carvers. Luke, after discussion with Peter, transferred the same number of lost sheep from the manorial flock to that of the Carvers.

Luke discussed with Matilda the question of a possible cult of pagan women developing in the village and passed on the comment of Tim Carver that his wife seemed to have gained possession of the goddess statue that was previously found by Matilda in a small cave on the western moors. It had found its way into the tunnel between the manor and the Carver pigpen. Mary Carver was the person so far identified as a cult member. Matilda promised to probe further.

She also told Luke that Tim Carver; his wife, Mary; and his sister, Emma, would be missing for most of the day as they would be interring Simon in the old cemetery beside the derelict abbey. Luke had offered to attend, but Tim considered it unnecessary.

One non-Catholic who did attend was Mother Harland, who returned later that day with the Carvers to the manor and immediately asked to see Luke.

"What brings you here at such a late hour?" asked Luke.

"It is in the interests of the dale that I make you aware of major developments past and present that might ease your task as lord of the manor and local magistrate."

"Could it not have waited until the morning?"

"It is not too good for business if the white witch of the dale is seen talking with the lord of the manor. Too many of my clients would feel uneasy, wondering what we had to talk about other than their own long-kept secrets. I only decided at Simon's funeral that I should reveal a major secret of the past to your lordship after one of Kit Jagger's men who represented his master there gave me some amazing news."

"What is this past secret that you now feel you can reveal?"

"My lord, from your first week here, you were obsessed with the decade-old case of Elizabeth Foxton. You were told many versions of what had happened, most of which stemmed from the imagination of individuals. Some, including my own account, were deliberate lies. Most people were not willing to tell you what really occurred. I know exactly what happened, but I gave an undertaking that my lips remain sealed until after the death of the girl's father."

"Of all people, why would you not tell the girl's father the truth?"

"Let me explain."

"May I call Matilda in to hear what you have to say?"

"I prefer not at this stage for reasons that will become obvious."

Luke reluctantly agreed.

She began her long disposition. "Much of the confusion arose from my late friend Grace Swan who claimed to have seen things that did not occur. Her eyesight had deteriorated, and with the intermittent fog and at the distance she was away from the scene, there was no way she had a clear picture of anything."

"I must admit Grace Swan's version strongly influenced me."

"And frustrated poor Matthew Foxton," added Mother Harland.

She continued. "Elizabeth approached the bridge riding on her new saddle. The first problem was that the saddler had simply slung the saddle over the horse and expected young Elizabeth to tighten the straps. For some reason, she had not done this or had done it ineffectively. On crossing the bridge, the horse stumbled on a raised plank and jolted Elizabeth and her saddle into the beck. Initially, when this happened, some of the boys in the area catcalled and threw stones, remarking joyfully on the inability of mere girls to ride. Ted Unsworth was the nearest to the accident and went to assist Elizabeth, who was struggling to climb the bank beside the bridge. Every time she tried to climb out, despite Ted's assistance, she fell back. Ted quickly assessed that the stream had two adjacent currents flowing under the bridge, one headed for the centre of the stream and then continuing at speed away from the incident. The other flowed at a more leisurely pace along the bank. Ted gave Elizabeth a big push into the slower eddy of the stream and then ran along the bank and, out of sight of the other boys, eventually pulled her to safety."

"Elizabeth was rescued alive from the beck," reiterated an incredulous Luke.

"Yes. The other boys, not wanting to be part of what they thought was Elizabeth's death, disappeared down the dale as fast as their youthful legs could carry them. Ted then half carried, half dragged Elizabeth to my cottage. I dried her and fed her over several days during which she made clear that she could not return to her father and cousin, implying that they seriously abused her. At this point, I discovered she was pregnant. I gave her medication that, in time, aborted the baby. She expressed the desire to go into service. I made the arrangements, and Kit Jagger had one of his men take her to a respectable establishment in Newcastle to start a new life."

"And did she?"

"Jagger's man who took her to Newcastle ten years ago continued to travel there on business for Kit and kept in touch. She had a good life as a servant and eventually married and had a child. Her husband died earlier this year, and the now widow Elizabeth Carson, on hearing of her father's death, has decided to return to Abbey Dale."

"That will not be easy for her if, as you imply, her cousin, now possessor of the land, was unkind to her as a child."

"I am well aware of the potential problems. For that reason, she will stay with me at Elderby while I try to find her employment. I intend to tell only two other people before her actual arrival—her cousin, Mark, and Ted Unsworth, who saved her life those many years ago."

Luke went to bed that night highly elated. Despite Mother Harland's reservations, Luke could not contain himself. As soon as he climbed into bed beside Matilda, he exclaimed, "The Elizabeth Foxton saga is solved! Mother Harland has explained what really happened. The girl is alive and well and will soon return to the dale."

The next morning, Mother Harland visited the rectory. Edward Unsworth's initial reaction was of a hard-line Protestant Christian to a purveyor of heathen magic and pagan beliefs. He berated the audacity that she should visit him in his home. Mother Harland smiled and said quietly, "I have some good news from your past, Ted. Let me come in as what I have to say is confidential for the moment. Only his lordship has been informed."

Mother Harland outlined Elizabeth's brief history and the fact that she would arrive in Elderby within the next few weeks. Mother Harland was touched by the rector's reaction. As she spoke, tears filled his eyes, and by the end of her narrative, his handkerchief was soddened. She placed her arms around him. "Now, Ted, the whole dale will know of your brave act in saving Elizabeth's life. You, Kit Jagger, and I alone have lived with the truth for a decade. With Elizabeth's approval, the full story can now be told."

"What will Elizabeth do in Abbey Dale? Mark will not welcome her back."

"I am aware of that. To this day, I do not know who, in addition to her father, abused her as a child—her cousin or a neighbour. One day she may tell us, and Sir Luke can then act. I will keep her at Elderby until a solution can be found. She can help me as an assistant as you and poor Simon did all those years ago. I hope that his lordship, with his expanding staff and affluent situation, might find a position for her at the manor. In his imagination, she certainly made an impression. Let's hope that in the flesh, she wins him over."

"Before her presence becomes widely known, I would like to visit her at your cottage soon after her arrival."

"As always, you are very welcome, Ted."

The reception from Mark Foxton was vastly different. Mother Harland explained the situation without detailing the pregnancy or his cousin's objections to him. She made it appear that it was in reaction to her father's abuse that she assisted Elizabeth into service.

Mark was livid. "I suppose you received a nice fee for what you did?"

"I am surprised that you have not thanked me for bringing your cousin from the edge of death back to life and, ultimately, in a condition to go out into the world and earn a living for herself."

"You say she has a child. He cannot be a Foxton and will therefore have no claim on my estates."

"Estates that were once her father's? I doubt whether she would be interested in returning to the Foxton property. It obviously had too many ghosts from her childhood, but if she did find a clever lawyer, her son or a future husband might develop a claim. In this dale, while only men can succeed, the line of succession can progress through the female line. I would have a talk to Sir Luke about the validity of your lease in such changing circumstances."

Mother Harland was upset with herself as she left the Foxton farm. She had created a very negative attitude in Mark regarding the return of his cousin, which might be harmful to the young woman. But Mark was developing unpleasant tendencies, similar to those displayed in later life by his uncle. As she made her way up the dale to Elderby, she was happy that both Sir Luke and Ted Unsworth had received her news with delight. Then an interesting thought flashed through her mind. If Mark Foxton was ever convicted for the murder of his uncle, his lease could be torn up and a new one issued to the widow Carson for her ancestral property.

Elizabeth Foxton's return in the persona of the widow Carson had a beneficial effect throughout the dale. From the Pilgrim's Rest to the confluence of Abbey beck with the Pickering, it appeared as if a heavy fog had been lifted. Luke realised that the accusation of guilt in the girl's murder that hung over many of the lads of the dale for a decade, and which he had reactivated in his examination of the case, had finally been removed.

THREE WEEKS AFTER HER previous visit, Mother Harland and the widow Carson with her young boy sat in the reception hall of Abbey Grange, awaiting a meeting with Sir Luke and Lady Matilda Tremayne.

Luke's first impression was so different from the picture he had formed of a thin, timid, weak young girl who had disappeared years before. Before him stood an almost stocky but reasonably tall young matron with a happy rounded face and short jet-black hair. She curtsied and spoke in an educated voice, which suggested that her Newcastle employer had attended to her education.

Matilda put the women at their ease, while Luke still wandered somewhere between his imagination and the present reality. "Please take a seat. I am very pleased to meet you, Elizabeth. For weeks, my husband was obsessed with you. He was convinced if he could solve what was widely believed to be your murder, he would also solve several of the more recent problems in the dale."

Luke finally gathered his thoughts. "You seem to have lost the accent of these parts but not developed the even more extreme dialect of the northeast. To be blunt, you speak like a gentlewoman from the south. Can you read and write?"

"Yes, my lord, I can read and also write. My mistress in Newcastle was a lady from the south, and when I surprisingly became her maid on the unexpected death of my predecessor, she decided to educate me in her image. I was educated above my class, and my mistress married me to a distant cousin of hers. Unfortunately, a year ago, an influenza epidemic hit Newcastle, and both my mistress, my master, and my husband died. My boy here only just survived. Recently, when I heard that my father had died, I decided to return to Abbeythwaite."

Luke listened carefully as Matilda asked a range of questions. He was highly impressed by the succinct, relevant, mature, and sensible answers that Elizabeth gave. Matilda brought the interview to an end by suggesting that Mother Harland take Elizabeth into the kitchen and have Emma provide them with something to eat and drink while she and Luke discussed the situation.

After the women had left the room, Luke said, "When you left Kent, many of your servants stayed with their families and did not come north. Offer the girl a position as second lady's maid."

Matilda shook her head in disagreement.

"No, Luke. Her mistress in Newcastle educated Elizabeth well above the level needed for a servant. It would be a pity if, on her return to the dale, her fortunes regressed. With your permission, I would like to offer her a position as my companion."

Luke agreed, and the women were recalled to the room. Matilda made the offer. Luke added, "You will be directly responsible to Lady Matilda. Your boy looks old enough to attend the school run by the rector, your saviour, Ted Unsworth. You shall occupy rooms within the manor close to her ladyship."

There was a gasp of pleasure from the widow and a series of repeated thank-yous from Mother Harland.

Emma entered the room, embraced Elizabeth, and led her and the boy away to arrange their accommodation.

Mother Harland remained behind, and Luke asked, "How is she coping? Her arrival seems to have created a positive feeling across the dale."

"Yes, the only one to suffer is me. Some are cross that I put so many people, and their sons, through years of torment when a word that Elizabeth still lived could have set everybody's mind at rest."

"She does seem to have had an excellent education, which has equipped her better than anything she would have accomplished here," said Matilda.

"Yes, your decision to put her into service proved very beneficial for her," added Luke.

"And she has remained, or rather become, an even more devoted Papist. As children, she and the then Mary Ogden were very devoted."

"After talking to Tim Carver the other day, the depleted Catholic community could do with new blood," Luke commented.

Three days later, Tim Carver approached Luke. "My lord, I seek your permission to convert the old priest's hole back into a Catholic sanctuary."

"What has led to this sudden enthusiasm?"

"The widow Carson! Elizabeth, in Newcastle, was subjected to many recent ideas from the continent and believes we should not allow our rituals to fall into abeyance. She has had an amazing effect on my wife and sister. Overnight, they have dumped their flirtation with the pagan goddess. Mary confessed that she and Emma have handed the statue of the goddess to their cult leader, who, I suspect, is my other sister, Alice Eades. Instead, they now resort to regular readings of traditional prayers from the church fathers led by Elizabeth."

"As both Elizabeth and Emma work in the manor, and you and Mary live at the other end of the tunnel, your request to restore the hidden chapel is granted," announced Luke.

The following night, Elizabeth, her friend Mary Carver and husband, Tim, dined with Mark Foxton, an invitation that surprised everybody.

As Elizabeth entered the Foxton entrance hall, she began to shake uncontrollably, and it needed reassuring words and a continuous hug from Mary to bring the panic attack under control. Elizabeth whispered, "After all this time, the house itself still terrifies me."

Over supper, Elizabeth made it clear to her cousin that she had no interest in the property and would in no way be trying to obtain a share in it or a place for her son in any revised lease. "If it was not now your home, I would burn it to the ground. It has so many evil memories."

Mark responded, "I did not realise when we were children together that you were so unhappy here. You father was a hard man. He beat me most days and at least slapped you on a regular basis. But all we children had a similar upbringing. It was part of a normal childhood, especially if we had parents or guardians who drank too much."

"It was a little more than a regular backhander. I will tell you my long-kept secret because eventually, the dale will want to know why I pleaded with

Mother Harland not to send me home and why she so readily consented. From when I was a very small girl, Father came to my room many a night and abused me. As I became older, this abuse became more frequent, and he began to treat me like a wife. That is why when I was tossed into the beck, I was quite happy to be swept away to my death. Fortunately, Ted saved me."

"I cannot defend what your Father did to you, but surely, you could have returned and told Mr Bates?" said Mark.

"After I was cared for by Mother Harland, I realised my situation was worse than I thought, and I pleaded with the witch to send me to sleep permanently. I was pregnant to my own father."

Mary could not contain herself and began to sob uncontrollably.

Tim was about to comment but bit his lip instead and put his arms around his distraught wife. Mark leant across the table and squeezed his cousin's hand. "I am truly sorry. I never knew that you were subject to such relentless and continued abuse. As children, we all heard of one off cases such as you describe but not such regular abuse."

"I am sorry too for bringing such news to your dinner table. Let us change the subject. I hear from Mary that you have left the church."

"Yes, and you must be very cross with me for having your father buried in the parish church and not amongst his fellow Catholics in the old Abbey churchyard."

"Not at all, Mark! A man such as Matthew Foxton did not deserve to be buried in sacred ground. No, my concern is with your soul."

Tim intervened, saying, "Elizabeth, during her time in Newcastle, was strengthened in the old faith, and received much information from our fellow Catholics in Europe, and even had visits from a clandestine Catholic priest. She is enthusiastically refitting our sanctuary in the old priest's hole in the manor. All she is suggesting is that you may wish to reconsider your decision and rejoin us in our worship."

Mark turned to Elizabeth half jokingly and said, "Ted Unsworth saved your body. He is delighted that he has saved my soul. At least with the current squire, you will be able to worship as you wish, and Ted has been prohibited from preaching against you."

"I have been invited to the rectory for refreshments next Monday afternoon," announced Elizabeth.

"Have you seen Ted since your return?"

"Only a passing encounter in the road outside the rectory when Mother Harland informed him of my return."

"All in all, Elizabeth, your return has been a very joyous event. People like Ted and myself and all the boys who were in the area of the bridge on the day you disappeared have been accused of being your murderer. Parents were so alarmed that most of us were sent away in case an investigation into what happened led to an arrest," concluded Mark.

Ted Unsworth gave Elizabeth a big hug. "Unlike the rest of the dale, I knew you were still alive, but while I was away in the army, I did not keep up with your situation. Since my return, Mother Harland told me of your good fortune in Newcastle, followed by the sad loss of your husband, and then more recently, of your imminent arrival. I am delighted you have been found such an elevated position. The new squire, although he was one of Oliver Cromwell's generals and fought in his day against Spanish and Irish Catholics, seems to have a soft spot for you English Papists. He has prohibited me from preaching against you on pain of being dismissed."

"He seems very enlightened for a heretic soldier," replied Elizabeth.

"I heard rumours that should the republic collapse, and the king is returned, the manor will return to descendants of the original owners, the Leighs. If that happens, Catholic supremacy will return to Abbey Dale, "commented Ted.

"Everything is in God's hands. I am sure it was God who moved you all those years ago to rescue me from the raging beck. At the time, I never thanked you as all I wanted to do was to die. I probably said some horrible things to you for saving me from my desired fate."

"You did, but Mother Harland explained your situation to me. I am glad that whatever she gave you to abort the child had no permanent damage and that you were able to give birth to your boy, who attended my school last week. He is fine lad and will clearly have a better childhood than you or I ever had."

That night, Ted Unsworth could not sleep. He continued to marvel at the fine person that little Elizabeth Foxton had developed into and felt immense satisfaction that he had saved the suicidal girl's life. But it was an even more disturbing issue that kept him awake.

34

NEXT MORNING, THE TROUBLED soul acted. Ted sought an audience with Luke on a matter of national security. An intrigued Luke immediately entered the reception hall, where he remarked, "This must be a first, you coming to the manor on your own accord to raise a matter with me. It must be serious."

"Sir Luke, you and I have never been close, and I live under constant threat of immediate dismissal if my sermons are not to your liking. We probably dislike each other intensely."

"Up until very recently, that was true. I detested your form of Puritanism and your intolerance of the local English Catholics,   but   revelations regarding your role in the saving of the young Elizabeth Foxton have dramatically changed my view. It is a pity that the current Edward Unsworth does not manifest all the personality of the younger you."

"Ironically, it has been your treatment of the returning Elizabeth that has modified my negative view of your lordship. Consequently, I am about to betray my best friend to a recent enemy. Since returning to the dale as rector, my strongest ally and closest personal friend has been the constable Robbie Dutton."

"Indeed, I still believe the two of you lead a campaign to rid the dale of Catholics," commented Luke.

Ted ignored the comment and continued. "Last week, I was complaining to Robbie about your attitude to me. He was very supportive and told me not to worry because before next year was out, the king would be back, and he would be lord of the manor of Abbey Grange, and my position would be safe."

"Did you question him on that statement?"

"No, I was so taken aback that I thanked him for his current support and changed the subject."

"So why are you telling me about it?"

"I do not care whether the lord of this manor is Robbie or yourself, but I do want to continue to worship in the way I desire. Robbie's elevation to this manor clearly depends on the return of the king. In my eyes, the return of the king means the reinstatement of the bishops and the cleansing of the Church of England of all of us who do not conform to their narrow interpretation of Christianity. Even if Robbie wanted to keep me on as rector, the bishops and probably the Parliament would have me dismissed, if not imprisoned. As Oliver Cromwell's former head of military intelligence, you too do not wish to see the end of the republic."

"The republic has brought a lot of benefits to England, although its current problems are not helping anyone. Why do you think Robert's manorial ambitions threaten the security of the state?"

"Simple! How does Robert know the king will install him as lord of the manor? He must be in contact with Royalist agents. It is a wonder he did not act when the Royalist troops were in the area."

"What is Robert's claim to this manor?"

"Just before Robbie was sent off to the army, he had been forced to marry one of the servants whom his father had impregnated. Only recently, I heard that that servant was a great-granddaughter of the Leighs, the former holders of the manor."

"Yes, I was aware of that. Even though in some dales, succession can devolve through the female line, that link would be so far back that most lawyers would not be able to establish a claim. Most likely, Robbie is relying on the fact that the king will reward him for his service to the crown over the last decade by simply removing me and allocating the manor to the Duttons. It would be much cleaner and quite within the power of any English government, republican or Royalist," explained Luke.

"Which makes my action in reporting this much more urgent. Robbie must have been acting for the king for years, even when he was an officer of the parliamentary army in York Castle."

"I agree. I will go to York. I will look into any records the castle might hold regarding Capt. Robert Dutton of Abbey Dale."

Over supper, Luke, Matilda, and Peter discussed the situation. Peter expressed astonishment. "I am amazed. I saw Robbie as one of us—veteran soldiers of the former lord protector, loyal to our dying breath. You do not express such surprise?"

"No, for a simple reason, I was forewarned by no other than the would-be king himself. Charles Stuart named his supporters in the dale, not for me to imprison them but to keep an eye on them to prevent their premature rising on his behalf, an action that continually undermines the Royalist cause. He knew I couldn't act against them simply on his word. Who would believe me? But I can act if I find independent evidence of treachery. I will leave for York tomorrow in search of any incriminating evidence."

Luke was received by Sir Evan Williams in the keep of the castle.

"I did not expect to see you so soon, Luke. Further trouble on the frontier?" he asked jokingly.

"Yes, and one that your records or men may have an answer to. I am investigating the career of Capt. Robert Dutton, who served here for almost ten years until two years ago."

"There are garrison books that list the soldiers, their rank, their rate of pay, their dates of enlistment and demobilisation, and any charges that may have been brought against them. Come with me. The documents are kept in an old cellar below the defunct kitchen of the semi-demolished main building."

The two soldiers entered the archives and were horrified. Papers were strewn across the room. Rats had eaten into some of the files, while an attempt had been made to burn others.

Evan reacted. "I am appalled. I have not been down here since I took up my appointment. Neither of us will waste our time putting this room in order. I shall send men down here to clean up and others to unearth all the material that they can find on Dutton. I hope that fire was not a deliberate attempt to remove certain records involving particular people. I am sure you have other things to do in York. If you return tomorrow morning, I should be able to have some answers for you."

Luke took advantage of his unexpected free time to visit Dutton's aunt, Lady Margaret Vernon. He thought she might be able to elaborate on the Leigh connection and on any Royalist tendencies in the family.

Over a repast of mead and cakes, Margaret was very forthcoming. "My brother-in-law, Giles, was an evil man. He got many of his servants pregnant and was delighted to discover one of them was a distant relative of the Leighs, who had fallen on hard times. Ever alert to possible gain, he forced his son to marry the girl in case further down the line, he could make a claim on the Leigh inheritance."

"A shrewd man, your brother-in-law. His son seems to be following in his footsteps. There are rumours that he is determined to have the manor I now hold."

"No chance. My husband looked into the matter when he was alive and found no court would uphold any such claim as it stretched across too many generations and depended on the female line on more than one occasion."

"I agree, but I expect if Robert takes over the manor, it will be as a reward for services rendered to the king. Are the Duttons Royalists?"

"At the beginning of the Civil War, most of North Yorkshire were Royalists. The exception was Abbey Dale, which, given a strong Puritan streak, and despite or perhaps because of its Catholic lord of the manor, sided with Parliament. It was quickly occupied by parliamentary forces from West Yorkshire. In York itself, a minority of merchants were for Parliament, and that included my husband. Brother-in-law, Giles Dutton, was also a stalwart for the Parliament, and young Robert was sent off to join Fairfax's parliamentary army and, consequently, spent most of the decade here in York as a member of the garrison."

"Would you be surprised to learn that Robert could have been a Royalist spy during most of that period?"

"Robbie inherited some of the nastier tendencies of his father and none of the gentle kindly characteristics of his mother, my late sister. Giles would do anything, including ill-treating his wife, to achieve his ends. However, he was so ruthless in his treatment of Royalist gentry and merchants that he would never be welcomed as a Royalist recruit."

"Robbie detested his father. Could his alleged later support for the Royalists hasve been to spite his father?"

"Quite possibly, but I cannot see how he could assist the king while being confined to a republican garrison all of his military career."

"At the moment, I have similar doubts."

Next morning, Evan received Luke with a cheerful countenance and announced, "I have some information that you will find both intriguing and worrying."

On Evan's desk lay several open volumes of documents. "What have you found?"

"During most of his time here, Captain Dutton commanded the unit responsible for guarding the prisoners of war, which, over the course of the decade, ranged in number from two hundred after the Battle of Marston Moor to three or four in more recent times."

"Well, that is one key factor established—opportunity. He had regular contact with Royalist officers who, on the whole, would return to civilian life or join the king on the continent."

"It's even more clear cut than you think. He was, on one occasion, charged with being too friendly with one of the prisoners."

"What came of it?"

"Nothing. The then commander, on hearing that the Royalist officer concerned had just been ransomed, saw no point in pursuing the charge."

"That's unfortunate. Some further detail would have been helpful."

"Don't despair, Luke. The man who brought the charge against him was Dutton's senior sergeant, who is still with us now as sergeant major of the garrison. I anticipated you would wish to question him." Evan nodded at an orderly, who left the room and returned immediately with a sturdy veteran soldier.

Evan introduced Luke as one of Oliver Cromwell's leading generals who had been the Protector's bodyguard and secret agent for years. The sergeant was suitably impressed but not in any way troubled by the presence of such a senior officer.

"How can I help you, sir?"

"I am investigating Capt. Robert Dutton, who was once commander of the unit responsible for prisoners of war. At one point, you laid a charge against him for fraternising with the enemy, which was dropped by your commanding officer. Can you elaborate on Dutton's relationships with the Royalist officers?"

"He was very friendly and went out of his way to deliver messages and parcels to and from the prisoners and their loved ones."

"Did he show signs of any Royalist political sympathies? Any political comments you may have heard between him and the Royalists?"

"No, his major concern was loyalty to fellow Yorkshiremen, especially those with wealthy relatives."

This reply disappointed Luke.

"Did Dutton show any especial concern for a particular Royalist officer?"

"I don't recall their names, but two badly injured officers were helped by Dutton, who paid for medical treatment at his own expense until the garrison's own surgeon was free enough to assist them. One was a Yorkshireman, whom I later learnt had joined a criminal gang that dominates the moors between the upper dales and Whitby."

Luke's interest piqued. It must be one of Kit Jagger's men.

35

LUKE HAD INTENDED TO confront Robert Dutton on his return from York with damning evidence of his treachery. This was not forthcoming. Dutton, during his employment at York Castle, had unlimited opportunities to converse with Royalists, who may have eventually sent relevant information to the king, but his activities in aid of Royalist prisoners seemed to be limited to fellow Yorkshiremen, driven by humanitarian rather than political reasons.

His desire for Abbey Grange may not have been based on a promise that the king might reward him for services rendered or through any hereditary claim of his wife. He may have been favoured because Charles Stuart had been approached by friends of Dutton's long-estranged wife, whose convent of exile may not have been far from the king's court.

Luke would talk to the Catholic community.

He did not need to.

The dale was rocked by the unexpected return of another woman expelled from the dale over a decade ago. It was Ted Unsworth who brought the news to Luke.

"Robbie has just told me that his relatives on the continent informed him that his wife is fully recovered and on her way back to Abbey Dale to take up her position beside him."

"You are a little sceptical of this development?"

"Not of the development but of the reasoning behind it. Did Robbie take steps to have his wife removed from the convent and sent back here? He has not considered his wife in over ten years. Maybe it is the Catholic relatives of his wife who are reactivating the Leigh claim with Charles Stuart. Perhaps Robbie is a pawn in the hands of his wife's relatives."

Three days later, Robert informed Luke formally that he would be absent from Abbey Dale for about ten days. He was travelling to Whitby to await the arrival of his wife from the continent. Luke saw his opportunity, pretending to know more than he did. "I imagine you will drop in on your friend from the days you were a prison guard at York Castle if you go by the Pilgrim's Rest?"

"Roly Jagger. That was a long time ago."

"Any relation to Kit?"

"A cousin. That is why I became involved with him as a prisoner. Kit heard of my role in the castle and asked my father if I would deliver goods to Roly to ease his time there. Eventually, I helped organise his release, and Kit found him employment. In recent years, he has been Kit's man in Whitby."

Luke noted this last comment. Roly Jagger, located in the seaport of Whitby, could be the contact between Dutton and the continental Royalists. The case against the constable was building but too slowly.

Another person who was unhappy with recent developments was the only remaining member of the abortive pagan cult of goddess worshipers, Alice Eades. While sharing the widespread joy at the return of the former Elizabeth Foxton, she was nevertheless cross that the returning woman had, at a stroke, cut Mary and Emma from her little band and reunited them with their traditional Catholic beliefs and allegiances.

As she clutched the little goddess in her hands and uttered a laudatory paean of praise, she was convinced that she must discuss the situation in the dale with her one-time mentor, Mother Harland. She was about to leave her cottage when there was a loud knocking on the door. Alice opened it to find a sobbing, badly bruised, and bleeding female neighbour, Nell Briggs.

This was clearly a sign. She took Nell to Elderby to be helped by Mother Harland, and while there, she would broach the big issues of the dale with the wise old woman.

There was another discontented woman in the dale. Robbie Dutton had made no attempt to explain to Janet Bates why his long-absent wife was about to return. He did indicate that Janet must find other accommodation as his spouse may not understand her role as mistress of one of his properties.

Ted Unsworth informed Luke that Robbie had an uninvited companion as he headed up the dale to the northern moors on his way to Whitby—Janet.

Ted did not think that the now discarded mistress was going on to Whitby to confront and embarrass the returning wife. She was probably using the trip to the Pilgrim's Rest to receive an explanation from Robert and perhaps hopefully renegotiate a relationship with him that could operate once his wife had returned.

Over supper, Matilda commented to Luke, "We were told by some that Abbey Dale was the dale of despair. I am inclined to rechristen it the dale of the Amazons."

"Why? We do not, in any way, resemble the jungles of Brazil."

"No, Luke. I mean in the sense of the dominance of powerful women. There are two in this house—Elizabeth Carson and Emma Snigg. There is the former mistress of this house, Janet Bates, Mother Harland, and that blacksmith's young wife, who is mature and knowledgeable beyond her years, Alice Eades."

"And there is the remarkable Lady Matilda Tremayne," added Luke diplomatically.

Matilda smiled and continued. "I wonder if Mistress Dutton will be of the same ilk."

"I doubt it. She was both physically and mentally unwell when she was put away many years ago. I cannot see how incarceration in a Papist convent on the continent would improve anybody," uttered the essentially anti-Catholic Luke.

A week later, Luke was surprised to find Kit Jagger seeking an audience. He claimed he was paying a social call while in the area. Luke could not help himself. He began questioning him on his cousin Rowland. "Your cousin Roly was the devoted Royalist in your family?"

"You forget, Luke, all my relatives, including myself, were Royalists. Some of us realised sooner than the others that that was the losing side and extricated ourselves. Now things have changed. There are rumours that the king will return within the year. Perhaps we should start to spruik our Royalist credentials. You could be left out on a limb, although you never quite explained why Charles Stuart sent his top man to visit you."

Luke ignored the comment.

"You gave Roly a job after his release from York Castle?"

"As I had paid his ransom, I expected years of service in return. Given his more acceptable Royalist connections, I made him my agent in Whitby, where he negotiates with local and continental Royalists on my behalf."

"After his release, did he maintain a close association with Robert Dutton?"

"No, not for years. Dutton was in York until a couple of years ago and Roly in Whitby. Since Robert's return to the dale, they could only have met if the constable has gone to Whitby. I know for certain that Roly has not been down Abbey Dale since his release."

"I could almost say the same about you. What special occasion brings you this far south?"

Kit chuckled, "You could almost say I have come to collect a wife."

Luke's jaw dropped. The answer was totally unexpected.

Kit continued. "She cannot be my wife as she is already married."

"Who is she?"

"Janet Bates."

Luke commented, "She has not wasted any time. Only a week ago, the rector was telling me how distraught she was as a result of Robert Dutton casting her aside."

"I know all about that. She arrived at the Pilgrim's Rest with Dutton. He continued on to Whitby. She stayed on for a night, and that night expanded into three days. I have always been fond of Janet from the moment my friend Tom Bates married her. Her reiver heritage makes her the ideal companion for a moorland brigand like myself."

"Kit, bring Janet with you, and we can have a farewell supper here tonight." On Kit's departure, Luke sought out Matilda to inform her of Janet's surprising change of fortune.

Two days later, Luke's life threatened to take a dramatic turn back into his past. Unexpectedly, his brother-in-law, Matthew Hatch, who, for years, had been a major agent for Oliver Cromwell's head of intelligence, John Thurloe, visited his sister, Matilda.

It was a cover. Hatch now worked for Thurloe's successor as head of republican intelligence, Thomas Scot, and he had been sent north to summon a selected group of loyal magistrates to an emergency meeting at York Castle. All he would tell Luke was that the king had ordered an imminent uprising across England but that the government had infiltrated the network of plotters and were aware that the date of the uprising was the first of August. The threat to the republican government was so serious that the competing factions buried their differences and the generals around London had mobilised a large number of troops to deal with problems in the south and John Lambert, the renegade general, was given full authority to mobilise troops in West Yorkshire and Lancashire. George Monk would cross the border from Scotland to deal with trouble in the far north.

"It has taken the king to temporarily unite the once-fractured army," remarked Luke gleefully.

Three days after Hatch's visit, Luke was in a chamber of York Castle. The door was locked, and a man whom Sir Evan Williams introduced as Thomas Scott addressed the gathered group of magistrates and military officers. He explained the situation, indicating that many of the leaders of the proposed insurrection had been arrested and a large majority of would-be participants, aware that the government knew of their intentions, had withdrawn their support. With the armies of Fleetwood and Desborough hovering in the south, Lambert in the Midlands and York, and Monk in the north, only the foolhardy or those who had not heard that the plot had been discovered or that the king had changed his mind would rise.

Scot believed that such ignorance might be present in the dales of North Yorkshire, especially those running south to north into the valley of the Esk, where government intelligence had picked up indications of Royalist sympathies. As a result, the government was calling back to duty Sir Luke Tremayne to command the local militia and, with the troops of the York garrison, to stay on alert until after the first of August. It was expected that isolated groups of Royalists might try to meet up to hold the area for the king. Should this rebellion occur and achieve any degree of success, then the troops of General Lambert would march to the rescue.

Luke asked why it was thought that Royalists in the dales and moors might not heed the king's change of plan. Scot replied, "Because we intercepted, and arrested as many of the couriers carrying the updated orders that we could, and replaced them with our own men giving the opposite advice. At least there will be confusion in these isolated Royalist groups."

Luke then asked Scott what his new role would entail. It surprisingly would not interfere with his daily life as lord of the manor or magistrate. He was given a list of the names of the cavalry to be mobilised within the dales and details how these men could be speedily gathered together.

Luke was delighted because this might be the opportunity for Robert Dutton to make a false step. He had to admit that he had missed intelligence work and military action and the current situation had created a positive picture beyond his own possible encounter with Dutton. The English army was once again acting together.

T ERESA DUTTON'S ARRIVAL IN Abbey Dale was a disaster. Luke and Matilda attempted to welcome the woman with an invitation for her and Robert to dine at the manor.

Robert diplomatically declined, claiming his wife's continued ill health and lack of confidence made acceptance inappropriate. Ted Unsworth successfully entertained the Duttons on the very evening for which they had declined the Tremayne invitation. He told Luke the truth. Teresa made it clear to him and his fellow guest that evening, Elizabeth Carson, that she would never enter Abbey Grange except as lady of the manor. Robert could no longer hide his intentions as his wife was shouting it from the rooftops.

Then Teresa attempted to shatter the religious compromise that Ted, Luke, and Elizabeth had established. Teresa made it clear to Ted that he must turn a blind eye to Catholic burials in the parish graveyard at night and that the Catholic community must cease attending the parish service. This completely ignored the fact that if that happened, her husband would be obliged to carry them all before the magistrate, and they would be heavily fined. Robbie tried to explain that such actions would be playing into the hands of their undeclared enemy, the current lord of the manor and magistrate, Sir Luke Tremayne.

Teresa appeared not to hear.

Ted continued to inform Luke of Robert's increasingly distracted state due in large measure to his erratic wife. Robert had not expected Teresa to be such a fervent Papist and, even more devastating, unwilling to take her husband's advice on anything. He had pleaded with Ted to persuade the devoted Catholic Elizabeth to talk to her about the need to fit in, especially if one day she was to be lady of the manor.

But Teresa listened to no one.

Ted was not the only informant of the Duttons' ambitions. Elizabeth, in her role as Matilda's companion, immediately reported the startling news that Teresa Dutton saw herself as the next lady of the manor.

Luke informed Peter and Harry of his meeting in York and immediately recommissioned them back into the army, Peter as a captain and Harry as a sergeant. Their first military task was to organise an around-the-clock watch on Robert Dutton.

Luke then, taking his role as lord of the manor seriously, decided to speak privately and confidentially with all the heads of household about their loyalty to the republican government. Peter strongly opposed any such intervention, claiming it would alert Robert Dutton to Luke's knowledge of an impending Royalist uprising. He suggested that nearer to the dreaded first of August, Luke should mobilise Harland, Briggs, Unsworth, Eades, and Carver under the command of Peter and Harry to protect the manor and the dale from the ravages of the returning marauders from the moors, a complete fabrication. Luke reluctantly agreed. If Dutton's potential supporters were already mobilised under the command of Captain Frost, they would find it difficult to join the Royalist rebel.

A week later, Luke was in his library, discussing plans to curtail any Royalist uprising with pro-government gentry from the surrounding dales. Their discussion was interrupted by shrieks and hysterical sobbing coming from an adjacent room where Luke knew Matilda usually sat with her companion, Elizabeth Carson. He put his initial concern out of his mind as the strategic planning continued apace.

In the early afternoon, the group broke for a meal, and as his guests entered the dining room, Luke sought out Matilda for an explanation of the wailing, shrieking, and sobbing. Matilda whispered, "There has been another death. Teresa Dutton has died."

"That unscrupulous bastard. Robert Dutton could not allow anybody, even his retrieved wife, to stand in his way. Did she have a needle through the heart like the rest of them?"

"No, come with me! Elizabeth and Emma witnessed the whole episode. They were in quite a state when they returned here. That is what you heard. They are much calmer now."

The two women were having a light meal when Luke entered the room. Matilda was direct. "Sir Luke wishes to know the details of Teresa Dutton's death."

"I don't wish to distress you further, but as it is the constable's wife who has died, I, as magistrate, need to investigate the circumstances rather than leave it to Robert Dutton."

"It was an accident, not a murder. Emma and I witnessed it all," answered Elizabeth.

She then gave an account of what they had seen. "The Catholic community was so shaken by Teresa's arrival and behaviour that we were asked to speak to her. We discovered from some of Robbie's workers that in recent days, to keep her out of trouble, she had been confined to the Dutton estate by her husband. We went to Dutton Hall. On arriving there, Robert directed us to several of the outbuildings where he said Teresa was making herself familiar with aspects of the property."

Emma intervened. saying, "We saw her in the distance in one of the barns. She saw us and began to move in our direction. To our dismay, Teresa suddenly began to sink and then disappeared completely. We could hear the shouting of workmen as they headed to the spot where Teresa had been seen. When we reached the scene, the tragic event was clear cut. There had been a large slurry pit at one end of the barn to hold the dung of the cattle housed there over winter. It was to ferment and dry out before it could be spread on the fields."

Elizabeth took up the story. "Given the spate of hot weather, the top of the slurry pit had dried and baked into a thick crust. Teresa was probably misled as two young boys had run ahead of her over the slurry pit. Her weight, increased by the heavy dress and plethora of petticoats, however, proved too much for the baked surface. She sank through it and drowned in the liquid slurry beneath. If she hadn't struggled and been so heavy, she probably would have been saved."

Matilda turned to Luke, saying, "Use your authority to persuade Robert to allow his wife to be buried in the old Abbey cemetery. Her faith was probably all she had for most of her sad life."

As Luke made his way back to his gentry companions, he convinced himself that devil was looking after Robert Dutton. Just when his wife threatened to derail his plans, she met a most unlikely death.

Matilda was proving a very popular lady of the manor. Her concern for her tenants, workers, and the dales women in general led to a constant stream of people seeking her advice and assistance. Luke was not surprised when Nell Briggs, the dales woman of ill fame, ran into his reception hall literally screaming murder.

Luke reached her just after Matilda had led her onto a cushioned bench. He plied the distraught woman with a large glass of strong spirits. Nell gulped it down, jumped to her feet, grabbed Luke's hand, and screamed, "Come with me, my lord! Poor Dick is dead!"

Luke realised something must be seriously amiss because Dick Unsworth's cottage that was normally full of Nell's clients was completely empty and the front door wide open. Nell dragged him through the door and pointed to the floor at the bottom of the stairs. There lay the twisted body of Richard.

Alice Eades, a neighbour, arrived and led Nell away. Luke examined the body. Was this a drunken accident? Dick was known to drink heavily. Indeed, his mouth reeked of mead. Luke climbed to the top of the stairs. There was no sign of a struggle or of any evidence of a desperate man trying to prevent his fall. He sent for Harry and also got a message to Mother Harland that her services were again needed to investigate another mysterious death.

Harry arrived and helped Luke place the body onto one of Nell's well-used beds. Harry would preserve the death scene until Mother Harland arrived. Luke informed Richard's nearest relative, his new friend, the rector, Ted Unsworth.

"How did the old curmudgeon die?" asked Ted.

"Mother Harland will make a thorough examination, but on the evidence available at the moment, death was due to a fall downstairs, which broke his neck. My manual examination of his twisted head seems to support this diagnosis. My immediate dilemma is whether he was pushed or fell accidently due to an excess of alcohol. Is it an accident or another murder?"

"Luke, I hope that if you discover he was pushed, you not take your investigation any further. Uncle Dick was a nasty man, a violent and sadistic individual. He beat young Nell relentlessly as he did me in my youth."

"How would you know about Nell? You are not one of her secret clients?" teased Luke.

"No, but many of her customers have raised the issue with me as both a relative and the rector. They asked me to have a word with Dick. Anything coming from me would have been counterproductive."

"If he was pushed, it could have been Nell, or any one of her customers, most of whom are very fond of her. It could have been a planned murder by one or more of these men," suggested Luke.

"I hope it was. I would have joined them if I had known" was Ted Unsworth's chilling response.

Luke left Ted and went along the road to Alice Eades's cottage, where he found Nell Briggs wrapped in a heavy blanket and gulping down a constantly refilled glass of mead.

Luke asked of her, "When did you find the body?"

"I did not find it. Alice did."

Luke was puzzled. "What were you doing there so early in the morning, Alice?"

"I was getting annoyed as some of Nell's clients were hanging around outside my cottage, waiting for Nell to open for business. It was late for her to commence work, so I went around to her back door and knocked. I received no response. So I went round to the front door, which was open, probably left so by a thwarted would-be customer. I peeped inside, called out, and then saw the body. At that moment, Nell appeared at the front door, saw the body, and ran off in the direction of the manor."

"Why were you late in opening, and where had you come from to find Alice and the body?"

"Dick was in one of his moods and would not let me dress or go downstairs until he heard knocking at the back door. By the time I reached the back door, the person knocking, that I now know was Alice, had gone. I decided to visit the herb garden to obtain some plants that I needed to lessen some bruises and others that I take regularly to prevent pregnancy."

"What happened to the clients waiting in the street?"

"They had looked through the open door and saw Dick lying at the bottom of the stairs and quickly disappeared," said Alice.

"Did one of them push him down the stairs?"

"I wouldn't think so," answered Nell immediately.

Alice was more aware. "If your clients did not do it, Nell, Sir Luke would have to suspect one of us."

"Yes, but at the moment, I have no evidence he was pushed" was Luke's diplomatic response.

Luke's initial assessment of events was completely overturned by Mother Harland. She examined the body and announced calmly, "Dick is another victim of our serial killer. His neck is broken, but he was killed by a needle into the breast. On the edge of death, he probably stumbled to the head of the stairs, and his lifeless body fell to its bottom."

"Four unsolved murders. Up until now, the victims were all Catholics. Richard Unsworth, on the other hand, was the most anti-Catholic man in the dales. These four men must have had something in common. Their deaths cannot be random," concluded a perplexed Luke.

Mother Harland suddenly had a horrible thought, which might explain everything.

For the moment, she would keep this flash of enlightenment to herself.

37

A S THE FIRST OF August approached, Luke became anxious. He convened an urgent meeting with Peter, Harry, and to their surprise, Ted Unsworth.

"Gentlemen, although the surrounding pro-government gentry are ready to act should a Royalist uprising occur in the dales, there are still major weaknesses in our local defence. I have just received news from York that Evan has been ordered to keep all his troops in the city. Thomas Scott believes that the target of the Royalists in the north will be York. He has even persuaded General Lambert to send a company of his troops from the West Riding to reinforce the York garrison. In other words, we cannot initially rely on the assistance of the York garrison in suppressing any local insurgents."

"We should be able to deal with any localised uprising, but if the local insurgents are reinforced by troops landed from the continent, then we are in trouble," observed Peter.

"It is the local insurgents that are our primary concern. How many of our friends and neighbours in Abbey Dale have been seduced by Robert to join the Royalist uprising?" asked Luke.

"I can guarantee that all the workers I have employed on this manor are loyal former veterans of Cromwell's army. None of them would help Dutton," answered Peter.

"As are mine," added Ted Unsworth.

Luke turned to Harry, saying, "You frequent the Three Roses. How do you think the inhabitants of Abbeythwaite would respond to a call to arms on behalf of the king if Robert Dutton approaches them?"

"Frankly, I do not think the government in London has much relevance to them. You as magistrate represent government to them. Whether you obey the generals, the Parliament, or the king is of little concern. The locals are concerned with how in your coming petty sessions you will deal with the several assaults that have occurred in the vicinity of the tavern and how lenient you will be with a couple of petty thieves. The overwhelming topic of conversation are crops and livestock and the effects of the weather on their condition."

"Ted, as rector, your parishioners must speak to you about their views of the world. Will many join Robert?"

"Most dales men would like to see the king back. Nobody, even his bitterest opponents, wanted the late king murdered. Now without the firm hand of Oliver Cromwell, most thoughtful people see the only possible future as the return of the monarchy but perhaps under conditions in which Parliament would retain much power. But whether any dales man at this stage would risk life and limb to bring it about is a different matter."

"I can't arrest the whole of Abbeythwaite to prevent them from joining Robert," remarked Luke.

"We can achieve the same result by a simple subterfuge," Peter announced.

"What was that?" asked Ted.

"On the eve of August the first, Luke will pretend to receive an urgent message that that band of marauding brigands have descended from the moors once again and are heading towards Abbeythwaite. He will order everybody to move into the manor for their own protection. If we provide enough food and drink, I do not think people will be unhappy. Once in the manor, I can ensure that none of the men can leave to join Robert," explained an increasingly enthusiastic Peter.

"It might work, but we do not know when the insurgents will actually come together. Will they be ready to attack their major objective on August the first? Will they start to muster in their local areas days before? Will that be one, two, or three days before the scheduled uprising?" queried Harry.

"We will have to rely on Robert's movements. You have had him watched these last few days. Immediately he acts in a way that can be interpreted as the beginning of an uprising, we can act," replied Luke.

On the evening of the thirty-first of July, Harry reported that Robert Dutton with five of his men had ridden off towards the western moors.

He was followed by one of Luke's men. Luke immediately had most of his workers run through the village, starting at the Three Roses, informing them of an imminent attack by some marauding villains from the north and a firm request that they all seek shelter in the manor. Harry assured the drinkers in the tavern that their drinking could continue as Sir Luke had an enticing supply of alcohol to sample.

Within the hour, Luke counted the local Abbey Dale inhabitants present in the manor. The only absentees of those within the radius that Luke's appeal covered were Robert Dutton and his workmen, Nell Briggs and Alice Eades.

Immediately, the gossip turned to these absentees. Luke lied about Robert Dutton. "In the circumstances, the constable and his men are shadowing the marauders."

The raucous and increasingly drunken assembly were less willing to accept the absence of the two women, especially as neither Alice's husband nor Nell's father could account for their absence. Luke came up with another lie, which seemed to satisfy most—they had gone off together to consult Mother Harland. This lie proved to be the truth, but for the moment, Luke had a bad feeling. Were they in some way linked with Robert and his Royalist rebellion?

Darkness fell late in the summer evening, and around midnight, the man whom Harry had sent after Robert returned. He reported to Luke, Peter, and Harry in the seclusion of Luke's library. "Where is Robert Dutton at this moment?" he was asked.

"Probably in a cave on the western moor" was the reply.

"You do not know for certain. You could not have been to the caves and back in the short time you have been away," announced an angry Harry.

"There was no need to, Mr Green. I was following the constable up the slope to the edge of the moor when one of Johnny Harland's men came running down. We knew each other, and he told me that his master wanted an urgent message taken to the squire."

"And what was that message?" asked Luke.

"Earlier this evening, two groups of horsemen arrived on the moors— one from the neighbouring western dale and the other from the northern moors led by Roly Jagger. The disturbing thing from Johnny's point of view was that Roly's group was openly displaying a Royalist standard."

Luke thanked his man, who was very pleased to join the drinkers with one clear instruction—he was not to mention what he had seen and heard. Luke was delighted. "At least we know that three Royalist groups are gathering overnight in the caves on the western moor. I assume that in the morning, they will head south. Peter, have our men ride through the night to inform our neighbours of what we know and that the government forces will muster at the confluence of Abbey beck and the Pickering to confront them."

Next morning, a group of some forty militia men led by General Tremayne waited at the bridge, which any group heading for Maldon and on to York would have to cross. The Royalists, who were not expecting any organised opposition, openly paraded towards the bridge with a beating drum and invitation for all to join the uprising on behalf of King Charles II. Two royal banners were waving defiantly in the rising breeze.

Luke kept the government's troops concealed until the Royalists set foot on the bridge. Luke noted that the command of the Royalists was in the hands of Roly Jagger and not Robert Dutton. Luke wondered if Kit knew of his cousin's activity.

Given his superiority of numbers, Luke's plan was straightforward. Three rows of government militia acting as musketeers opened up relentless fire into the advancing Royalists as they attempted to cross the bridge. Two smaller groups, remaining on their horses, crossed the stream and took up positions on either side of the suddenly panicking Royalist rebels.

Roly continued advancing as those around him were cut to pieces. Luke ordered all his musketeers to direct their attention on the Royalist commander. After an intense fusillade, he was cut down. Luke then noticed Robert Dutton galloping away, back towards the southern edge of the western moor. While Peter took over command of the main group, Luke led a detachment of six men after the retreating Dutton.

When Luke's posse attempted to climb to the moorland along a narrow valley, Dutton's few men were in an ideal position to hold up their advance. If Luke and his men attempted to climb any further, they would be cut down by musket fire.

After half an hour, the defensive fire ceased, and Luke cautiously recommenced his ascent. He quickly realised what had happened. The defensive fire, which in the end might have been limited to one man, was designed to provide time for Dutton and the rest of his men to disappear. Dutton had escaped, but where would he go?

Two days later, Luke and his comrades were informed of the failed Royalist uprising across the country. Only in Cheshire and Lancashire had troops commanded by Sir George Booth put up any resistance, but they were effectively defeated by Gen. John Lambert, whose army of veterans had displayed some of the old fervour of Oliver Cromwell's troops.

Luke wondered if Lambert's renewed popularity and effective army would tempt him to try and impose his authority on the government in London. When news of the insurrection spread through Abbey Dale, most were surprised that the only local participant was Robert Dutton. Luke wondered now if any of the locals were harbouring him.

He was intrigued to receive a visit from Kit Jagger.

Luke was blunt. "I am sorry, Kit. Your cousin took up arms against the government, and my men cut him down. He was openly displaying a Royalist standard."

"No, Luke, I have not come to discuss my cousin's foolish behaviour. I suggested to him months ago that he need only to stay quiet, and within two years, the very army that executed the last king would bring the new one back. I thought George Monk would have taken advantage of George Booth's uprising and joined forces with him."

"If Booth had held out longer and defeated Lambert, that might have happened," admitted Luke. "Why are you here then?"

"On his way to participate in the uprising, Roly brought me a letter from Whitby, a letter addressed to me. It contained some very happy news. It was from Tommy Bates, sent from outback Massachusetts six months ago. He has found his daughter, a happily married wife of a frontier farmer with two children."

"That is happy news. Is he about to return? How will that affect your situation with Janet?"

"That is even better news. Tommy fell in love with a widow who is his daughter's mother-in-law. He used his legal skills to persuade the local authorities to grant him a divorce. I have come here to ask you as magistrate to come up to the Pilgrim's Rest and marry Janet and myself."

38

Two Days Earlier

AS ROBERT MADE HIS way north across the western moor, he contemplated the disaster in which he had just participated. How could the government have anticipated their uprising and have troops ready to combat them at that strategic bridge? He had been very careful, refusing to seek allies, even amongst his neighbours, many of whom he knew held Royalist sympathies.

Only his friend Ted Unsworth knew that he expected the imminent return of the king and of his desire to become lord of the manor of Abbey Grange. But he had made clear that he expected such a result because of his family link with the previous and rightful owners, the Leighs, not for any services rendered to the king.

He had hoped, however, that his participation in a general uprising of Royalists across Britain, which should have brought the king back, would hold him in good stead when making such a claim. He had been lucky. A draw from a hat determined the Royalist order of battle. Roly Jagger had won and led his Whitby group into what amounted to a suicidal advance that virtually annihilated his whole unit. The dales men from the west formed the second wave of advancing Royalists, whereas Robert and his men brought up the rear. This gave him an opportunity to assess the situation, and as the overwhelming numbers and firepower of the government troops became evident, he made the correct military decision and beat a retreat.

He could not believe that his departure from the battlefield had been noticed by a government officer. A body of government cavalry was clearly tracking his withdrawal. He had badly underestimated the government's response to the uprising. He had seriously underrated the ability of Sir Luke Tremayne and the local government establishment to get troops into the field. After all, Tremayne had been head of the government's military intelligence and an experienced battle commander. Had he inadvertently betrayed himself to Sir Luke?

What would he do now? His men could hold off Luke's detachment to give him plenty of time to escape. He would return to his farm and collect the wherewithal he needed to disappear. For a moment, he considered staying put on his farm. He could claim he was misled into joining Roly, and he did not know that it was a Royalist uprising. If Sir Luke was not a neighbour, he might have a chance of bluffing his way out of trouble, but he could not risk it.

Sir Luke had a reputation of being a ruthless operator. Robert could find himself murdered in his bed, and the act would be covered up as act of state security. He had to flee and to the continent. Would it be through his aunt in York and onto Hull, or would he seek out his estranged brother in Whitby and travel from there?

His aunt actively disliked him and blamed him for the ill treatment she felt her sister, his mother, had endured. She would most likely inform on him to the authorities, although he need not tell her why he was leaving for the continent. She may be able to send some of her senior servants to run his properties while he was away.

He had not seen or communicated with his brother since the death of their father. The brother had received no inheritance, was not a party to any of Robert's many leases, nor a beneficiary from Robert's will. It would not be a friendly encounter.

In the end, he decided that he could more safely get to Whitby than York as the former could be accomplished essentially across deserted moors. Would he call in on Kit Jagger and tell him of the death of Roly? Kit and Sir Luke appeared to be on very friendly terms, and if Roly had told his cousin that he would be accompanied in the Royalist uprising by Robert Dutton, there was no telling how Kit would react. It would be safer to avoid all contact until he reached the safety of urban Whitby.

His lonesome journey across the moors gave him time to plan how he would deal with his estranged brother, whom he still disliked intensely.

He arrived in Whitby having second thoughts about involving his brother. He found accommodation in a low-grade inn. He was dressed well beneath his status; the wealthy gentleman farmer adopted the appearance of a down-on-his-luck labourer. This decision was fortunate.

A day after his arrival, the news of the abortive North Yorkshire uprising reached Whitby with the disastrous news that Roly Jagger and most of the locals who joined him were dead, largely due to the desertion by the Royalist rear guard of Abbey Dale troops led by a Robert Dutton.

Robert could not believe that this lie so quickly circulated in the Whitby alehouses. He did not desert. It was a tactical withdrawal. Fear nevertheless started to eat away at him. Now that his name had been mentioned, the government authorities would put him on list to be apprehended and arrested, maybe alive or dead. A price on his head would not help him escape the country. In addition, local Royalists would also be out to get him for apparently betraying their local hero, Roly Jagger.

Robert found some solace in the unusual black Whitby ale with its strong infusion of liquorice. He eventually found his way from the drinking chamber up to a tiny bedroom, where he fell into a deep sleep. When he awoke midmorning, he decided his only option was to seek his brother's help.

His brother, Roger, was at work and did not immediately recognise the dissolute, ale-infused drunkard who appeared before him. Robert pointed out he was not drunk and was indeed his elder brother in disguise.

There was nothing but disdain in Roger's eyes. "You betray your country by taking up arms, and then you betray your comrades. I had stones thrown through my window last night because they know my name is Dutton. I had to allow local vigilantes into my house to prove that you were not there. Roly Jagger was a popular figure in this town. If anybody recognises you, you will be stoned or hanged on the spot. How can I possibly help?"

"Make arrangements for me to board a ship for the continent, and you must then return to Abbey Dale to take over the family properties in my absence."

"Robbie, you are unbelievable. You inherited all the family property and did not divert even the smallest plot to me as I am sure Father intended. I do not benefit from your will, nor am any part of the leasehold agreements for the many properties that you have accumulated."

"If you help me, I will remedy some of these unfortunate oversights."

"No way. I am not a fool. You will remedy these oversights first, and then I might help you."

"I promise to make you my heir and to add you as the next holder of my leases, most of which are ninety-nine-year tenures."

"Your promises are worthless! You will write a letter immediately setting out two things, that I have your authority to take over all your properties and that I will be incorporated into your leases as soon as this can legally be achieved. Above all, you will draw up a new will now, making me your heir."

Robert was reluctant, but he was trapped. He could always renege on his word when circumstances changed in his favour.

"I will do that for you, brother," he grudgingly conceded.

Roger provided paper and quill, and Robert wrote. Eventually, he handed over a letter and will. "Great," replied Roger. "Now let's go next door to my company's solicitor, who will witness both documents as we sign them in his presence."

Robert's final request was that Roger hide him in his house until he was ready to set sail.

Roger seethed. His mother had suffered greatly from Robert's lack of sympathy, and he, Roger, had been cast out. Now when this wealthy landowner was in trouble, he expected an estranged brother to come to his aid. He would help but at a high price. On Robert's death, Roger would now inherit his brother's many properties.

Over the next few days, Roger made enquiries regarding a boat to the continent. A small cargo vessel was sailing for Hamburg the next day. Roger took some of Robert's money to pay for the voyage, three times what was needed. Robert was furious. Hamburg was too far north, hundreds of miles away from the royal court in the Spanish Netherlands. Roger's retort was direct. If he wanted to go to Flanders, then he would need to take a coastal ship down the coast towards the Thames estuary and take passage from anywhere south of the Humber to his preferred destination. This would add to the risk of discovery. At last, Roger found a small cargo ship that was heading for the Netherlands, the *Whitby Waif.*

The following night, as midnight approached, Robert waited on the wharf beside a bollard adjacent to the *Whitby Waif.* The late hour was determined by the tide, and Robert watched in admiration as the sailors raised sail in blustery conditions. The ship would soon confront the North Sea, and he would be safe.

As he waited to be called aboard, he did not notice two bulky individuals emerge from the shadows. In quick succession, he was hit on the head and his limp body tossed into the harbour. The two assailants whistled cheerfully as they headed back into Whitby.

Roger headed for Abbey Dale at first light the next morning before any news of Robert's disappearance could have surfaced. Weeks later, when the *Whitby Waif* returned to port, its captain reported to authorities that he believed Robert's assailants were not random troublemakers but supporters of Roly Jagger, who had somehow been given the identity of the lonely figure on the waterfront.

Roger had had the ultimate revenge.

On arriving in the dale, he presented himself to Luke, who asked, "What drags you away from Whitby? The last time we met, you hinted that you would never return to this godforsaken part of Yorkshire."

"I bring you distressful news. My brother fell into Whitby harbour, although his body has not been recovered. I have come to take up his estates as his heir and ask you to update all the leases he has with you. This is the documentation you require."

"Welcome back to Abbey Dale. I will get my steward to draw up a new set of leases. There has been a spate of returning inhabitants, many of whom were thought to be lost forever. You would be aware that your brother was a wanted man. Did he throw himself into the harbour, or was it a frightful accident?"

"I don't know" was the smug answer.

"Whatever! It saved the state a trial and execution," added Luke with a knowing look.

Both men understood each other. Luke would get on better with the new master of Dutton Hall than he did with the late but not lamented Robert.

Roger was nevertheless a Dutton, and Luke wondered if he had played any part in his brother's demise.

39

AS SUMMER COLOURED RAPIDLY into autumn, the rhythm of life in Abbey Dale was dominated by harvesting and the distribution of young livestock, a tenth being demanded as a tithe by the church and significant proportions taken in rent by the lord of the manor.

Luke was alarmed when he received news that Gen. George Monk was about to enter England with his English army of occupation from Scotland and was heading for London. The constantly changing Parliament had dismissed Generals Desborough and Fleetwood and appointed Monk commander in chief. Luke feared that the temporarily united army would now be ripped asunder by a major battle between Monk as he headed to London and the popular and recently successful army of John Lambert that gathered to stop him.

The victor would march on London and control the government. Although Lambert's men had tried to kill him, Luke's sympathy was with Cromwell's former deputy. Lambert would restore a military republic as England had been in the early days of the protectorate. George Monk had been a twister, and with him in control, the return of the king was more than likely.

The latest good news was that Monk remained at the border.

The dale was a happy place, and following Kit Jagger's marriage to Janet Bates, a number of couples announced their intention to wed. Luke received Ted Unsworth once a week to discuss church matters. Ted broke the normal routine with the shock announcement. "Luke, I resign my position as rector forthwith."

"That's a sudden decision. You and I got off to a rocky start, but I thought you were very happy now as rector of Abbey Dale parish."

"I am, but unlike you, I believe that the return of the king and his bishops is imminent and that despite any desire you might have to keep me, I will be removed."

"I have the advowson, the right to appoint to this living."

"That is true, but you can only appoint clergy who have a bishop's licence to preach and administer the sacraments. A returning king would revoke my licence, and therefore, your appointment of me would be null and void. And I want to start my new life sooner rather than later."

"And what would that new life be?"

"With the death of my uncle, I inherited the family property, which he let fall into rack and ruin. I will lease further land and develop a viable farm. But there is an even stronger reason for me to resign."

"What would that be?"

"I am about to ask you as the local magistrate to perform my wedding ceremony."

"Who is the woman of your dreams?" asked a surprised Luke.

"At the very moment, she is asking Lady Matilda for permission to marry me. It is the widow Carson, my long-lost school days' friend, the former Elizabeth Foxton."

"A fervent sectarian Protestant such as yourself and a very devoted and pious Catholic—it does not augur well for a successful union, my friend," said Luke gently.

"No, but not being rector will make it much easier for me to accommodate my wife's beliefs. In addition, she could, if she and Lady Matilda desired it, remain her ladyship's companion, whereas as the rector's wife, she could not."

"Congratulations! I wish you both well."

At that point, Matilda and Elizabeth entered the room, and Luke began to pour drinks and summoned a servant to bring them some refreshments. Matilda spoke. "Luke, this is not the only good news. Our household may have to undergo several changes. Emma has just told me that Mark Foxton has become her suitor, and marriage there may not be far away."

Later that evening when they retired for night, Luke commented, "The dale is indeed a happier place than a few months ago. The despair and depression that seemed to dominate when we arrived around Easter seems to have disappeared in the eight months since. Christmas is indeed a season of good cheer."

Matilda took Luke's head in her hands and passionately kissed him on the lips. "It will be an even happier place for you and me. When Mother Harland was here to check on the young livestock a week ago, I spent some time with her. I am pregnant. We are expecting a child."

Luke was beside himself with joy. He had always believed that Matilda was unable to bear children. Perhaps after all these years, he would lay the basis for a powerful family dynasty. He already had a name should the child be a boy—Oliver.

Even national news was positive. The imminent conflict between the armies of Lambert and Monk did not occur. Monk waited in Northern England, while wiser heads managed to convince large sections of Lambert's army to defect. When this army was reduced to an unviable remnant, Monk marched through England to London, where he, the commander in chief of all armies in Britain, literally began his career as kingmaker.

As winter approached, the almost idyllic life in Abbey Dale was plagued by what began as a minor irritation to a small group of male inhabitants. Since the death of Dick Unsworth, his housekeeper, Nell Briggs, no longer made herself available to cater for the sexual needs of a few males. As the weeks progressed, this minor annoyance to a few became an increasing disruptive social problem. Frustrated males began to proposition respectable women in the Three Roses. Their husbands, fathers, and brothers took umbrage at this behaviour, and several tavern brawls followed.

Tim Carver, who had been appointed constable to replace the late Robert Dutton, had a busy introduction to his new role. As more of the villagers appeared before Luke for affray and riot, the cause was clearly related to the disrespect towards women and the retaliation of their relatives.

Luke called in Harry, who frequented the Three Roses for further information. "Why has Nell stopped providing her services? Surely, the death of Dick Unsworth would have given her more freedom. She could now even sleep with Catholics."

"Two reasons from what I can ascertain from the gossip. First there is no suitable venue. Dick's old house is now owned by the retiring rector, and he is about to move in as soon as he is married. Secondly, and much more important, is the rumour that Nell has lost her interest in males and now prefers females—one woman in particular, Alice Eades."

"Doesn't Nell now live with the Eades?" asked Luke.

"Yes, and that has added to the tension in the Three Roses. Initially, William Eades had to put up with good-humoured banter about how he was the luckiest man in Abbeythwaite with both Alice and Nell to service his needs. More recently, it has turned nasty, and William is being called a cuckold, implying that his wife is having an affair with Nell."

"Our blacksmith would not take kindly to such jibes."

"No, he will kill somebody one night soon. He loses his temper at the slightest comment regarding himself, Alice, and Nell. Mother Harland has concerns that in a fit of anger, he might also take this ribbing out on Nell and Alice."

"There is not much I can do about that specific situation, but the general absence of harlots in the dale is a problem that should be rectified."

"It could be sooner than you think. You sent me to the Pilgrim's Rest last week. Kit Jagger's new wife, the former Janet Bates, is restructuring Kit's household and business. She is very unhappy about some of Kit's servants providing favours for visiting travellers and perhaps for even Kit himself. She told him he must sack several of them, including your friend Elinor. I mentioned the problem we had here, and Kit thought Elinor and a workmate would readily move to Abbeythwaite. The problem is from where would they operate? I thought of the Three Roses, but James Harland was not too keen given the opposition of the women in his family to Nell's presence there before she moved in with Dick Unsworth."

"I will have a word with James," said Luke.

Luke chatted with James Harland in terms of law and order and the need to curtail the constant fracas and affrays emanating from the Three Roses. James had clearly changed his mind. "Sir, I have in the past tried to keep such women away from my tavern, particularly under pressure from my daughters. They have now completely changed their views. After weeks of being propositioned by the unrulier of my customers, they want an end to this plague of predatory males. I will go to the Pilgrim's Rest to discuss the situation of these women with them and Kit."

Luke was just about to leave the Three Roses after downing a light ale with the publican when the main door of the drinking chamber burst open, and the bulky body of William Eades burst through. He staggered a few steps into the room and then crashed to the floor. On a quick inspection of the prone body, Luke could see a gash and large bump on the back of his head. William had been hit by a rock or hammer or even an axe.

A more detailed examination could find no other obvious injuries, and Luke and James carried William into one of the rooms and placed him on a bed.

"We will have to wait until he recovers consciousness. I don't think we need call your sister. If he does not regain consciousness, then it will be a different matter. I will inform his wife."

As Luke approached the Eades property, he could see that the doors to both the cottage and forge were wide open. He called out but received no response. He entered the cottage and ascertained that there was no one there. In moving onto the forge, he immediately found a blood-stained hammer and drops of blood on the floor, which he surmised he could follow to the tavern. William had been hit from behind in his own forge by his own hammer. The immediate suspects were Alice and Nell. Where were they? Had William's constant badgering by the drinkers at the tavern about his wife's affair with Nell finally forced him to act against these two women, and had they retaliated? Had they fled after their assault on the blacksmith?

As Luke left the forge, he met one of the neighbours and asked, "Did you see Alice or Nell this morning?"

The reply intrigued him, "Yes, my lord, about an hour ago. They were going to Elderby to see Mother Harland. Nell Briggs is pregnant."

Luke was frustrated. What he expected to be the simplest of enquiries never got off the ground. William regained consciousness and, ignoring James's request that he stay in the tavern until he could be questioned by Luke, made his way back to his forge. Luke, on hearing of this, went to see William, only to be stopped at the forge door. "Your Honour, this is not a matter for the magistrate. It is a mild domestic squabble that Alice and I will sort out."

Luke eventually intercepted Alice and Nell on their return from Elderby. As he approached the women, a concerned Alice asked, "Sir, is William all right?"

"Yes, apart from passing out for an hour and bit, he returned to his forge with little more than a headache."

"What did he say happened?" Alice asked,. probing

"He refused to tell me, claiming it was a domestic matter, and you and him would sort it out."

"That is correct. William made a mistake, and I overreacted. He was completely misled by village gossip. When the truth is explained, all will be well."

"Yes, I understand that William has faced considerable riling in regard to the relationship between Nell and yourself."

"That relationship is simply that of a friend who could not allow Nell, who is pregnant and homeless, to face both problems alone. I took her into our house and have just come from Mother Harland with potions to help her pregnancy, but I have already said too much."

N ELL WAS DELIVERED OF a healthy boy by Mother Harland, and both mother and son were welcomed back into the home of a proud grandfather, the miller Briggs. William and Alice Eades were reconciled. Elinor and a friend arrived from the Pilgrim's Rest and were relocated in an outbuilding of the Three Roses, where nightly brawls and consequent disruption were now reduced to a minimum.

As the New Year dawned, Luke could look back on his first nine months as a married man, civilian, local landlord, and magistrate with great satisfaction except for one overwhelming problem—four unsolved murders. His search for a common motive had failed. The killing of Unsworth destroyed his original hypothesis that it was an anti-Catholic plot and also his fallback position that it was an attack on manorial officials.

He refused to admit that these were four unrelated murders, a position he justified by the identical method used to kill all four victims. They were disabled, and then a narrow blade or long needle pushed into their hearts. He remained convinced that there was one murderer.

The breakthrough came from an unexpected source that initially provided the missing link—a common motive behind three of the murders and a closely related link with the fourth.

Mother Harland was on her monthly visit to check on Lady Matilda's progress. As was now the practise, she stayed overnight and joined Luke, Matilda, and Peter for supper. After a few French wines, Mother Harland addressed Luke. saying, "My lord, I do not often praise my superiors, but your time here has been very beneficial to the dale. You have admittedly been helped by the departure of several unpleasant types and, conversely, the return of several able people, lost to the dale for years. Your one failure is the lack of progress on four murders."

"I agree. If only I could discover a common motive behind them, I could complete the enquiry very rapidly."

"I can help you there. For weeks, I have been thinking about what I am about to say because if I am right, the implications that can be drawn are shattering. To me, all of the murders relate to one issue—the shocking and extreme abuse of young children and women. Three of the murdered men were gross abusers and the fourth, an unfortunate result of such abuse."

"Do you know for certain, or is this dale gossip?" asked a sceptical Luke.

"I know for certain and, apart from the victims, was often the only one who knew. Young girls were often brought to me to help conceal their bruises and abort their pregnancies. Charles Ogden was a constant offender. He sexually abused his daughter, Mary, from a very early age until almost the eve of her marriage to Tim Carver, even after for all I know. She thought it was normal and never complained. Charles was also guilty of incest. He slept with his sister, who had married the then bailiff, the older Snigg. The product of that incestuous union was poor Simon. The person who murdered Charles was overcome with pity for Simon as his condition reduced him to little more than a cabbage. The murderer put out him of his misery and, in the process, freed Emma to lead a normal life. Matthew Foxton embarked on similar abuse of the young Elizabeth, who, as a result, as you know, refused to return to her family. Dick Unsworth was another monster who carefully hid his outrageous behaviour. All that vandalism just before your arrival was his work. He was doing his best to paint Tom Bates and the Catholic officials on the manor in the worst possible light. His attack on the property of his nephew, the then rector, was pay back for what the younger Ted did to him a decade ago. Kit and I long suspected Dick of being the contact man for the out-of-town abductors of young children. He gave these kidnappers the information they needed to abscond with dales children. I am sure it was Unsworth who targeted Tommy Bates's little girl. More recently, he beat Nell Briggs relentlessly and abused her sexually with all sorts of painful implements. It is lucky that the pregnancy was not aborted."

"Was it Dick's child?"

"No, but Nell was clever enough to claim it was. If Dick thought the child belonged to one of her clients, he would have killed her."

"Does she know who the father is?"

Mother Harland smiled. "She says she does—an unmarried young man with promise, her father's apprentice."

"If you are right as to motivation, do you have any idea whom the avenging angel might be?"

"This is where I make my confession. As the person responsible for the health and well-being of women in the dale for several decades, and someone with a knowledge of what has happened to many of them and with superior knowledge of potions and poisons, I was in the perfect position to remedy the situation. It was my neglect of the problem that in the end forced the murderer to act. In many ways, I wish I could simply confess to you now that I murdered those three evil men and put Simon out of his misery."

"But you are not our murderer," commented Matilda.

"No, but I wish I was. I could have got away with it, especially in the decade when we were without a lord of the manor and any local magistrate."

"And you also know who the murderer is," Tadded the astute Matilda. continued

"Yes, but I have no evidence that would stand up in court."

"What have you got?" asked Luke.

"By a process of elimination, it can only be one person. There is one young woman who is much brighter than her ilk, who absorbs everything she reads. This woman has convinced herself that she is obeying a Norse goddess, who protects and brings justice to women. She believes she has a divine mission to avenge her female friends who have suffered such abuse. For several years, she was my assistant and, during that period, picked up information about such abuse and certainly has an advanced knowledge of potions and poisons that might incapacitate her victims."

"I found evidence of a local cult worshiping a Norse goddess. Initially, I thought that you were its leader," admitted Matilda.

"No, originally, it consisted of Alice Eades, Emma Snigg, and Mary Carver, but with the return of Elizabeth Carson, Emma and Mary reverted to their Catholic faith, leaving Alice alone as the guardian of the goddess. She may have recently converted Nell Briggs to her beliefs and half a dozen other young women. I am not even sure that my own nieces have resisted her evangelising zeal."

"You think these murders were carried out by a group of women led by Alice Eades?" asked Luke.

"No, they are the work of onely one woman who has an endless supply of sharp blades and needles."

"A blacksmith's wife," uttered Peter.

"Alice Eades, a cold-blooded killer. It is hard to believe," muttered Matilda.

"But it does fit all the facts," noted Luke.

"Will she avoid trial and execution?" asked Mother Harland. "She was doing what the state should have done. Unfortunately, Alice did not have enough life experience to realise that a great proportion of what riled her was accepted behaviour across the centuries. In these three cases, the abuse clearly went too far, but without the strong force of the goddess, this young woman would not have had the strength to act."

"What are you going to do, Luke?" asked Matilda.

"What the law obliges me as a magistrate to do. Gather the evidence to prove that she is a murderer and have the case put before the Assizes. She will be tried in York and executed. But first, I need evidence to convince the judge."

Luke went to question this very intelligent yet naive and superstitious young woman. He would try to bluff a confession out of her. He knocked on her cottage door. She answered with a direct rebuttal, "If you have come to reopen the disagreement William and I had some time ago, I have nothing to say."

"No, Alice, I have come on a much more serious matter. I have evidence that you murdered Dick Unsworth."

"I doubt that" was the confident reply.

Luke lied, "A witness, one of Nell's eager clients, claims you knocked on the back door, entered the house, and hid in the back entry until Nell walked past you to go into the back garden. You then mounted the stairs, stabbed Dick, and as he staggered to the top of stairs partially incapacitated, you pushed him down. Whether he died first from the needle wound or from the broken neck, we will never know, but you were responsible for both. And you had an unlimited supply of needlelike implements to inflict on your victims. A broken piece of the needle was found in Dick. It was of the same inferior composition as most of your husband's iron implements."

"Why would a sensible and important man like you waste time and sympathy on a monster such as Dick Unsworth? Justice has been served whether by me or another."

"Alice, I understand why you did what you did, but it is against the law no matter how worthy your motives may be. I must gather the evidence for this and the other murders, and when I have what I consider sufficient to convict, you will be arrested, tried, and hanged."

"You are not going to arrest me now?" asked a somewhat surprised Alice.

"No, I know you are guilty, but I need more evidence to convince our legal system." This was another lie. Luke hoped that now that she was exposed as the murderer, she would eventually confess, or she might, in fear of being hanged and publicly shamed, take her own life.

Three weeks later, William Eades arrived at the manor, clearly upset. He requested to see Luke immediately. "My lord, Alice confessed to me last night what she had done and why. When I arose this morning, she was gone, but she left this letter for you."

Luke absorbed a long confession and read aloud her final paragraph.

> *English law is written by men for men. Until we return to the rule of the goddess where women had rights we will continue to suffer vile abuse from the very men who should cherish us. I am going to spend eternity with the goddess. With her, clasped to my breast, and after consuming a mixture of potions that will soon allow me to enter the next world, I will walk the western moor until the goddess takes me home.*

William asked, "My lord, would you have arrested her and taken her to York to be tried and hanged? You have killed many more men in your time than my Alice."

"Very true, William. Unfortunately, women are not soldiers, and the relationship between parents and children is not considered war. If it were, as a soldier for justice, fighting a war for a better life for women and children, her actions would be applauded."

"Will you send a search party out to find her?"

"No" was Luke's spontaneous and surprising answer.

Later at supper, Matilda asked, "Why have you not sent a search party after Alice?"

"To what end? I am convinced that a strong personality such as Alice will carry out her intention of suiciding by poison. There is part of me, the old soldier rather than the current magistrate, that hopes she will bury her principles and that her letter and disappearance is a simple ruse to escape my clutches and leave the country."

Matilda was more direct. "I hope she lives and starts a new life in the Americas."

Luke sighed. "At least I hope we never find her body. Then we can both believe in a happy ending."